Calabrinia Falling

Pilar de Ovalle

Calabrinia Falling

A Fantasy
by Pilar de Ovalle

The Crossing Press
Freedom, CA 95019

Cover art by Mark Johnson
Typesetting by Karol Franklin

Printed in the U.S.A.

Library of Congress Cataloging in Publication

De Ovalle, Pilar.
     Calabrinia falling : a fantasy / by Pilar de Ovalle.
       p. cm.
     ISBN 0-89594-434-0 -- ISBN 0-89594-433-2 (pbk.)
     I. Title.
PS3554.E592C35 1990
813' .54--dc20   90-40973
                                           CIP

Preface

This work is intended as pure fantasy: that is, without social, political or psychological ax to grind. Realism is as far from the author's mind as making a living by writing. The entire world of Calabrinia is contained in a crystal sphere, as the historically minded reader may remember was once the case with this world; the Empire which bulks so large in the minds of the *dramatis personae* would measure approximately the equivalent of 800 by 500 miles, excluding the frozen northern mountains and the volcanic range to the east of the Desert of Death.

The reader is therefore encouraged to regard the novel to follow as an elaborate Christmas tree ornament, or a Russian Easter egg: "such a form as Grecian goldsmiths make." Those who wish may crack it open like a fortune cookie to see if there is a moral inside; but it will be a more satisfactory artifact if lightly tossed from hand to hand so that it glitters in the sun.

For this is a fairy tale (although it is not about fairies), and there are dragons in it, as there should be; but the reader who hopes dragons are only to be found in fairy stories will be much mistaken.

The quotations at the head of each chapter are mere literary jilladandyism and may be disregarded.

One

...these are the Inner Lands, the lands whose sentinels upon their borders do not behold the sea. Beyond them to the east there lies a desert, forever untroubled by man: all yellow it is, and spotted with shadows of stones, and Death is in it, like a leopard lying in the sun. To the south they are bounded by magic, to the west by a mountain.
— Lord Dunsany

THE imperial dragon counted on the five claws of each foot, tearing creamy petals one by one from the flower of the Moloquat, the tree that bears fruit with no stone. As each petal parted from the golden heart of the flower, she spoke a name. The petals span away slowly on the bright blue airs of heaven, and the names echoed softly back in the enclosing crystal sphere.

"Alina," said the dragon, tearing off the last petal. "Alina it must be."

In the languorous blue evening light of the Court of Turquoises, the spray of fountains fell brighter than diamonds into brazen basins set on veined marble pavements, around which mosaics depicted all the nations of earth. In the center of the court grew a great Moloquat tree whose branches, bowed under the weight of snow-white doves, arched over resting panthers tethered on steel chains.

This particular evening, the last night before spring burst into summer with lily-heads heavy on their stalks, one bough was bent almost to the pavement with the hanging body of Korab Khan, unsuccessful revolutionary.

There it hung, for three days a testimony to the scandal and the resolution of it.

"For who," said Meerkat Lobum, the Second Vizier, "would wish to ignore the manifest will and decree of his Benign Supremacy?"

"I would," muttered Alina, where she sat biting her embroidery floss, youngest of the nine hundred and eighty-two princesses domiciled in the Courtyard of Royal Princesses. Since her conformity was assumed without being sought, no one paid any attention but the lean ivory-white hound bitch at her bare feet.

This princess Alina had no mother in the Queen's Quarters. Apparently she had never had a mother, and was in consequence the most willful and wayward of all the nine hundred and eighty-two princesses. These ranged from portly maidens of fifty with fat white tresses braided with pearls, through haggard greying harridans of forty much given to magicks and ill-wishing, superb sloe-eyed sirens in their thirties still hoping for the rose-decked matrimonial litters of ambassadors to call for them, to moon-faced demoiselles of twenty-five who competed at handball and the archery butts like hoydens.

In theory the princesses were for export. They learned no history or mathematics, only languages, dancing, music, fine embroidery and the chase, to fit them for royal marriages. But in fact none had been betrothed for a number of years.

And since the three hundred and eleven queens seemed to have left off bearing offspring of either sex, the tally of princesses increased in years and accomplishments, but the number remained stable.

Their chief domestic employment was interminable ceremonial dances in the Temple of his Benign Supremacy: with veils, with swordblades, with candles, with full goblets, with batons, with every accouterment but shoes; so that their most serious occupation was daily drill with

2

the dancing-master.

Sometimes Alina thought she would like to be married in some barbarous foreign land to confirm a treaty; sometimes she merely wanted to burn down the whole palace (first opening kennels, stables and mews) just to see the leaping flames instead of princesses, queens and the staff of 3,500 directly under the Second Vizier that ministered, waited on, guarded, rewarded, trained, punished and amused them.

But of late—she had just attained her fifteenth year—her mind had been otherwise occupied, very much so.

It so fell out that this third day on which the body of the aforementioned royal revolutionary Korab Khan hung like an overripe fruit in the Court of Turquoises, was the eve of a holiday.

When she spoke, Alina was mending the border of her best ceremonial veil, torn on a previous occasion when she made a slight misstep, for everything must be perfect for the Feast of the Moloquat.

The Moloquat tree was the symbol and emblem of Calabrinia throughout the known world, stamped on grain bags and silk bales, engraved on instruments musical and astronomical, drawn in gold ink on parchment rolls of poetry and philosophy, branded on purebred chariot horses, tattooed on the left shoulder of each royal princess of the blood.

The Moloquat then grew nowhere but the courts, boulevards, squares and ramparts of the imperial city, having no related species, wild or domestic, anywhere else. Its form was large and spreading, with a twisted silvery-grey trunk, very thick and branching low into wide boughs of dense evergreen foliage. Each leaf was the size and shape of a hand with spread fingers, deeply textured, showing a dark green shiny surface and a pale, almost silvery underside. Its huge beautiful flowers, wide as a face, creamy-white with the faintest carmine blush on the outer petals, opened to massed gold stamens like a royal crown; but the tree set seedless fruits, so must be

3

reproduced by rooting cuttings in the month after the intoxicating fruits fell.

In or out of bloom, the influence of the Moloquat was such that it was death to sleep under it at night even for a few hours; but during the day the aromatic fumes of the gum exuded from its bark heartened and enlived the body better than food or strong drink. It was believed that the first Moloquat sprang from a single holy seed presented a millennium since to his Benign Supremacy by a celestial dragon.

Therefore, given the significance and bustle of the occasion, it was not surprising that the well-punished though ill-defined case of Korab Khan ceased to occupy the women's wing of the Palace. The Court of Princesses was busy as a beehive, echoing with peafowl shrieks: for this slave, for that one, for henna, curling-irons, jasmine-oil, ankle-bells; for white arsenic, chalk, belladonna and aromatic vinegar; for chamois-cloth and emery-boards and pumice-stones.

All day little eunuchs trotted back and forth with their eyes rolling like marbles, bearing triple-embroidered silk veils, so stiff they stood of themselves, from the laundry; caskets of jewels from the treasury; tiny vials of scented oils from the perfumery.

All day maid-slaves in double yokes hauled pails of asses' milk to the baths and poured them into wooden tubs steaming already with boiling water in which bergamot and germander steeped; they scrubbed green slime off the edges of the ancient marble Great Bath in which cold spring water had bubbled since before the Palace was built, and made head-high piles of clean towels beside it.

Princess Alina, meanwhile, finished mending her border and shrieked for her own maid Aysha. Although her turn in the baths corresponded to her place in the roster of princesses—that is, last—she was late even so, and found herself and Aysha alone. The two exchanged a look, and Aysha put out her thumb for her mistress to prick with a bodkin in order to moisten a small folded napkin bearing her glyph. The maid winced, sucked her thumb, and left the napkin on the floor in plain view.

Alina prepared for her bath. She was of no more than middle height, with blue-black hair shiny as a crow's wing that hung to her knees unbraided. Her eyes were amber, but turned black with belladonna, or fury, or dim light. She had a high-boned nose, thin and curved, a mouth full-lipped and inclined to sullenness, with teeth like almonds if she smiled, and a sharp-cut chin. Her particular beauties were thin black winged brows and skin the color of cream and cinnamon.

As to the rest, visible above the steaming milky bath-water, a round slender neck joined elegant thin shoulders, the left one marked with the royal Moloquat in black, and continued to breasts rather more pomegranate than peach, surprising in one so young. Her waist might once have been spanned by two hands (and had been, more than once) but latterly had thickened. She had a dancer's long-muscled legs, and graceful arms, and hands with long henna-colored nails.

The arms were ornamented with several fine bruises, some days old and more yellow-plum than blue-plum in color; but still needing careful cosmetic-work. Her brows drew into a straight line over darkened amber eyes as Aysha toweled her dry and smoothed flesh-colored salve over the bruises.

She was late again to the huge common room, the Hall of Princesses, where a eunuch impatiently held the door for her. The Hall was paved with tiles, cool underfoot between islands of multi-patterned rugs and heaps of cushions, all under a vaulted dome of sky-blue enamel set with crystal stars. The only windows opened high under the cupola, above walls of marble plaster carved like lace that seemed to ripple in the light of a hundred and fifty cressets.

The hall was full: royal princesses and their maids, slaves, musicians, guards, messengers, apothecaries and eunuchs with trays of supper. The task of getting themselves ready for the Feast of the Moloquat would take all night, the procession to the Temple starting at two hours before dawn.

Alina was immediately served a tray of white wheaten cakes, conserve of quinces in honey, tiny strawberries with curds, and walnuts crystallized in brown sugar and ginger. She ate hungrily if daintily, with her long-nailed fingers and her double-edged silver knife. Under cover of the music of kettledrums, bells and copper flutes, she whispered to Aysha, pounding colors and perfume essence in a mortar.

"Tomorrow, then?"

"Tomorrow it must be or not at all, Princess," replied the maid, trying the color on her wrist. "The head eunuch frowned when I fetched your tray—said how fat you are getting."

Alina dropped a quince and crossed her arms quickly over the slight curve of her stomach.

"Go ahead and eat it. One way or another, it may be the last you'll have for a long time."

"What do I care!" Alina's eyes filled with great salt tears, but she sniffed them back and swallowed them with a draught of raspberry brandy iced with snow from the subterranean vaults of the Palace.

Aysha, looking over her shoulder, signalled with her left ear, and Alina composed her face like a painting on gesso.

It was Meerkat Lobum himself, Second Vizier of Calabrinia, come to address the royal maidens on the eve of the Moloquat Feast. His person was surrounded by the tallest and broadest eunuchs of the Guard, each with a panther on a chain, since it was not unheard-of for even a Second Vizier to be torn into unidentifiable scraps in the Hall of Princesses in times of emotional turbulence.

However, the princesses' energies were directed to competitive bedizening for the coming public appearance, so he was safe for the moment. He exhorted them all to their finest efforts on the morrow, so that the ugly stain of—treason, he might say—might be washed from the royal family and the gods never cease to smile upon Calabrinia in the person of his Benign Supremacy.

After the peroration the musicians resumed, and he strolled about the hall listening to complaints, refusing favors, keeping his ears pricked and his eyes sharp. He paused where Alina sat on her private cushions having her hair braided with strings of black pearls.

"Ah, little Alina," he remarked. "How you've grown! This will be your third time in the Moloquat dance, won't it? I seem to remember you forgot the sequence of the Sixth Hour, last year—I trust it won't happen again?"

Alina turned a dusky mulberry-red. She remembered her ankle-bells jangling out of time, jeering faces turned towards her, stinging red weals across her backside afterwards. How Meerkat Lobum had enjoyed that—"No, Excellency, I assure you it will *not* happen again."

"That's what I like to hear." As he turned away, his small, opaque black eyes lingered thoughtfully on the painted breasts, more matronly than maidenly. Both girls held their breath. Over his padded shoulder he said, "You need a better maidslave than this sluttish Rat. Tomorrow you shall have one."

"May all the gods and his Benign Supremacy keep you," Alina murmured politely. "Keep you on a red-hot grill with scorpions and rock-vipers," she hissed at his fat brocaded back.

Aysha dropped a string of pearls slithering over the tiles. "Oh, Princess," she whispered, "may I be shod if he doesn't know."

"He suspects, certainly. We must take our chance." With a hand that trembled like a leaf in the first fitful gust of storm, Alina took the pot of cinnabar and savagely reddened her mouth.

"Escape or the bowstring for us," said Aysha. "Let fear lend us courage!"

"*You* may fear, of course!" exclaimed the princess in an undertone. "But the hand of one of *my* blood does not tremble at the thought of a bowstring!"

"I shouldn't think you'd care for it, Princess, with all respect. Are you finished with your supper?"

"I fear only to fail of my true love's mission, with which he entrusted me, only me—bring me the emerald-carver's box. It's in my sponge-bag, and don't let anyone see it."

Aysha touched her forehead perfunctorily to the tiles and scurried away for the box.

It was a round sandalwood casket no larger than the palm of her hand, curiously carved all around with the figure of an imperial five-clawed dragon; there were no hinges or visible lock. Alina touched it here, there and again with her long russet nails, and the two halves of it slid apart like the halves of a walnut shell. As she did so, her bone-white lean hound at her feet disappeared under the cushions.

What the box held, amidst camphor, orrisroot and sea-salt, was a withered dry object like a prune-persimmon, or an old leather pouch, stiff and weathered, or...

"What is it?" whispered Aysha, pretending to untangle strings of garnet and turquoise beads.

"Ah!" said Alina, impressively. "What is it? *You* think his Benign Supremacy is immortal, king forever, ceasing never, and so forth?"

"So they say."

"Korab Khan, prince of the blood royal, by his consummate science and magick perceived that the godking is not one but many; long-lived indeed, but not immortal, following one on another for a thousand glorious years of History. A seamless web, the warp of which is the dynasty and the weft the science, arts, commerce, philosophy and wealth of Calabrinia! But now," continued Alina, remembering words not her own, "the pattern is cut, and must be strung anew on the loom of Time."

"Yes, yes, they say—they whisper—everywhere the same, something is wrong at the center of things."

"And Korab Khan knows what, and means to mend it with my help!" cried Alina in a triumphant undertone. "Who but he! Impossibly handsome, incredibly dashing, a superb fencer, reckless horseman, nonpareil dancer, past master of all grammarie!"

"But my Princess, do you not forget...?"

"In this box I have the heart of his Benign Supremacy, who lies dead in the snow cellars under this palace, in a cask marked 'smoked eels.' My lover found it and took the heart to publish the death to all the city and the

8

world. Now I must do what he told me and bound me to with many oaths, (and beat me to make sure I remembered): for he had doubts of the loyalty of the emerald-carver, and you see he was right."

"But, my Princess, his Highness is dead, be his talents all that you say!"

"I will cut down his body before the tenth day, put this charmed ruby in his mouth, and so he will return to life!"

"Ooh! Can you really?" Aysha spoke through a mouthful of hairpins, her fingers flying as she braided Alina's hair, fine as silk, into plaits no thicker than her little finger.

"Certainly I can," said Alina, angling the mirror to see. "I am a royal princess, and this ruby is very ancient and magickal."

"And then?"

"Ah! Then we shall take horses, and loyal men, and seek the lost Prince of the Isles (whom Korab Khan shall find and force by his arts to aid us), forge an alliance with some people called Barak-Shar (I do not know who they may be), and ascend the throne in a twinkling! The empire will again prosper and I shall be queen above all queens!"

"Are you sure you want to do all that?"

"Of course! What else was I born for?"

"Oh," replied Aysha doubtfully, pinning up a plait. She knew that the stupider you seemed, the more you would be told. "But is it not called the Dragon Throne? What of the celestial dragons?"

"What of them? Probably another foolish myth. Have you ever seen one?"

"No, but...speaking of myths—perhaps it is not so that the Moloquat tree is under the special protection of dragons?" asked Aysha, after a pause. "That they are—um—around and about, for the Feast of the Moloquat?"

"Highly unlikely," Alina returned.

Aysha was still doubtful. "Now that we are come to it—these plans. Did you mention to his Highness that you...that he...that is...?"

"That I find myself, um, slightly with child?" Alina

frowned and made a point of hauling the dog out from under the cushions. "Here, you Lula, come out. Well—yes. Actually that was why he beat me. But we'll work it all out when we are on the Dragon Throne."

Then a eunuch came for the tray, and Aysha made herself very busy with hairpins.

Two hours before dawn, the desert chill lay coldly inert on the stiff leaves of orange-trees and still water under dry fountain-nozzles. On the beaten earth of the parade-ground, the procession formed.

The royal princesses were draped in white robes against the chill, the common gaze, and the Evil Eye; they were mounted on nine hundred and eighty-two white donkeys (some of which were more docile than others), led by little pages in green velvet short pants embroidered with the Moloquat emblem in black and followed by maidslaves with combs, hairpins and smelling salts.

Princess Alina, naturally, was last. And here was plain Meerkat Lobum's eye to detail, for the maidslave at the donkey's tail was not Aysha but another.

No doubt Alina was offended, for she did not speak to the new maid or nod to her sisters, only sat her mount stiffly, sidesaddle, bare feet on the padded velvet footboard and reins of satin ribbon slack in her hands, so the page had much trouble to guide the donkey.

The procession of ghost-grey donkeys in the dark, bearing sheeted figures from which came the occasional muffled clang of bangles from wrist and ankle, uncoiled itself in the vast square and snaked under the double arch into the Avenue of the Temple. It trailed an air of musk and bergamot, and left small piles of donkey-dung for the gardeners to collect later in barrows. The dull plunk of little hooves changed to a sharp tip-tap on the cobblestones, joined by the heavy soft tread of bull-hide boots as the Guard fell in on each side, carrying flaring torches.

The avenue was wide enough for a troop of cavalry ten abreast, cutting a broad zigzag swath through the city from the Palace against the eastern wall to the Marketplace fronting on the Temple above the river. Where streets led into it were plazas, large and small, planted with Moloquats around marble basins filled with water-lilies and copper-colored carp.

At this hour the carp slept, the lilies were furled tight, and even the great open blossoms of the Moloquat were sad-colored in the light of the smoking flares.

Crowding doorways and courts, side streets, alleys, roofs, and the garlanded hanging balconies of the tall houses, the commons of Calabrinia silently watched the procession of shrouded princesses. The men wore Molo-quat flowers stuck in their hats—the women (bright shawls grey in the pre-dawn murk) had each a single ivory bud nested in her hair.

The procession made its slow reptilian progress through the city while overhead the stars faded and the indigo sky washed into pale gray-blue. As they neared the golden-domed Temple and the statue of his Benign Supremacy gilded with soft pure gold, the invisible sun injected the low clouds in the east with rose madder and crimson.

At last the tail of the procession coiled into the crowded, silent Marketplace, facing the broad steps of the Temple. Donkeys and princesses ranked twenty abreast were led and pushed up the steps into the odorous, gong-vibrating half-dark of the atrium just as the sun's red disk showed above the horizon.

In the Market, fireworks went off, sparkling wheels and rockets and artificial comets with the deep-mouthed yell of the populace: noise enough to reach his Benign Supremacy dead or alive.

The donkeys capered nervously in the rain of sparks, and the people surged after them up the steps with deafening cheers, all according to custom.

But in the Temple murk, under the frowning bronze stare of minor godlings, the solemn rhythm of ritual broke in a flurry and whirl of motion: one of the princesses fell off her donkey. There was a press of bodies in the gloom, a wail from a page as someone stepped on him, an unhallowed remark by a guard stooping to lift the fallen

11

princess and hitting his head on the donkey-saddle.

When more torches were brought, however, there was only the thick white sheeting, rucked and rumpled on the colored pavement. No princess, barefoot, bejeweled and painted, hung with brilliant silks and clashing bangles, was to be seen!

The remaining nine hundred and eighty-one princesses in the Temple (hastily counted off) screamed; eunuchs and maidslaves milled and wailed; the guards formed up and lowered their twelve-foot pikes in a barrier across the atrium; Meerkat Lobum rushed up and down the ranks; but the missing princess was nowhere to be found. Princess Alina had vanished.

Presently the captain of the Guard thought of counting the maidslaves as well; there were exactly the nine hundred and eighty-two there ought to have been, since by that time the extra one who had worn the empty sheet had slipped into the crowd on the steps and disappeared in the maze of alleys behind the Temple.

But of necessity the ceremony must continue, and at last the gongs began again.

When she heard them clanging, faint and far, Alina crawled out of the straw of Lula's kennel. The dog-runs were deserted, since the kennelman, for devotion, and his underlings, for the holiday, were gone to the Marketplace.

She pulled out a leather pouch containing some useful items, which she slung over her shoulder. She had on a groom or garden-boy's costume of red headrag, blue woolen smock and clogs. Unlike most princesses, she could walk in clogs. Dressed so, she used to steal to the Old Garden, to the half-ruinous kiosk where the brook flooded in winter and no one but the secretive old emerald-carver ever went—no one but herself and her lover Korab Khan, he dressed like a gamekeeper, with red earth rubbed on his smooth olive cheeks and powdering his thin mustache and silky black love-locks.

How they had laughed to see each other like that! Even in the seriousness of illicit love and plots against the

12

headless state, they had laughed. Also they had spoken, in exalted terms suitable to their rank, of stagnant waters and fire of youth, the necessity for young blood, the dusty Dragon Throne.

They spoke also of themselves, naturally. To Korab Khan had Alina confided her mysterious horoscope:

> *Earth, Air, Water, Fire:*
> *One shall hold my heart's desire;*
> *Air, Water, Fire, Earth:*
> *One be foredoomed from my birth.*
> *Water, Fire, Earth, Air:*
> *Two be foul yet two be fair.*
> *Fire, Earth, Air, Water:*
> *'Ware the bane of Godking's daughter.*

He could make nothing out of it, but assured her she was marked for a high destiny, and all would become clear as glass after the fact, as was often the case with prophecies, amulets, portents and such associated with noble and royal persons.

He himself possessed a talisman, a balas ruby as big as a pigeon's egg. It was proof against ensorcelment, lightning and erysipelas—it would even buy off the black boatman who plied the subterranean dark UnderCa, river of death and twin of great Ca that watered the city of Calabrinia.

Alina did not doubt Korab Khan then, and now she could not hurry fast enough in the clumsy clogs to revive him, all through echoing empty passages and courts to the Court of Turquoises. In one hand she clutched the warm ruby he had given her for safekeeping, in the other flashed a double-edged blade to cut him down.

Headlong and breathless she burst into the silence of the deserted courtyard. The cord parted at the first pass of the blade—the body, like a too-ripe fruit, slumped squashily to the pavement. The unburdened bough shuddered and lifted, dropping a dark, hand-shaped leaf to land silver-side-up beside the body partly preserved—but only partly—by the oozing resin of the Moloquat.

Alina did not hesitate. Prying open the black lips, she

13

forced the ruby between them, then rocked back on her heels to await the result.

The sun was burning high over the city when she admitted the operation a failure. Clearly the ruby was at fault, since she was as royal a princess as might be to administer it, youngest and last of her line as she was. No doubt some secret enmities of enchanters had sucked the virtue from the stone; or conversely, it might be due to the strange decline of magick lately noted, whereby spells were weak and wavering at best, and at worst failed utterly. She had heard of such things.

That being the case, the sad heap staining the marble at her feet resembled so little the gallant figure of her lover that she felt a strong impulse to leave the Turquoise Court at once and never return. She was then sick into the nearest basin, which cleared her mind as well as her stomach.

What was to be done? Korab Khan was unarguably dead. His plans for rebellion and conquest must then fall to the ground as the body fell...Alina was almost sick again, but lacked the wherewithal. But what of her part in it? She had arranged a particularly dramatic public disappearance—she could not now simply turn up, claiming to have overslept.

No. To say nothing of the other matter, her gravid belly (about which something was bound to be said soon if not already), she had come too far to turn back. She must go on, although Korab Khan had fallen (no, not that image again). It would be best to leave the city alone, take refuge in the provinces, and consider.

Alina rose from her knees, spitting and wiping her mouth. She turned her back on the heap under the Moloquat tree; beyond the pearly cupola of the Hall of Princesses she could see neither the green fields nor the desert beyond, but only the snowy peaks of the Blue Mountains, seeming close enough to touch in the clear air. She had a vision of herself mounted, streaking like a hawk over the intervening wasteland traversed by no-

14

mads, to those mountains, bearing...proclaiming...what? Her own troubles? No, princesses must be above such matters. But why should she herself not carry out what Korab Khan had begun? Why not seek the lost Prince of the Isles, propose alliance to the—whatever they were, the Barak-Shar—and all the rest of it?

She would show the mummified heart, she would proclaim the challenge in Korab Khan's own words!

There were a few details yet to be settled, perhaps even a flaw in the major premise, but Alina must do something at once; and a veneer of rational purpose is better than none at all. She whistled up her hound Lula nosing about the courtyard, and made for the stables as quickly as might be.

She painted on her memory in enduring colors the image of Korab Khan, raising his javelin as the lioness leaped; Korab Khan outdistancing all the princes on his white-faced red stallion; Korab Khan rolled in a silken mantle, laughing at the comic song she sang him in whispers; anything but the dreadful heap in the Court of Turquoises.

The sooner she left the Palace, the whole stifling smelly leering city, the better—she could not breathe until the walls were behind her—the distant clanging of gongs was hateful in her ears.

At one moment she thought she was caught—a sliding or rustling sound, not an echo, came from a passage behind her. Turning, she saw for an instant a scaly flicker, as of a tail—but there was nothing there and she hurried on. Perhaps it had been a stray peacock, trailing its feathers?

The stables were abandoned this day, like the rest of the Palace. Alina found her own mare by the simple expedient of calling her name: "Braseli, Braseli!"

A whinny answered, and she ran to the sound. The mare nosed her down for lumps of honey-nougat while Alina attempted saddling, a thing she had never tried before. She held up the bridle, with copper noseband and braided silk reins, in puzzlement; Braseli, who knew a good deal more about it, put her head into it properly.

15

The light hunting saddle, with pointed stirrups lined in green velvet, was fitted with a short stiff bow and quiver of envenomed arrows, a bag suitable for carrying comfits until the slaves brought the luncheon-baskets along; and a copper canteen for a day's gazelle-hunt in the stubble-fields.

As she led the mare out of the stable and mounted, she thought of the small party of loyal warriors that Korab Khan was to have procured for their start at dawn, equipped with long swords and longbows, travel-rations of dried meats and fruit, water-bags on a pack mule, maps and flint and tinder.

But she had no way of acquiring any of those things, and the whole morning was lost waiting in the Turquoise Court; by mid-afternoon, the rituals completed, guards with panthers in leash would fan out from the city in all directions. She could only hope the noon sun might lift her fresh trail quickly. She trotted to the horse-gate opening directly on the fields beyond the city wall.

"Hola, there!" said the guard, waking cross and suspicious from his doze in the shade of the pillars. The gateway was open, but he dropped his pike across it.

"Hola yourself, you lazy squash," said Alina with tart emphasis. "Get moving, do you expect me to saddle both at once while you sit in the sun?"

"Dragonfewmets? What, both what?"

"Horses, gourdhead! The black stallion at the end of the third row is supposed to saddled and ready. B' is B'nign Sup', move or it'll be in the bowstring for you!"

The guard's duty was to let no one pass without presenting a doorstone of white jade. Alina's demand entirely confused him.

"The stablemaster..." he hazarded.

"At the Temple," Alina said crisply, flashing a fire-opal on her thumb as though it were authorization. "The horses to be there immediately, and half an hour ago better."

"Dragonflukes! All right. Hold the gate for me. And— give me the ring in case."

Alina shrugged and tossed him the ring. If it brought

him luck, he was going to need it. "Haste! I can't wait all day!"

As soon as the leather cuirass disappeared around the stable, Alina backed Braseli three paces and drummed on her ribs with the heels of the clogs. The high-mettled mare sprang like an arrow from the bow, clearing the barrier as a gazelle clears a thornbush, and sped over the fields beyond at a headlong gallop. Lula slipped under the pike and followed.

The clumsy clogs fell off and the blue woolen smock bellied out like a flag as Alina rode northwest, through green fields of amaranth. She looked back on all she had ever known with a scowl of repudiation as wide as the beatific smile on the great golden face of his Benign Supremacy's statue. The sun on the gilded dome of the Temple flamed like a torch.

Field workers shaking clappers to scare birds stared dumbly as she passed, but Alina did not heed them. She was clear away, escaped, off on a high mission to fulfill her great destiny! Perhaps she was not quite sure of either, but it was exhilarating to be free of the tyranny of viziers, the tale-bearing of slaves, the endless tittle-tattle of idle princesses.

The tasseled rein-ends flew wide in the wind, as Alina gave the well-fed mare her head and urged her with bare heels to greater speed. She wanted to leave behind the muddy fields with patient donkeys plodding around the water-wheels, the flocks of cawing crows that rose as she passed. She put the mare at a wide ditch of thick green river-water and felt like a swallow on the wing.

At last Braseli slowed from a gallop to a canter, then to a trot, and finally down to a walk. Lula loped behind with her tongue lolling. They were beyond the watered fields, far into the rough sheep-grazing. When they came to a well all pocked about with little cloven gazelle-prints, they stopped to drink and rest a moment.

The desert proper was not far away. On the dry thin air shivered a rising and falling cadence: the mad laughter of hyenas. Lula's ears stiffened and her hackles rose; the mare lifted her muzzle dripping from the cool, metal-flavored water, and Alina, wringing out her headcloth, put a hand to the bow and poisoned arrows on the saddle-bow.

Now she noticed calceous white droppings of hyenas ringed the well. Thoughtfully she tied the wet rag around her head. She had a packet of fig comfits, but no other food, nor had she thought of bringing any. Mundane considerations these, unbefitting high courage and noble birth. She dismissed them.

The first day of summer, scented with the promise of apricots, it became general knowledge in the ancient, wise and wealthy city of Calabrinia, that the Princess Alina had vanished; whereupon the wildest speculations circulated.

Rumors ran from the Palace to the Marketplace, from the Guard barracks to the Temple, from shops to the docks on oily, slow river Ca. All Calabrinia, city of eternal sun, wherein dwelt (or not, as the case might be) his Benign Supremacy, beloved of dragons, was aware of the scandal and had opinions. These opinions were given out, with greater or lesser freedom according to circumstances and the rank or lack of it of the individual.

Meerkat Lobum the Second Vizier rolled his eyes to heaven (already brassy and white-hot) and invoked the—mercy—of the gods on the poor princess, undoubtedly driven insane by the treason of her half-brother.

The Master of the Royal Stables discovered the mare missing and insisted that the princess must have been eaten by lions on the occasion of the last court hunt, unnoticed in the crush. The Head Eunuch publicly accepted that explanation.

The nine hundred and eighty-one princesses remaining had each her own theory, and sustained it at the top of her voice, so that the Courtyard of Royal Princesses sounded like a cageful of peahens.

The queens in the harem, all but mad Queen Elyse of the Isles, who had not spoken for ten years, also pronounced severe and various judgments.

The commons, supervising the huge slave-tilled fields of amaranth and buckwheat, the orchards of peach, pomegranate, date, apricot, walnut, fig, melon and raspberry, attributed the princess' disappearance to the jealousy of magicians; or possibly she had been snatched up to heaven by a celestial dragon in order to protect her from the same.

Even the Rat people, poling their barges loaded with seaweed, offal, oyster-shells and fishbones from the southern sea to enrich the fields upriver—even they, in their low and primitive minds, formulated some idea or other about the matter, but it was not likely that people so despised for their low office, a reminder of the dark boatman of UnderCa, would be asked.

Perhaps therein lay an error. As that fatal day spread over the vast sky, a Rat crew, caring nothing for the Moloquat festival, had shoved off from the crumbling wharf and poled their barge into the slow strong current midstream, with a downriver cargo of amaranth flour, tin bars and apricot jam. With them went a runaway slavegirl who spoke the river patois with a certain hesitation and whose flat features were the creamy white of indoor life.

She had with her a bundle of strictly contraband shoots of the Divine Moloquat, wrapped in silk; and the hem of her fine smock was as lumpy with jewels as a blacksnake full of pigeon's eggs.

Only the Guard had no opinion. It was their duty to believe nothing but what their officers told them, and these merely turned them out at sundown to search the proximities of the city walls and beyond.

A few untoward incidents occurred: The venerable emerald-carver Rijak Majum committed suicide with a chisel in the antechamber of the Great Audience Hall, in the presence of the First Vizier—a thoughtless proceeding for whatever motive, as it was well known that the First Vizier abhorred the sight of blood ever since the operation he had undergone to fit him for high administrative office.

What his Benign Supremacy thought, if he thought anything, was not known. An older and less immediate

19

rumor (not without foundation) had it that his Benign Supremacy was dead these ten years. However, since on a previous occasion he had circulated a false report of his own death to see what reactions might ensue—this occasion was still remembered by many—everyone, from the First Vizier to the boy who led the blindfolded donkey around the sweep of the water-wheel, behaved as though the all-seeing eyes were very much open.

In this wise Calabrinia continued exactly as it had for many years: Crops were harvested, taxes gathered, offices sold, ceremonies performed, barbarians bought off, flood and drought endured, all under the aegis of his Benign Supremacy, for whom the city of eternal sun flourished by its slow green river, a lighthouse of knowledge, a beacon of commerce shining out to enlighten all the world, even to the borders of the cold, salt, infidel sea.

Two

. . . liken to a laidly worm
that warps about the stone.

—Child Ballad

A PHALANX of six scouts moved across the desert at a fast running walk. Their small ram-headed mounts were dun and mouse-colored, liver chestnut, brindled fawn and rusty black. The riders on high-piled sheepskin saddles were small also: lean, bowlegged, leathery little men with narrow eyes and straight black hair shiny as licorice. Whip-like mustaches were braided into their earlocks.

They had crossbows slung on their shoulders and flat skin water-bottles hanging at their horses' flanks; their only other provisions were a handful of dates. The horses, even more abstemious, made do with what fodder the desert offered and its alkaline infrequent wells.

Always hungry and always alert, the dun stallion of the leader pricked his black-tipped ears and raised his muzzle towards where buzzards wheeled in descending spirals. The phalanx shortened stride and turned in unison, picking up a high-headed lope to the ground center of the buzzards' circle.

They found a horse in the last stages of dehydration, a mere hide stretched tightly over a framework of bones held up more by the natural bracing of joints than any active effort. In the meagre shadow cast by the standing horse lay a person and a dog.

In silence the phalanx split and formed a circle around the buzzards' find. It was an anomalous situation, and must be examined before proceeding recklessly. Buzzards must live too, but if there was anything worth stealing, the Horse Nomads had first rights to it.

The leader, shorter than the others and younger, chewed the ragged edges of his mustache and fingered the hilt of his dagger. He dismounted, leaving the reins on his horse's neck, and cautiously edged down into the hollow. The person had a bag—he pinked it with the dagger-point and drew it gently towards him.

The dog raised its head and emitted a dry husk of a bark. The person clutched the horse's knee convulsively and sat up, mouthing unvocalized words through perfectly dry lips.

That, naturally, changed the situation. Kyril sheathed the dagger and took his skin water-bottle from his saddle. He held it out at arm's length—that committed him to nothing, and perhaps the person could then speak and explain itself.

Alina sucked, swallowed, choked, coughed, and finally got down a therapeutic dose. She turned her amber eyes, deeply sunk in blackened sockets, on the phalanx. The barbarous Horsemen of the desert. There was some important idea uppermost in her baked brain, and she clambered to her feet with Braseli's shoulder for support.

"Greetings, Horsemen," she croaked. "You arrive in good time, but pray to the gods through whose hands run the sands of the desert, that our message may not be too late."

Kyril snapped to attention. "What message?" he said. "Who's 'we'? Who are you and how do you come here?"

"We are the Most Excellent Prince Korab Khan, late subgovernor of the Isles; Alina, Princess Royal of Calabrinia; and suite," she answered with a ghastly simulacrum of full court manner. She waved her dry, jeweled hand with russet nails gleaming through dust. "It is imperative that we all be conducted at once to the presence of your chief, be he who he may."

Kyril glanced sidelong and laid a nervous hand on his

dagger. The grayest and most wolfish of the scouts murmured to him in a gravelly whisper, "Better do it. In case."

"Very well," said Kyril aloud. "We will take you, and your mount if she can travel." He ran his eye over the mare and found her a little weedy for her height, but with good bone. Worth keeping.

At sundown Ca-Shemam sat moodily on the tongue of his principal wife's caravan. Its gaudy blue and yellow paint, his own plume of scarlet horsehair and white horse-leather shirt and leggings embroidered with glass beads, all marked him as an important man. He gazed without joy at his son, come to report. "What now? You found no grass—no water—you got lost?"

Kyril was as impassive as his horse. "There is no pasture to the south this year. The water is bitter and there is little of it."

"Hah. So what is this, another mouth to feed?"

"I was delayed bringing this emissary from the City."

"Another one? They already paid the tribute...he looks dead, anyway."

"It is a she, and alive but crazy."

"Oh, very well. Never mind my grey hairs. Take your emissary to your mother, and if you are late, you won't eat. Go away."

Kyril wheeled the pony and trotted around the caravan to the other end, where a fire of chips smoked and sparked under a fragrant pot presided over by a square woman. Through nearly closed eyes Alina saw her approaching amid plumes of bitter smoke.

She must have fainted. She woke much later in an oblong wooden box painted blue and yellow—under her was horsehide laid over sweet-smelling dry grass that rustled. She tried to wake up several times, convinced that she must be dreaming, until she realized that she was awake, alone, in a caravan of the Horse Nomads. Above her head, almost touching her nose, was a row of china cups painted with pink dragons—everything else she could see was made of leather or horsehair or bone.

Lula her dog was curled up on her feet, eyes open and bright. She herself was naked, oiled liberally all over with a scented oil that eased the pain of her sunburned skin. In fact it was healing. In fact, she felt well, although disoriented.

She kept wanting to turn to Korab Khan, and remembering that he was dead (trying *not* to remember how dead when last seen). Had he not escaped with her into the desert and been rescued? No. But of course, she nearly died before the Horsemen found her; she must have been with Korab Khan on the banks of UnderCa but called back before the boatman came for them. She was certainly alive now—the blood beat in her wrists and temples with the regular thub-dub of her heart.

She levered herself to her elbows, but fell back half rolling; she must not be as well as she thought. Then the cups swung over her head on their bone pegs, back and forth, and she realized that the caravan was moving.

She got to her knees in the cramped space, and found her clothes had been under her head: unwashed, but meticulously smoothed, brushed and folded. She put on the silk shift she had worn under the gardener's smock, and wound up her braids (which had also been oiled). Under the clothes was her bag, with the handsome Temple jewels she had been issued for the Feast of the Moloquat, and—the box. Her mind cleared like the sky after a thunderstorm.

She was, after all, more than just a runaway.

Encumbered by Lula under her feet, Alina stumbled and lurched towards the front of the caravan. She saw daylight around the square back of the woman she remembered tending a fire.

The squat woman, without turning, said, "I'd go back where I was, if I were you."

Alina pressed forward to argue and Lula leaped up and knocked her backwards. At the same moment she heard the long snarling cry of a hunting panther, and the team of six desert ponies shied violently. The leaders reared

24

and backed as the woman reined them up facing the squadron of the Guard.

Alina flung herself back into the box-bed, and looked about wild-eyed as a hare. But there was no better place to hide than the painted wagon—to break and run in the empty desert was certain capture. She crawled under the pallet and lay as still as a fawn in cover.

Through the wooden boards of the wagon she could hear the coughing snarl of the leashed panther, and also a quick patter of unshod hooves.

"Soleba!" said a mournful voice she remembered from the night before.

"Ho," responded the squat woman.

"The City Guard halts us. Always something. Now they want a lost princess. Have you seen such a thing, wife?"

"A princess. Hmmmmm. What sort of princess?"

"The usual sort, no doubt. Tall, golden-eyed, of unearthly beauty, dressed in jewels and brocades."

Alina shook under the horsehide. The Horsemen were famous for their honesty—they never lied. Now she must be betrayed without remedy. She drew her double-edged dagger from her shift.

Soleba took her time. "No, husband. Nothing like that. I would have noticed."

"Anyone would," agreed the mournful voice. "Was she riding a dragon, oh unballed one, to travel in the desert where only we Horsemen can live?"

"A bay mare," snapped the guard.

"Ah, a bay mare? We found riderless bay mare yesterday."

The panther's snarl rose almost to a scream. The pitch of the guard's voice rose too. "Where was that?"

"Exactly forty-three *terks* hitherward, by sixteen *baithin*, approximately, whither. Sighting by yestereve's moon," responded Ca-Shemam helpfully.

"And where in this desert cursed by all gods is *that?*" demanded the guard. "Use civilized terms, can't you?"

"If I were civilized, your City would not need to pay me tribute. Look, I will point the direction, if you are not too citified to follow my forefinger."

There was a scuffle and shuffle, as of feet, hooves and paws, a ring of metal, a quick patter of more ponies surrounding the caravan. Alina kissed her knife-blade instead of breathing.

The caravan lurched suddenly as the ponies jumped into the rawhide harness and trotted on. She peered through the curtain of knotted horse-tails and saw them galloping back along the wagon-track on tall piebald horses, panthers loping alongside in leash. They must be under orders to search and find, not embroil themselves with Horsemen.

Alina pressed the cold steel of the knife to her mouth to stop her teeth chattering, and wondered why the panther hadn't caught her scent and found her. It must be the aromatic oils all over her—she must smell more like a herbolarium than prey.

She made her way forward to the box again. "Thank you, mistress Soleba!"

"For what?"

"For telling the Guard you hadn't seen me..."

"Ho. Seen *you?* They were asking for a royal princess, covered with silk and jewels. I saw only a bundle of rags, with a girl in them my son dumped here. Ca-Shemam told them about the mare when they asked. Whose fault is it if they ask the wrong questions and don't understand the answers?"

"Oh! So you didn't lie."

"Never," smiled the squat woman, showing a three-tooth gap and a dimple in each leathery cheek. "Who are you, in case anyone else asks?"

Alina shot a glance backwards, where the dust of their passing mingled with that of the Guard.

"Don't worry," remarked Soleba. "They only caught up to us because we just came from the Tribute Stone. By tonight we'll be far beyond where their fat piebalds can carry them. And if we meet with the Barak-Shar, there'll be no names asked or given, you may be sure of that."

"Oh," said Alina. "Well, then—I am a princess, in truth. But perhaps I should—state my business to—your chief persons."

"As you will," nodded the woman. She spat through the gap in her teeth, and guided her team around a dry wash. "Tonight will be soon enough."

So all that day Alina perched on the hard seat of the wagon in the shade of the leather top, and around her blew the eternal dry wind of the desert. Soleba watched the horizon and the tracks of the caravan ahead with narrow eyes, and answered such of Alina's questions as she thought worthwhile.

The scouts, Alina found out, rode ahead to hunt for grass and water. The caravans trundled along at a steady pace, just in sight of one another; Soleba indicated her married daughter's wagon, with a thrust of her lower lip. She herself, although to Alina she looked at least ninety, was actually not over thirty grasses and had borne sixteen children. She was quite proud that three had lived to grow up: Kyril, leader of scouts; Ryn, who had married into another clan and traveled with his wife; and Raisa, who had a child of her own that was the most intelligent, lively and remarkable creature ever seen. There was a yellow foal marked out for him already.

The dust cloud following the caravans was the main herd, mares and foals and loose horses herded by children, who learned to ride before they could walk. Horses were all in all to the nomads: pulled their wagons, carried them on forays, gave milk and hair and dung for fuel; were their most prized possession and their only means of survival.

When the sunset stretched like a stubble-fire along the horizon, Soleba checked her team of dun mares and swung them into a circle with the other wagons. Alina could see no advantage to the site, but when the mares were unhitched they nosed their way to the spring of bitter water the scouts had pointed out. They stayed biting the harsh scrub around the water while the main herd was driven up into the wagon-circle.

Alina perched on the tailgate of the wagon and watched. The women wore *boots*, clumsy rawhide shoes and leggings like men's—it was almost obscene. She wrapped the blue smock around her shoulders in the sudden chill of the evening, curling up her toes, and saw how the women built fires and set pots on them, balanced on iron tripods. Others fetched water from the spring in skin buckets, and took sacks of barley from the wagons. Apparently the whole grain was put into the sacks with two or three smooth stones, and was ground into coarse meal by the jolting of the wagon in the course of a day. An ingenious shift—Alina would hardly have thought of it herself, being accustomed to sending Aysha to the kitchens when she fancied something.

A toothsome smell rose presently on the sharp dry air, and the men straggled in to claim wooden piggins of stew. There seemed to be no particular etiquette—the women and children were sampling spoonfuls already—so Alina picked up a piggin and with gracious condescension addressed herself to the nearest pot.

She was astounded, too surprised even to resent it, when a large wooden spoon cracked sharply across the back of her hand. A stout young woman with apple cheeks and angry brows wielded the spoon.

"No work, no eat," she enunciated clearly, as though to the deaf or half-witted. She nodded towards a pair of buckets.

"Now, Raisa," said her mother Soleba. "Perhaps the poor thing doesn't know how to fetch water. Drinks wine and bathes in milk, mayhap."

Doubly stung, Alina drew herself up to stare down at the square nomad girl, shod like a plow-ox in spring. With an air of pleasing herself, she picked up the yoke, studying to carry it as gracefully as the heavy brazen disks in the Gong Dance of the Temple.

She followed a trail of hoofprints to the spring. The horses had muddied it, so she waited for the slow-welling water to clear. It was so shallow that she could only half fill the buckets dipping them sideways. Hyenas were laughing at the quarter moon when she staggered back to the caravans under the yoke, and received her supper.

It tasted remarkably good, for tough horsemeat seasoned with smoke and bitter herbs. A mount too old or weak to keep up was slaughtered for food, but the stew made from it was called by the animal's name, in gratitude: this supper was Whitefoot.

Shooting her eyes from side to side, Alina identified Kyril and Ca-Shemam, squatting around the fire gobbling stew as though they hadn't eaten all day, as in fact they hadn't. All the men, when they finished, carefully wiped the piggins on their leather shirt-tails and rubbed their greasy hands over their mustaches and braided sidelocks. Evidently that kept the plaits solid and shining, like black garden snakes.

"Now," said Ca-Shemam, clapping his hands so the glass beads on his shirt and leggings rattled, "let gather all the clan, and let us hear the tale of this nameless person who is many people at once."

Alina straightened up, wishing she had prepared for the moment better. The raggle-taggle clan of nomads gathered around the frugal fires stared at her with unwinking black eyes: matrons, horsemen, children, babies, youths her own age and a few elders. She felt as though she had forgotten a dance figure in the Temple.

"First may I know how is Braseli, my mare?" She meant it for simple arrogance and to gain time, although she was truly anxious about the mare, but it turned out a stroke of diplomacy. It was evidently proper to put the welfare of her horse before any official embassy.

Ca-Shemam's face realigned in less lugubrious wrinkles. "A fine mare, hardy and docile. She does well. For tonight the herdyoungers have blanketed her and fed her a mash of yogurt and barley-meal and crushed dates."

"But what is she doing here at all?" hissed Raisa, bronze baby on her lap. Her brother Kyril elbowed her, and her husband looked another way.

"Why don't you start by saying who you are?" prompted Soleba.

"I am the princess Alina of Calabrinia," she began.

"Is that Korab Khan?" Kyril struck in, pointing to Lula at her feet. "And the rest?" His father elbowed him in turn.

"No. No, I spoke of a—a former companion, being then delirious with the sun and thirst. I am alone—I came alone on a desperate mission." All the beady black eyes, reflecting firelight, were fixed on her. The wind whistled through the hide coverings of the caravans and puffed acrid smoke in her face. She gathered her ingenuity. "Lord Ca-Shemam, you who hold your wide desert lands under his Benign Supremacy, know then..."

"I, hold land, under whom?" broke in the chief with gentle surprise. "The sun has melted your wits, has it? The golden godking pays us, the Horsemen, so he can keep his City. We are none of his, neither squatters nor traders, but herdfolk."

Out of the saddlebag on which he sat he pulled a flat bone with incised markings on it. "This shoulderblade is one *tyrie*, that is grazing for sixty-three horses. I, Ca-Shemam, hold ten such, and the other chiefs in proportion. Once a year we meet beyond Hath and adjust claims. I have never heard that the Golden Statue claimed even one *tyrie*."

Alina was taken full aback, like sitting down on a cushion that wasn't there. She was sure she had learned in her lessons that his Benign Supremacy owned all the world and leased it out to everyone according to his desserts. But the Horsemen did not lie (no wonder they weren't traders) and Meerkat Lobum, who saw to the education of princesses, certainly did.

Ca-Shemam went on. "The yearly tribute we receive is very useful. With it we buy caravans from the wheel-wrights of the wooded mountain valleys, pots and stirrups and iron bridle-bits—but we plied the desert from the sea in the south to the headwaters of Ca long before his Benign Supremacy, as you call him, and will always."

"Ah!" cried Alina, seeing her opportunity and diving into it. "But you need wander no longer! His Benign Supremacy is dead! I have his heart, in a box, preserved in salt and orrisroot and camphor! Why should you not conquer the city and take it for your own?" She left a dramatic pause. "I, Princess Royal, will lead you!"

Ca-Shemam stroked his mustaches. No one else did anything, except Soleba, who spat sizzling into a camp-fire. The wind whistled in the silence.

"Is he dead?" inquired the chief mildly. "The Golden

Image seemed much as usual, and the profile on the coins we received was uncorrupted—unaged, even."

"Of course! But in reality, in the flesh, his Benign Supremacy is dead, I will show you his heart!"

"Ah well. We only know him from the coins, which have no heart. Yes, we could overrun the City. In truth, we dream of it, think and talk of it around the fires while the sad air of the empty desert chills our feet. It is the dream of all the horde.

"We think of hooves pounding down the white-paved avenues between pillars of malachite and chains of gold. We think of jewels filling our saddlebags, of wine in goblets, spiced soft meats and white wheaten bread, dishes of pale porcelain like the moon, and silver bowls to water our horses." He fell silent, and all the Horse Folk sighed in his silence.

"But all of that can come true! I tell you the godking is dead, dead, dead! The Guard will crumble like stale crusts under the forefeet of your horses!" Alina spread her arms so that the woolen smock made blue wings behind her. "Will you not take it if I lead you to it?"

Ca-Shemam became even quieter and more melancholy. "No. Because then the City would be no more. Always the Horseman yearns for the City, but he can never possess it, only approach and retreat again. He can destroy the City, but not keep it. The Horseman is stronger and older than the City, but not its master."

Alina swept an unbelieving glance around the circle of faces. Soleba looked monolithic. Raisa scowled. Kyril's obsidian eyes glittered on her, but he said nothing. The others swayed a little, like shadows of horsehides blown in the wind.

Alina held her tears with royal pride. "Then I shall leave you and go on as soon as may be," she announced.

"Don't be a fool," said Soleba. "You wouldn't last a day. The hyenas would gnaw your bones—that's all there is to you anyway. Have some more stew."

Ca-Shemam pronounced. "I suppose you must stay with us now, because you have to. Can you do anything useful at all?"

Alina answered, each word distinct as though pricked in thin metal. "I can embroider silk in cross-stitch, crewel and blackwork; make lace with the cushion, pins and hook; do drawn-work, faggoting and smocking. I speak the six languages of the known world, excluding the guttural grunts of the ice savages to the far north. I compose classic modes of poetry and ballads in three languages, with exquisite calligraphy. I perform all the ritual dances of the Temple, court pavanes, and popular round-dances; play the sitar, tambourine and bone flute. I can bring down marshfowl with envenomed darts at a hundred and twenty paces. I also make sweetmeats with rose petals and white violets and angelica, love-apple marmalade, and take portraits."

The chief raised his hand and sighed heavily. "These graces are of little use. Can you milk a mare or bleed a stallion? Flay a carcass? Tan a hide? Stitch bootsoles? Poultice fistulous withers, treat whooping cough or pull a tooth? Can you tell direction by the stars and weather by the leaves of thornbushes?"

"No," she returned. "But if those things are accomplishments suitable to principal persons among you, I shall learn them!"

Ca-Shemam sighed still more deeply. "You could go to the shaman for instruction. You have knowledge, and perhaps discipline, to an exquisite degree. We have neither, but depend upon good sense and remember what is useful to us."

Alina was not sure if she was a pet or a prisoner, an adopted daughter or a burden—she seemed to be all of these by turn, but nothing of importance. The Horse People accepted her news, but they altered the seasonal routes of the caravans no more than the flocks of migratory birds that sometimes flew overhead.

The clumsy wagons trundled across the desert, from the Southern Sea where they wintered, towards the summer grazing of the grasslands to the north. As summer wore into the hottest moon, they moved along far into the night, but stopped for several hours in the heat of the day. Always the wind whistled, near and far and lonesome, so that Alina hardly knew any more that she heard it, unless she awoke from dreams of lying abed in silken sheets in her room, with the fountains playing on the honeysuckle vines at the lattice.

She learned to file her nails short, oil and butter herself against the sun, tie a handkerchief over her nose and mouth against the blowing dust, even to wear footgear among the thorns of the desert.

With other unmarried younglings, she drove the herd. She learned to quarter the desert on horseback looking for the slight signs of ephemeral water: the appearance of vegetation, the movements of animals, even the aspect of the horizon above moist ground. She learned principally from Kyril, who appointed himself her mentor.

At first she was surprised at the frequency with which water holes turned up along their line of march—but Kyril explained that the horde followed the changing course of an underground river to survive.

"Do you mean UnderCa, the river of Death?" she asked him.

"It is under Ca, but we live by it."

"What do your dead do, then?"

Kyril shrugged. "What they ought and what they must—that will be clear enough when I die."

Alina put the same question later to the shaman, the only person with much time for questions. He was lame, too twisted of spine to sit a horse, which was why he was shaman. His name was Jas, and he was cheerful and full of chatter. He drove seven grey mares to his caravan stocked with packets and bags and bundles of herbs and worse things.

"Yes, yes, yes, a good question. Particularly in your own case. These adoptions are always a problem! Well you may wonder how to get to the proper afterworld. It is told in one ballad that..."

"But what do the Horse People themselves do?"

"Yes, yes. I hadn't forgotten your question. Do you see the sky?"

It was night, and the desert sky was immense, horribly so for Alina, accustomed to see it limited by walls and roofs, sliced into sections by tall cypresses; the moon was stridently full and the stars blazed like Meerkat Lobum's diamond waistcoat. Alina nerved herself to keep staring, lying back on the wagon seat to see the stars. She felt neither happy nor sad, only present; time did not seem to pass, as the desert flowed backwards around her and the sky swung around its crystal sphere.

"Yes, yes," murmured Jas, "See, do not look. The long spiral runs there, too many stars to count—you there, Kyril, stop skulking behind the wheel and come here to be educated. Yes. That is the Last Road, wide enough for all the Horse People to ride abreast forever."

"Then what?" Alina demanded, sitting upright and rubbing the small of her back. She had taken a fall breaking a filly that day, and it hurt.

"Isn't that enough? Yes, yes, that's enough. But a good question. You're a bright girl, more brain than last year's bird's nest, which cannot be said for Kyril. A good youngling with a bow, if you show him exactly what to shoot and what not—I wanted a horned viper alive, and he brought it to me shot through the head."

"Why did you want a horned viper?"

"For potions. Spells are well enough in their way, though lately they don't last the way they used to when I was a youngling, seem to spoil somehow—maybe it's the weather. But give me a sackful of live horned vipers and I'll brew you a potion to raise the dead."

"How long dead?" demanded Alina.

"Not long, yes. Depends on the weather. The potion doesn't keep well, either. You can dry it, though, and it's still good for headache, if it doesn't kill the patient. You never know. But I like to have some at hand. Why don't you and Raisa hunt up a horned viper or two tomorrow noon?"

So the next day the two young women set out—Raisa with the tiny solemn child bound to her back—to look for vipers during the noon halt. Kyril made an excuse to go too, lounging behind them on the dun horse in the baking sun.

Bent double in the straggling thornbushes that clawed at her borrowed coarse robe, Alina turned over stone after stone with a forked stick. Raisa, less assiduous and encumbered with the baby, sat on a rock and gazed around her sullen-eyed.

"There," she pointed. "See if your Highness can catch that one."

There was a tracery on tiny claw-scrabbles in the dust, and the minute furrow made by a tail; following it with her eye, Alina caught a flicker of movement like the shimmer of heated air. She darted her stick and pinned the creature behind the head.

Lula, nosing after, leaped back and barked, a shrill yip of alarm, but too late.

The trapped creature, jewel-green and gold, flipped its flexible tail over and stung Alina's wrist before she could help it. She cried out with the sudden sharp pain and put the back of her wrist to her mouth.

"Yiiii! Did it sting you? Donkey, didn't you see it was a thorn dragon after all?" wailed Raisa, scrambling farther away with the baby. "Jas! A thorn dragon!"

Kyril spurred the dun to Alina's side in three bounds. He hauled her over the saddlebow and galloped for Jas's caravan. "Oh my princess," he groaned, "does it hurt?"

"Not now," she murmured drowsily. "I feel nothing—I can't see..."

The horse leaped wildly to the spur, but when Kyril laid her on a horsehide in the shaman's wagon-bed, Alina was already senseless, rigid and flushed, pulse pounding.

A bunch of yellow dog-violets bound to her wrist withered at once. The inert body responded to none of the convulsives and revulsives applied by the shaman, nor yet to the pleadings of the distracted Kyril. At last Jas sent him to gather a certain rare and powerful herb, one Jas was reasonably sure he wouldn't find, in order to have quiet.

After the first pain of the thorn dragon's sting, Alina felt as though a gentle warmth suffused her veins. Muscles and ligaments softened, as though she were dissolving in a warm and perfumed bath to the sound of wind instruments playing. Her scratchy horsehair robe and shameful boots were gone, as were her bruises and scratches—even her still-small but swelling womb seemed to have been abandoned with her clothes.

Then a girl came and sat on the edge of the bath (which was of translucent green stone like chyrsoprase, and had no bottom) and poured scented oil into it; she gave Alina a great soft sea-sponge to wash with, and almond-milk soap. She was beautiful, with short burnished-gold hair and eyes green as beryls, seeming no older than Alina herself. She laughed pleasantly when Alina thanked her.

"Those greasy horse-blanket things must be unbearable," she said. "Isn't this better?"

"Oh, much better. But I don't altogether understand."

"That's all right," said the girl. "You may not, at first. But you must get out of this, and the sooner the better. It is all a mistake, we are waiting for you in the city!" She smiled a most enchanting smile, showing white little kitten-teeth.

And then the bath vanished and the two of them were walking in a walled garden, the girl in the same straight shining white shift as before, but Alina found herself clothed in a magnificent gown of peacock-green with an iridescent train of sapphires, emeralds, opals and turquoises trailing behind her and a tall crown of gold wire and diamonds on her head.

They strolled through the garden bright with caged singing birds, past pools of still water and heavy flower-heads bending to the marble walks with the weight of their perfume. Tapestries of blooming vines hung on the sunny walls. But then Alina noticed great cracks in the walls from foundation to coping, and that the basins too were cracked and draining, the goldfish floating belly-up in stagnant dregs; fat black slugs gnawed the roots of the lilies.

She turned to the girl pacing daintily beside her like a

tame gazelle, and all seemed again as it should be, only a little blurred as if by distance; but the girl's figure was as sharp as colored glass.

"You are the princess," she said, "which is to say, the centerpiece of a mosaic cemented in place. It is not for you to think of being otherwise, as a bird, a leaf, a fish, a pear. Come now to the Court of Turquoises, and you will see how in the mosaic of the nations of the earth a space gapes, the missing piece, linchpin and keystone..."

Alina stopped, spoke with a terrible effort, as though her tongue and teeth and jaw were locked: "No. I will not look on the Court of Turquoises ever again. When I am queen I shall have it destroyed. No."

Three

As a last resort, kill or cure, Jas funnelled the last of his powdered viper-potion into a quill and blew it delicately into the large vein at the bend of Alina's elbow. Then he left her.

Two days later she woke, furious, and hungry as a moulting hawk.

"Yes, yes. From the sting of the thorn dragon comes madness and, commonly, death. Survival is not unknown, but rare. Hallucinations? Yes, yes. Very likely. I wouldn't doubt it. Anything of general interest? No? Purely personal application? Ah! Yes, yes. No, how should I know whether they were true visions or a figment of your imagination? I am a barbarian but not a fool—you must wait on events to find out. Raisa is sorry to mistake the track of a thorn dragon for that of a horned viper—she must have been thinking of something else. Yes, you may get up. In fact, you must, to satisfy Kyril. For two days he has been dogging my wagon and making my old mares fidget."

Alina rolled over just as the front wheels hit a rut and she half fell out of the cupboard bed. Jas's bent back on the seat wavered in her vision, but she clutched the wooden edge of the bed until her sight cleared. She was light-headed, irritable, shaky—but in her right mind and her own body, familiar but maltreated. And yes, the secret contents of her hard little womb, all present.

She staggered to a hatch and pushed it open, directly over powerful sand-colored haunches and a long thick tail oiled as glossy and black as the rider's mustaches and plaits.

"Kyril!"

The horse bounded like a stag and danced sideways at the canter, as Kyril essayed his idea of a courtly salute. He achieved a certain utilitarian grace, if not elegance. A smile like a water course opening in the desert crossed his saddle-leather face.

"Thank you, Kyril, I'm all right now and you can't hang around the caravans all day. Go make yourself useful somewhere."

Even that pleased him. He waved, spun the stallion around like a dust-devil, and galloped ahead. The wagon-team shied and Jas muttered. Alina noticed Kyril sat a high-piled war saddle with crupper and breastplate, and carried a small round shield at his saddle-bow; he wore a leather helmet shaped like a coffee-pot.

"Is Kyril showing off?" she said aloud.

"No more than usual," returned Jas over his crooked shoulder. "We have crossed Hath. From now on we keep the caravans close together, riders armed for battle, and scouts well ahead and to the sides.

"Oh!" said Alina, sitting suddenly back into the cupboard bed. "Do the Guard come so far from the City?"

"The Guard! I'd like to see which of their fat pintos could follow within 300 *terks!* But from Hath northwards we may meet Barak-Shar."

Jas said nothing more for the moment, quieting his lead mares. Alina lay back on the hard pallet, her bag under her head. Barak-Shar—the mysterious Barak-Shar which figured in Korab Khan's scheme. The word sounded ophidian, a slither and a hiss, but attractive. She had learned nothing of such people in the schoolroom, and tried more than once to draw out Jas on the subject in the days she lay recovering strength.

But the shaman eluded her questions with the same agility he showed getting his twisted body up and down from the wagon seat. "No, no. You have trouble enough, carrying around a dried godking's heart. Dissension and strife, that's what it brings. You don't need Barak-Shar, not you." Or again, "Ask Kyril, why not—for all the time he wastes riding at the tail of my wagon, he may as well make himself useful. Now it is time for the midday halt, so you can continue telling me about harchitecture, which interests me greatly. Now what sorceries hold your harch from falling?"

"It's 'arch,' not 'harch.' And it isn't magick at all, that's what I was trying to explain. Look." Alina got up and squatted on her heels on the floorboards of the wagon. "Take these blocks of dried mud. See, alone each falls, wanting to reach its mother the earth. But I can make two piles—like this, so each rests on another. And then I take these five like this," (laying them side by side on the back of her hand) "and fit them between the piles. Each still desires to fall, but since no one block will cede place to the other, the impulse must run sideways to the pillars and perforce the arch hangs in the air."

"Yes, yes." Jas narrowed his eyes to mere wrinkled crevices, delicately poking the little arrangement until it fell and building it up again with brown bony fingers. "And will it work in large?"

"The size makes naught. Except that levers and pulleys must be used with heavy stones. The arches that hold up the dome of the Temple are higher than the height of ten men; each block is bigger than this wagon. I do not know how it was done, because only the theory is a proper study for princesses."

"Is that what it is to be a princess, to know and be unable to do?"

The tone was colorless, but Alina felt a criticism. She pulled the coarse robe from her left shoulder to show the royal Moloquat emblem.

"Yes, yes. We do that with foals. But a brand shows age, ownership and breeding, not what the horse is good for."

Unable to think of a good answer, Alina asked, "Why do you want to know these things, when the Horse

People have no desire but to trek endlessly back and forth across the desert?"

The shaman moved the blocks around again. "Ah well. Yes. Yes. You can speak only out of your own mouth. But knowledge adds no weight to the packsaddle, and may come in handy some day." The blocks fell and bounced on the floorboards.

"I shall ride now. The swaying of the caravan makes me sick," Alina announced. On the heels of her pettish words came the clangor of Soleba's steel triangle, the signal to move off.

She whistled up Braseli, who came cantering to the tailgate, tossing her head and nickering. Alina fed her a date and mounted bareback, guiding the mare with her knees to where her saddle and bridle hung on the side of the caravan.

She tried the exercise of bridling and saddling a horse while riding at a canter, which she had been practicing before the thorn-dragon sting. A nomad twelve-year-old could do it faster, but she did it.

The terrible sun was huge, a red ball filling the western sky, but the heat of the oblique rays dispersed in the dust-laden air instead of striking straight down like hammer blows. The wagons went three and four abreast at a brisk trot, with scouts before and herds behind; already the trampled camp-circle and the blackened rings of fires were invisible in the wind-combed sand.

There was nothing to see but the train of caravans painted red, apple-green, orange, bright yellow and blue. The desert was the same from camp to camp, no tree, valley, pond, house or field, unchanging as the sea. If this was to be her portion, she did not know whether she must go mad with the monotony and dreary discomfort of it, or be ravished by the austere beauty of the infinite horizon, the beryl-green sky above, and the thin wisps of burning cloud between her and the sun. For a moment, she felt balanced on a point, about to choose—but Braseli shied sideways, rattling her copper nose-chain, as Kyril's sweat-darkened dun stallion shouldered up beside her.

"Princess, will you ride with me ahead of the dust?"

asked Kyril. "I am scouting three *baithin* whitherwards, and would be glad of your company."

The moon rose, yellow as apricots in the orchards of Calabrinia, and the desert was bright as day but all changed. The dusty grey-green foliage of the stunted thornbushes, hardly distinguishable from the ground under the flattening weight of the sun, reflected a pale brilliance like opals and cast jagged black shadows in the moonlight.

Every stone, even the wheel-ruts cut by the wagon-wheels of another year, were laid out in black and silver calligraphy, as though empty desert were written all over in subtle inks invisible by day.

"How lovely!" Alina said aloud. "They never let us go but a little way into the desert, hunting—they said it was death for nightfall to catch you."

"For the princes of the City, whose blood is lukewarm bran-mash, it would be. But you don't still think of returning? You can't, you know."

Alina shrugged. "I wish I could paint this."

"Paint it, like a wagon? Where could you get enough paint to cover the desert?" Kyril turned his face, like a silver and black enamel mask, to her.

"Paint—oh!" She had seen no pictures among the nomads, though they loved bright colors and patterns; she had thought it must be a taboo, as the Rat people would not eat the river sturgeon. Perhaps they never thought of pictures?

"I mean, draw lines on a surface, like that outcrop of rock, and color in the outlines so it looks like the real rock."

Kyril obviously was still bewildered.

"Some time I'll show you."

"You've shown me so many things," said Kyril, warmly and huskily. "So many. I...I..."

Alina watched him out of the corner of her eye as the horses jogged gently. "Nothing to what I could show you and teach you," she said in silken tones. "Perhaps you don't agree with your father that the old ways are the only ways? Perhaps it is you who can break out of the old rutted wagon-tracks?"

"With you I could!" Kyril cried so that his horse jumped and snorted. "I will buy you a blue caravan with red wheels and beds of pure sheepsfleece and enameled tin drinking-cups! I'll..."

Alina was disconcerted. She wished to goad Kyril to action, but not, precisely, to the immediate purchase of a bridegift.

"By this time next year, I will be of age to claim my share of the Citygold and take a wife! You shall have the finest caravan of all the clan, and a hundred chestnut mares all with white blazes and stockings!"

By this time next year I'll have a child—whatever else happens, thought Alina. What shall I do with Kyril? She looked sidelong through her lashes. Truly, after weeks spent in the desert, the oily, wiry, warm-hearted little man was not unattractive. The obvious course had many advantages, especially for a fifteen-year-old stray princess notable more for warm blood than a cool head.

"Why wait until next year?" she whispered. "Painted wagons and white-faced mares are well enough. But there are other ways to please a woman, even a princess." She touched Braseli with her heel and set off at a gallop for Kyril to follow, leaping a thornbush to show off.

But in a quarter mile she heard only the drumming of her own mare's feet and the screech of a disturbed burrowing-owl. She drew rein and turned. Kyril stood where she'd left him, the dejected droop of his shoulders visible even at that distance.

Then Alina set spurs to the mare in good earnest and galloped her temper into the moon-shadowed ground. It took her a long time. Before the fit of outraged pride was quite over, Lula dashed in front of her with hackles a-bristle. Braseli slid to a stop on her haunches and fetched up foam-covered and sweating.

They had come to a long spur of the Blue Mountains reaching out into the desert. It was black and featureless, casting a shadow so deep it looked as though you could fall into it and never hit bottom; but in the middle of the blackness was a tiny red tongue of fire.

Now the eternal wind carried the smell of wood burning and the high thin whinny of a horse. Braseli raised her head, nostrils wide, and answered with the shrill call of a lonesome mare.

Too late Alina slid to the ground to cup her hands over the mare's muzzle; a chorus of deep howls broke out of the darkness, and humped black shapes crossed the winking eye of fire once and again. They could not be Horse People, who fed no dogs and burned no wood. Might they be merchants traveling to some reasonably civilized outpost? Might they be the fabulous Barak-Shar? Should she risk approaching the camp to see who they were and what her chances might be?

The mastiffs were loose and running. She must either ride boldly into the camp at once, or flee. She hesitated one more moment, listening, then mounted and whisked around the way she had come. She put spurs to Braseli and the mare bounded forward, hard little hooves striking sparks from the flints. Lula fled before them like a ghost-dog, making (Alina hoped) for the caravans.

They galloped a mile, two miles, three—no horse could keep up that pace. Braseli's breath whistled in her throat, sides going in and out like a bellows. Were the hounds loosed just to frighten strangers and called back? No, they were baying steadily on her line, deep-voiced and bell-mouthed, and gaining—they were hunting her!

She tried to force the mare on at speed, but Braseli put up no more than a jog, and the hound-music was closer. Alina turned in the saddle, called Lula to heel and halted.

Tongue between her teeth, she took one of her little envenomed bird-darts, made of peeled ashwood and fletched with hoopoe-feathers. She spat on the steel point like a pen, nocked the arrow to the stiff short bow, and waited. The moonlight mocked distance and perspective, but she could make out a loose line of wolfish shapes. The hounds did not see the bow, or thought it of no consequence; they divided as though to take a man with a sword, attacking from both sides.

Alina emptied her mind of distractions, according to the precepts of her archery instructor, and let the arrow fly when it wished. It took the lead hound in the throat as he ran. The second stopped to tear at him, so it was the third hound that got the second shot in the chest and fell rolling.

Three more came on together, but she pinked two of them and the last turned tail letting out a high whine of defeat.

Alina remounted, and made the mare keep the best pace she could behind Lula. The moon set and the night turned velvety black. As the cool dew dropped down, the desert came to life, with peepings and chirrupings, buzzing drily. Yellow eyes regarded her thoughtfully from a hole. A bat flittered down the wind above her head.

With no moon and no dogs, she thought, I'm safe. Lula will find the caravans.

Just then she realized the regular pad-pad-pad she heard was not an echo of her own animals' footsteps—one slow, silent-running hound still followed his quarry, and his hoarse panting sounded like cloth tearing.

The spent mare stumbled in terror and fell to her knees; the dog pressed forward. Lula leaped back to slash his dewlap, but the mastiff brushed her aside with his heavy shoulder, not even troubling to snap. Bravely she worried his flanks, but the huge dog came on like Nemesis.

Alina jumped from the saddle as the mare struggled to her feet; she groped on the ground for a stone, a thorny branch, anything, but sand ran through her fingers. She stood up, futilely putting out her hand against the enemy, and—

"Take this," said a cool voice over her shoulder, and a hand laid the thin shaft of a poison dart on her palm. Alina put it to the string of her bow and shot directly into the panting maw of the dog. For a moment she thought she had dreamed arrow and shot, as the padding feet bore the bulk onward still—but it was a dead weight that knocked her to the ground as it fell.

Lula flung herself on the carcass, and it was several

minutes before Alina could drag herself free and look to see who had spoken. There was no one in the huge dark; but the remembered voice wore the form of a slim girl with a cap of burnished hair and cool green eyes, and now it seemed as though the voice said also, 'Everything must be paid for; everyone pays. Hurry now to the cart-folk, before the bill falls due.'

There was nothing, no track or trace; except a curious mark, burned black, like the prints of four fingertips close together on the click hot shoulder of the mare. It looked like the Moloquat brand.

In the last dark before dawn, leg-weary horse and slumping rider, bone-thin hound with tail between her legs, stumbled into the night-circle of caravans. The embers of old campfires, like nests of glow-worms, gave her a tepid welcome; and Soleba perched on her wagon-tongue grumbled, "So late chasing jackrabbits? It's almost time to hitch!"

"No," said Alina, a raw catch in her voice. "I discovered a camp—they had terrible dogs that hunted me all night!"

"Dogs? Dogs?"

Heads were thrust out of caravans. Bachelors sleeping rolled in horseblankets around the fires woke and jumped up. Soleba struck three blows on the sounding steel triangle to call up the herders. "Barak-Shar!"

"Kyril, take this mare," said Soleba with deadly calm. "Raisa, some tea. You, Chaka, find Ca-Shemam."

In the time it took Alina to drink a cup of sage tea and catch her breath, most of the Horsemen gathered around her asking questions.

It must be the Barak-Shar. Only they had such dogs—merchants would not be so far from the roads, and they kept only cur-dogs. Who else but the Barak-Shar?

"Where exactly was the camp?" Ca-Shemam asked for the fifth time. "The Blue Mountains have more spurs than a troop of Horsemen. There are gullies. And draws. And saddlebacks."

Alina could not tell him. She could have given accurate directions to a stranger in the hundreds of labyrinthine corridors, underground passages, halls, stairs, galleries, chambers, balconies, courtyards, towers, closets, dungeons, kitchens, amphitheatres and hidden cubbies of the royal Palace; but the desert was a blank to her. She had not yet mastered the Horsemen's elaborate oral tradition of pathfinding.

But she could see the place clearly in her mind's eye, floodlit by the moon; they must know it. She seized a dead coal from the edge of the fire and sketched roughly but accurately on the hem of her robe.

"Look," she said, making the details with a sharp edge, shading with the flat of the coal. "Here is the descending ridge of the mountain, with three twisted pines like arms. Here is a dry watercourse with boulders like a wall."

The Horse Folk stood around and stared as though she had gone mad. The outlines of mountain, trees, stream and boulders to them were random marks on a piece of cloth.

Jas said, "Up too soon, out too late, yes, yes. Too soon. The poison of the thorn-dragon is long and subtle."

Soleba took her by the shoulders and pushed her into the wagon, onto the pallet and horsehide.

Outside, Kyril raised his voice unasked. "The seeing enchantment failed and we saw nothing. But perhaps the princess saw what she says. The arrows are gone from her quiver, and the mare is most strangely marked on the shoulder."

"She may have been seeing things," grunted Ca-Shemam, "and shooting at them, too. But who's to know what things or where? All the same, we will swing sunward as far as possible, keep sharper watch and closer formation."

"Lula," Alina whispered to her tight-curled dog on her feet, "I told so many lies to all of them in the Palace—from Meerkat Lobum down—and they nearly always believed me. But now I tell the truth no one believes it!"

Then the deathly sleep of exhaustion fell like a shovelful of sand on her puzzled brain. She did not feel the wagon jolt into motion.

Alina awoke at the noon-stop, a short and apprehensive one. Kyril came for his ration of date-meal mush, but neither sought nor avoided her company. She thought him less clownish in his offended dignity, but had no stomach for reopening the business just then.

Until far into the night the caravans rumbled at the fastest pace their clumsy wooden wheels could be forced, with two extra horses to each team bowing their sweating necks into the breastcollars. Alina stayed in Soleba's wagon, pounding strips of meat thin. She pinned them to the top of the caravan, to parch in the sun.

Soleba pointed to a line of clouds on the horizon. The mountains. They must turn toward them again, because they were headed for one of the few fords by which a wagon could cross Ca—he ran in rocky gorges for most of his course until Bel joined him, to become a broad and mighty river washing around three quarters of the City and her fields.

Of course the Barak-Shar also knew the ford—but the Horse Folk had no choice but to cross it to the northern grass-plains, until winter rains brought green to the desert again in spring.

They detoured a prudent distance around a waterhole where lions were resting. The Horseman and the lion respect each other, and leave each other strictly alone. But the horseherd stampeded as soon as it got downwind of the lions, and time was lost gathering all of them up. Not even for fear of the Barak-Shar would they abandon the herd.

Kyril, wooden-faced, brought Braseli up to his mother's caravan on a rawhide tether. It was she, heedless of the cries of the herders, who started the stampede. Alina tied her securely to the footboard of the wagon; the mare jerked her head back, switching her tail and sweating.

By then the mountains could be seen, a dark line under the piled clouds.

When at last they stopped, Alina fetched her share of water, then went looking for Jas. Kyril was with him, about to leave on night patrol—when he saw Alina he rode away.

"Jas," she said. "Who are the Barak-Shar, really? Did they set their dogs on me? Why?"

Putting aside the bones he was arranging, Jas gave her his sidelong attention. "Barak-Shar? Oh, yes. I think so, yes, yes. As for why, they do that. Because they are Barak-Shar."

"Who *are* they?"

"Why, any common skulking bandit so ill-advised as to follow your cousins, Princess," said Jas kindly. "In fact, you are by way of being a Barak-Shar yourself."

"What?" gasped Alina.

"Oh, yes," said Jas, giving up entirely on his little bones, "it is well known that the royal house of Calabrinia needs to spit forth its more rebellious offspring from time to time. They become outlaws. Not if Calabrinia can catch them first, naturally."

Alina thought of Korab Khan.

"Those quick of foot and eye, lucky or foresighted, more blessed with henchmen or less burdened with scruples, escape and gather bands of like-minded persons about them."

"Do you mean I'm not the first to leave the city?" demanded Alina.

"Not at all. Nor the first to attempt to enlist us as allies. Nor is it unknown for the blood of Calabrinia to ride with us for a season, to improve its seat on a horse. But it is not common, I will say that."

Alina took this in. "What do the Barak-Shar do?"

"Plunder and murder, chiefly. With rape, arson and slave-trading if the opportunity offers. We try not to offer."

It was an uncomfortable conversation, with the eternal wind blowing, blowing words who knew where and to whom. Alina lay on her thin pallet, with her bag under her head. Perhaps it was the atmosphere of apprehension that had hung all day over the Horsemen—perhaps it was the hard lump of the rosewood box under her ear.

At any rate, Alina slept and dreamed she was waking, with the round solemn eyes of Raisa's baby looking through and through her, while Raisa took up the robe Alina had sketched on with charcoal. In the distance she saw the fabulous Barak-Shar riding gryphons with feet of gold and the ghost of Korab Khan at the head of them, shivering and complaining that the wind blew through him.

Then all these things vanished away and Alina dreamed again of the girl with eyes of green beryl who said, "Remember there is a price to pay. Everyone has to pay the price, everyone but myself."

In her sleep Alina asked, "Who are you?"

"You may call me Anthea," said the girl, smiling with small pointed teeth as white as milk.

Meanwhile, a pair of burrowing owls, hunting together, skreeked in rage; they objected on principle to any predation but their own. Under their flight lay a fresh-killed horse, a tough little mouse-colored horse of the nomads; the rider lay beside it, dead too. He had been husband to Raisa, of the clan of Ca-Shemam, but the owls cared nothing for that. They kited up a long updraft over another rider on a dun stallion, making the horse blow softly out his nostrils and the hair on the rider's neck prickle.

The dun stallion pointed his ears as the owls glided away with their skreeks. Kyril listened, with the keenness of desert-bred ears and the sharpness of fear. He uttered the high yip of a kit-fox, once, twice and again, and got no answer.

Then he heard it: the chink of metal. Iron shoes scraping flint; iron bits jingling in unquiet jaws; the clank of spur against stirrup and the faint ring of rowels. The pocketful-of-coins jangle of chainmail. The *chkkk* of a sword loosened in the scabbard.

Without seeing or being seen, Kyril knew they were the tall reckless-hearted warriors of the Barak-Shar, armed with steel and probably half-drunk on white maize brandy or worse.

He made his horse circle step by step; not soundlessly, but making no sounds that the ear could interpret as the measured gait of a ridden horse. Not until he was out of earshot did he ask the stallion for all the courage and wind and speed that he could give, and more if possible.

Alina woke from bad dreams to the reverberating clangor of the triangle beaten feverishly, and the booming voice of Ca-Shemam: "Circle, circle, circle! Saddle and arm!"

The caravan swayed and almost overturned as the team plunged violently and pulled up short; Soleba stood on the box with the reins in both hands.

"Shut the tailgate!" she cried.

Alina scrambled to obey. With sleep and the night chill numbing her fingers, the leather thong would not go over the peg. She lost it altogether. She leaned out. The wagons were drawn up facing in, their high sterns forming an overlapping palisade in the shape of a weir; in the center women were turning the teams and unhitching them, men running and shouting, panicky horses rearing and backing. Alina climbed out on the tail gate and came face to face with Braseli, all eyes and nostrils, throwing herself madly against the tie-rope.

Alina pulled the loose end, snapping out the knot, and leaped on the mare's back. She set her knees into the muscles behind the shoulder as Braseli reared and whirled. She felt like a bird on a strong updraft; it was her chance to escape from the Horse Folk, yet she was reluctant.

But she was not unnoticed.

"Alina! Get into the circle! Go back!" shouted Kyril, in the act of saddling a fresh horse.

"Traitoress!" cried a shriller voice from a caravan. "Go to your kin you brought down on us!"

A pebble took Alina on the cheekbone and she put her hand to it. The mare threw up her head, jerking loose the halter-rope.

"Alina!" called Kyril, galloping on the fresh horse out of the wagon circle. "Come back!"

But his father rode his stout grey across the opening and blocked the dun stallion.

And then a trumpet-blast over the thunder of iron-shod hooves announced the coming of the Barak-Shar like a winter hailstorm, and Alina on her bolting mare rushed into the darkness like a spark fleeing the fire.

Four

Think, in this battered Caravanserai,
Whose portals alternate are Night
and Day...

—Omar Khyyam

THE sun rose redly through the smoke of burning. Braseli had run far on her breeding, remarkably far with a steel arrowhead in her flank, until her heart stopped between strides and she pitched dead to the ground.

The fall, partly softened by the bag, stunned Alina and she lay still. Lula whimpered about her and licked her ears, until at last she shivered and opened her eyes. But when she tried to get up, her right arm and shoulder would not bear her.

Swaying to her knees, right arm clasped in left hand, she faced the sun rising out of the smoky wall to the east. She had come too far to see the glow of the flames, only dark and oily smoke blowing on the horizon.

Her dead horse lay stretched beside her, neck and head stretched bravely to the west. The price, a voice echoed in her memory, had to be paid. The four-fold black mark on the sticky dull shoulder of the mare—was Braseli the price? It was a high one. Braseli had been hers as a foal; always answered her call high-tailed and prancing, carrying her onward when even the huntsmen tired; always biddable and easy-gaited, faithful to the end.

Careless of her present plight, Alina put her head on

the unmoving flank and wept. As she had not for Korab Khan—but that was different. Obscurely she felt it to be so, although only the Horse People would understand.

But she couldn't go back to them now. Even if the clan of Ca-Shemam survived, even if they did not blame her for the attack (she was not sure on that point), she would never be able to catch them up on foot. She turned away from the east wind, on which greasy black cinders rode like bats.

Many leagues to the south lay Calabrinia; but even if wishes were hippogryphs and would whisk her there in an instant, she dared not return without an army at her back.

Northward also the desert stretched for league on league. But to the west the lower hills of the Blue Mountains knelt on the horizon, promising at least shade and water; perhaps even, if she won so far, roots and berries to eat. The thought of wild cloudberries, tart and cool, pale red like drops of spring's blood, got her painfully to her feet.

"In any case," she said aloud to Lula, "we can't stay where we are."

And can we stay where we're going? inquired the mournful brown eyes; but Alina made a sling for her right arm from the halter-rope, and hitched the bag over her sound shoulder. For the last time she bent to caress the mare's neck and almost fainted when she straightened up.

But already buzzards assembled above her head, and hyenas would soon be on the blood trail—she must be gone. With her left hand on the dog's neck to steady herself, she began walking due west, the sun squarely hot on her back. It was not a hopeful project, but Alina was not willing to lie down and die.

Hours or minutes or days spun around her, until it seemed as though she trod a ball always spinning away under her feet and never advancing—she thought once that the golden-haired girl wanted to walk beside her, but Lula kept between them and showed her teeth.

She was terribly thirsty.

Then Lula was not with her; puzzling over this—she

knew her horse was dead, but thought she still had her dog—she staggered on. Presently Lula came under her hand again, but pushing steadily against her, so that each off-balanced step shifted her path to the side.

A few paces more, and shade fell around her like cool water. Still the dog nosed and pushed her, down a narrow ravine; and now she could smell water. In a shallow cave or grotto, hardly more than an overhanging shelf of rock, ferns grew around a tiny pool of clear water.

Drops trickled out of the granite and collected in a hollow scooped in the rock by the dripping water, brimming but not running over the lip.

Alina and Lula drank without troubling themselves to explain the phenomenon. The water was good, cool and faintly flavored with iron and copper. When they had drunk they lay on the sandy cool floor of the grotto, out of the sun.

"What have we here?" said a voice. It was a hoarse voice, almost a whisper as if long out of use, but kindly, with an underlying amusement.

"I am Princess Alina of Calabrinia!" she cried. She tried to get up, forgetting the shoulder. "I pray your name and condition."

"Why then I am King of the Painted Rocks," returned the voice, with gentle amusement patent.

Alina struggled to half-raise herself and look at the speaker. He was tall and stooping, burned black with the sun; of any age, but his sun-whitened hair was thick, and the beard was dark where it grew from lip and chin. His face was thin and beak-nosed, and wore an expression Alina could not fathom. His rank was equally a mystery, for on his lank big-jointed frame hung only a spotted yellow hyena-skin.

He had a basket on his arm, which somehow reassured Alina, although he carried also a stout and knotty staff.

"Your Highness is welcome," he said with the sketch of a bow, speaking the tongue of the city with a drawling accent that Alina could not for the moment place. "Make my humble dwelling your own. As you have already done, with exquisite sense of what is due to your Highness."

"I...thank you."

"Don't be afraid, little sister. I won't hurt you, or the dog either—don't growl so, cousin," he added to Lula, who immediately clamped her jaws and lay down. "Do you search for something, run from something, or, like the moon, do you make a change for the sake of changing? Not a fair question," he answered himself. "You are hurt. Perhaps your appearance has some relation to the battle of the wanderers and the bandits last night, or rather, early this morning?"

Alina nodded, with caution. "Do you—know anything of that?"

"No, not I. There are charred wagons east of here, and half-roasted bones; also tracks leading north and east. I might have asked my four-footed cousins the hyenas, whose tracks and whence? But they are too courteous to answer with their mouths full."

As he spoke he put his staff and basket down on the sandy floor. His long cool fingers went directly to the point of jagged bone and swollen hot flesh jutting under the sleeve of Alina's shift. She grimaced, and he said, "That wishbone won't heal for many days. Unsuitable as the accommodations may be, I fear they will have to serve. Matter is such a small matter after all, is it not. And yet will have its due."

He sorted through the basket, then thought better of it. "I was not expecting a guest. I must make a few arrangements, so if your Highness will excuse me..."

"Wait, please, who are you? I don't even know what to call you!"

The lanky figure paused, half in sun and half in shadow, a fantastic piebald scarecrow. "Since there is no one else here, it hardly seems necessary to call me at all. But if you must or you will, I am the hermit of the Painted Rocks.

"I meant, what is your name?"

56

"My name lies buried a long way away." With the same half-graceful, half-burlesque sketch of a bow, he went out. She saw then that he was slightly lame, missing three toes on the left foot.

Alina pulled herself to her feet and stared around her. Now she saw a few things—an empty gourd, a flattened pile of dry grass—which must be the hermit's, but by no means did it look as though anyone lived there.

She tottered to the mouth of the cave and looked out. The shadowy purple mountains looked very close, with night pulled as high as their shoulders. The shadows were long, each stone and spike of vegetation underlined with inky black. All around the ravine reared tall standing pinnacles or rock, weathered and carved fantastically by the stinging wind; they looked like towers, waves, fountains, trees, castles, ships, glowing with the hot colors of the desert; ochre, sulphur-yellow, vermilion, umber, a veined coppery verdigris and dull black. The Painted Rocks.

She heard the whoop and giggle of hyenas, not far away, but by now her broken collarbone was pulsing like a mad hummingbird, sending waves of sickening pain through her whole body. Whether the hermit was sane or not, disposed to help her or eat her, she could go no farther.

She sank down in the corner again, her bag under her head, utterly forlorn. The grotto smelled of water and bitter greenery and stone—after a moment she realized that for weeks, waking and sleeping, she had been surrounded by the smell of horses, and she missed it.

The collarbone healed badly. The jagged bone-ends knitted fretfully in a large tender knot at the juncture; Alina found the arm painful and almost useless.

The hermit, with a certain exasperated patience, applied plasters of mud and leaves to the shoulder, and fed her; for the first day or so, nothing but a broth of meat boiled without salt, and after that berries, seeds of many kinds, occasional starchy roots and a drop of wild honey.

He went out gathering daily, and must have eaten his own rations then—at any rate Alina never saw him eat. Lula kept her company during the day and went out at dusk to catch short-tailed rats away from their holes.

They all three drank the rusty water that filled the stone cup in the grotto four times a day. It was not very much, and man, girl and dog spent the heat of the day lying or sitting on the damp cool floor. Alina tried to teach the hermit chess, using pebbles on the sand, but he either could not or would not learn. So they talked, about many things.

Uppermost in Alina's mind—and a safe subject—was her mare Braseli.

"Travel afoot is slow and laborious. I noticed that when I lost my toes. But perhaps you feel as the wanderers do about their horses?" Alina nodded. After a little while he half-sang, half-spoke the following words:

> *Four hooves shod with air*
> *Are stones unmoving.*
> *Nostrils that breathed speed into the wind*
> *Are closed.*
> *The mane full of light is furled forever.*
>
> *Flesh is light, speed and wind*
> *For a season.*
> *Earth calls, falls to earth.*

Alina found a grief shaped and sung easier to bear, and was grateful.

"I was once a singer," he explained as if apologizing. "It needs the whistle and trapdrum, really. He drummed a hasty breathless rhythm with his fingers on the empty gourd. "The heart-beat of the hunted deer, so—." The beat changed to a rolling blunt-fingered gallop. "The ram-headed desert horses, hard-ridden—." Abruptly he stopped. "I dwelt once in gardens of bright images, plucking metaphor ripe and simile fresh from their stalks. I said then that metaphor is truth—and truth metaphor as well."

"And now?" Alina prompted.

"And now I shall go and see what my private pantries, granaries and stewponds provide for this day's nourishment," he replied, unfolding his bony length and rising.

At another time she tried to find out more about the Barak-Shar, but he said he had no interest in them beyond avoiding their notice. "I do not make a study of piles of dead leaves the fall wind sweeps into any corner that will hold them. I would rather walk in the woodland paths, a garden, or even this desert that seems bleak at first glance; to see how the living things comport themselves: root in soil, stem, leaf, flower and fruit. I watch which insects frequent each plant, which animals eat them; I learn their properties, oils, juices and essences, what soils and weathers favor each."

Such strange ideas attracted Alina; but something else was more important. "All this talk of woods and gardens—when did you see such things? Have you not always lived in the desert, I wonder?"

"Your eyes narrow, oh clever Highness. I do not ask why. Yes, I came here from another place, a short time past as the Chronicles of Calabrinia count the years in decades, but a long time to myself—I will even tell you where. I was born in the Green Isles, I and my brother, downriver from the city. There Ca spreads as wide as a small sea and divides his slow stream among the islands. There are singing birds there, and pigmy mammoths with long ivory tusks; the apples served you in Calabrinia, golden red with a freckling of green, are from the Isles."

"Oh, now I place your speech! You sound like Elyse, the old Queen of the Isles."

"Since the Treaty of Al, queen in the Harem of Calabrinia—of course. Dear Elyse. How was she when you saw her last?"

"Quite mad," Alina replied, still watching the open humorous face closely. "She spoke only with her birds."

"I am sorry to hear that. Or perhaps, she may have made the better choice. My brother also spoke with birds, but I have spoken with no one for years."

Alina touched possibilities quivering under the urbanity of the surface conversation. Sitting cross-legged in her shift, the worse for much wear, she could see her own arms and legs the same color, and nearly as thin-boned, as the toasty-brown gazelles of the desert. The hermit was knottier, thinner and browner still, and more uncouth of dress; but she thought she could see the shadow of what he must surely have been. She waxed diplomatic and perspicacious.

"Since news of Calabrinia interests you, my good— hermit, perhaps I should inform you that, while on the surface all runs smoothly as a water-wheel, his Benign Supremacy is dead. Has been for ten years." Alina drew herself up, crook-shouldered.

The hermit slouched as comfortably as before, and a friendly grin divided his skull-like face. "That is news indeed, although not altogether unexpected."

"To prove it, I have his heart with me, dried and preserved."

That wiped the grin from his lantern jaws. "Have you?" You'd better leave it at the hyenas' rock. An ill trick to play them, but better than keep it! Even if you had..." His hand went to where the scruffy fur pouched at his rope belt.

"I had thought rather, my lord Prince of the Isles, to propose an alliance..."

"Absolute nonsense! Who put that idea into your head? No, don't tell me! Absurd!" He got up and paced the tiny cave-floor, neck bent to avoid hitting his head on the low roof.

"I take it my offer is refused?" said Alina, hiding her disappointment under a haughty tone.

"Unreservedly. Make no mistake about it. And do me the courtesy to drop the 'lord Prince.'"

"Do you not wish the freedom of the Isles? That might be easily done, a condition of alliance."

"No, not that either. Freedom cannot be proclaimed, peddled or foisted. If they won't be free of themselves, they can't be made so."

"I think you are madder than Queen Elyse," said Alina through stiff lips.

The hermit stood still and silent for so long a lizard

popped out of a crevice and ran across his foot. It caught a gnat and ate it, then paused, throat pulsing creamy-white under its jaw.

"Little sister," said the hermit finally. "Here in the desert the air is thin and pure and the food dry and scanty. There is little to confuse the mind, and to speak at all is to speak truly. But a true answer sounds foolish if given for the wrong question. And it is less use still to answer questions that are not asked." He gave her a look between desperate and considering, then appeared to reach a decision.

"Still, you are no longer a fat and glossy princess bathed daily in perfume and ass's milk—come with me a little way. We will go slowly."

He dipped the gourd into the stone cup, and balanced it half-full on his palm. As he ducked under the lintel of rough stone, Alina followed, cradling one arm in the other.

There was a sort of path among the standing stones, lightly traced by bare feet. It led to a hollow at the base of a jagged orange tooth of stone, where a handful of soil had collected out of the everlasting wind. In the pocket of soil grew a plant of modest narrow foliage, grey-green and hairy. From the center of the whorl of leaves rose a slender stem with five bell-shaped flowers, the tenderest sky-blue and most delicate recurved form that Alina had ever seen.

"Oh, how beautiful!" she cried, dropping to one knee to see it on a level. "I never saw such a flower! What is it called?"

"No one calls it," said the hermit, tipping the half-gourdful of rusty water into the dry soil around the plant. "It grows here only, and is called nothing at all. You have never seen it, you say. But if it grew everywhere, in the gardens of the city, Princess, among purple lilies as tall as a man, drifts of orange blossom, perfumed curtains of honeysuckle hanging armslengths thick, under branches laden with gold-crowned, narcotic Moloquat flowers— would you see it then?"

"I might," insisted Alina. "But all flowers have names,

even if no one cares about them. What is the name of this one?"

"Oh, as to that, I suppose dragons know. If you find out, you can tell me. Provide it be soon."

"And how would I find out?" Alina returned, more for the sake of the argument than in hope of information.

"What you wish to know, you will find out. The first step is always to decide what you wish. You can choose to float with the current or oppose it, but if you merely set out to swim, you will be swept downstream willy-nilly."

Alina turned abruptly away. "Oh, if it's only a matter of wishing! I wish there were a basketful of Moloquat flowers here, so my shoulder would ache less!"

The hermit offered her his stick to lean on. "Would not Moloquat essence harm the child you carry?"

Alina stopped as though a chasm had opened in front of her. At three months—less!—she couldn't show that much! "What makes you say that?" she asked.

"It is obvious. Otherwise you would not have got this far. There," he added, pointing, "is the hyenas' rock, in case you are inclined to take my advice about that heart. The packs pass often to leave and receive messages."

Alina shook her head.

"Well, then, a little farther on there is a thicket of hareberries."

In silence they picked and ate tart blue berries, until Alina, reaching awkwardly to the back of the ledge, froze.

A thorn-dragon, green-gold and shimmering, had also come for hareberries. It shot its forked tongue in and out nervously, its stinging tail coiled, enormous dragonfly eyes flashing like cut sapphires in the sun.

"Don't be afraid," murmured the hermit. "You have survived the sting, now you are immune. Hold out your hand and see if he'll come to you."

Holding her breath, Alina uncurled her fingers; not so much trusting the hermit as fearing that if she snatched her hand back suddenly it might provoke the creature to fly at her face.

The thorn-dragon, no longer than the hermit's bare foot, arched its spiny back and cocked its head; when she made no further movement, it stepped toward her dirty, purple-stained hand, going more sidelong than straight, with a absurd high-stepping gait. Alina kept still by a great effort. The thorn-dragon hopped onto her hand, turned around three times whisking its tail, then ran up her arm to the injured shoulder.

Alina felt the tiny claws where it perched—then a warmth seemed to radiate from it, not a surface heat like the sun on her back, but a blood-heat from deep inside, like a strong soup. Sweat broke out of her skin in huge drops dried instantly by the desert wind.

The pain left her broken collarbone; not dulled and tamped down as by the hermit's poultices, but absorbed, sucked out of the marrow and torn muscles and swollen flesh by the mysterious heat. She saw the livid color fade from her bruises and half-healed cuts closing to fine white lines; finally the calceous lump on the collarbone dissolved like sugar in hot tea.

The hermit, watching closely, said, "Has he done you a courtesy? Then prick your finger with a thorn and offer it to him."

Her extended hand lay among the armed branches of the hareberry. With the other hand she bent a twig and pressed a sharp blue-tipped spine into her thumb. All the while the strange warmth coursed through her, until the thorn-dragon ran down her arm again and darted its forked tongue at the bright red drop welling out of the ball of her thumb.

Just as suddenly it tired of human society and scuttled back into the crevice behind the ledge of rock.

Alina joyfully stretched her thin brown arm out, up, way above her head. "It's all cured!" she cried. "But how? Why did the thorn-dragon cure it?"

The hermit shrugged. "Who knows why dragons do anything, from the tiny thorn-dragons to the great five-clawed imperial dragons of the spheres? They keep secrets. It is known they like brass, and gold, and copper, and meddling. Silver and tin repel, but magick attracts them."

"I don't believe in the great dragons," said Alina.

"Where do they come from, and why?"

"It is said," the hermit replied reluctantly, "that they come here for the sun, because it's very cold, the other place. What other place? Why is it cold? I don't know that, either. All answers raise more questions, anyway. Now what about these berries? Tomorrow the ripe ones will have burst, and wasps will come for them."

After that Alina grew daily stronger, while the hermit, curiously enough, seemed thinner and more skeletal with each day passing. He took her on his gathering expeditions, showing her how it was he lived where it seemed no one could survive for a day. He taught her to find her way in the desert, avoiding the notice of larger predators and conciliating smaller ones, like serpents, who were aggressive when provoked.

Food-gathering itself was more laborious than difficult: it was a matter of stripping a few seeds from a stalk here, picking a tiny prickle-covered sour fruit there, scraping the hairy peel from a small tuber somewhere else. His desert was very different from what she had seen from the back of a horse or the seat of a caravan.

At first Alina wanted to set snares for gazelles, or at least for the huge-eared hares, but the hermit would have none of it.

"If you made a kill, the hyenas would take it. Besides, where would you set the snares? Why should gazelles walk into them?"

"I would find a water-hole."

"Each water-hole belongs to a lion. He does not dispute a drink with a passing caravan, especially if a sick colt is left for him. But you could not expect a welcome as a permanent tenant."

"Is this a wasteland or a royal palace? The etiquette seems fully as complicated!"

"The more you know about anything, the less simple it seems. I came here to gain wisdom, and I know less than ever."

Alina asked another question. "If it is against the rules

to eat meat, what about the stews you fed me when I first stumbled into your grotto? For which I thanked you then and thank you now," she added, not to sound ungrateful.

"You needed it then to live. And it was your mare, in any case."

"Oh. I ate horsemeat with the wanderers. But not my own Braseli. And you made such a lovely song for her!"

"She carried you loyally while she could. Do you think she would grudge her flesh when it served her no longer? Would you grudge a friend in need some old cloak of yours you had already discarded?"

"No. I suppose not. But the Barak-Shar, do they follow these rules?"

"They don't live in the desert, only make forays at the edges."

"Where do they live?"

"In the caves that honeycomb the Blue Mountains—look, here is the twelve-fingered foliage of the chia—see, it is nearly ripe. One teaspoon of chia seeds keeps you on your feet for a day's march. Hold the basket while I cut the stalk."

Alina held the basket steady, but inwardly she was restless; the new things she learned and new ways of seeing old things sat uneasily on her stomach. And she did nothing, nothing, as though Korab Khan died for naught; and his Benign Supremacy ruled still as though his own death were nothing; and she feared that she, Alina, might be for nothing either.

In this fretted state the year rolled over the peak of high summer and began its invisible slow decline. Alina was well and healthy, but more than before resembled the gazelle of the desert: her eyes huge and unquiet in her thin face, her brown limbs fleshless so that each ligament traced a clear path over the bone, the braids of her hair like fine dried grass.

But the hermit was failing. Finally one day he stretched his skin-covered skeleton out and stayed in the grotto. He refused the sparrow-rations of food that Alina, all in a

65

fright, brought him; Lula laid fat rats anxiously at his side; but nothing availed.

He did not appear to suffer, and would talk, about anything but himself, but he would not get up. He would not taste even the pure wild honey Alina had gotten with no few stings.

"You will die!" she accused, eating the honey herself with fingers mud-daubed over stings.

"Most probably."

"It is an offense to the gods!"

"What gods? There are so many. Made of stone, of gold, of leather and cloth, even of flesh. Some I have heard of are invisible, clothed in volcanoes or whirlpools. Some like a sacrifice of fresh butter, some prefer blood. Each rules a village, a tribe, a patch of territory. But which has jurisdiction over the others? Which claims the desert?"

"And what is the answer to all that?" asked Alina, exasperated.

"How should I know? But shall we not now ask questions of you, princess that you are? You must take your nasty little bit of dry meat, that heart, somewhere. Also your bellyful of imprudence. Where? You have tried the wanderers' hospitality and cost them dear. Do you think of going north, to Lake Tal? It is a long way. The villages of the Hopgangers are closer. They are stolid as cheeses, but with their greed for a lever you may move them to your purpose. There are also traders on the roads, sharp men and awake to their own interest—but they are few, and not fond of risks." He paused, breathing so shallowly that his chest hardly rose.

"Beyond there are only the Four Ports of the Western Ocean, whose fisherfolk are willful and stout-hearted; the bread the women there bake is salty as tears. I do not know if you would care for it. But I advise you not to take the heart of his Benign Supremacy among the Barak-Shar. They are easily excited, and I can't answer for the consequences."

"Who asked you to answer for them?" she snapped, and curled up with Lula in her own corner of the grotto.

When morning came she was no longer angry. But

there was no one to be angry with except herself, for the hermit had died in the night—probably early, since the body was stiff and cool as the air of dawn.

"Oh, Lula, didn't he make a sound? A gesture, even? Couldn't you have waked me?"

The dog flattened herself to the ground and whimpered. The hermit had had the last word.

Alina wept then: a weakness she had learned to avoid since she had taken her first tottering steps on the marble pavements of the Courtyard of Princesses. But here there was no one to batten on her weakness, and she wept as long as she had a mind to do so.

But even tears end at last, and the problem remains as it was. As a first reaction, she though of staying in the grotto and contemplating the little plants that grew amid the Painted Rocks.

But it being the general custom of pregnancies, once begun, to proceed, hers advanced as steadily as the sun inclined to the meridian. Counting on her fingers, she calculated that she must deliver in the second raw month after the cusp of winter. And then what?

Picking up her bag, she felt the hard lump of the rosewood box within it, and a revolution of feeling seized her. Could she so lightly consider sending the Empire of the Sun rolling like a child's hoop? What of her promises to Korab Khan? So far she had done nothing but cover a few leagues of wasteland. Was she a princess of the royal house of Calabrinia, heiress to the Dragon Throne, or a wandering beggarmaid? The grotto seemed no longer a refuge but rather a shameful retreat. Of course she must go on.

She drank off half the water in the hollow stone and left Lula the rest. A handful of chia seeds, hairy-husked without and pale and sweet within, she wrapped carefully in a mullein-leaf and stowed in her bag along with the gourd. Already the grotto looked uninhabited again.

She was ready, too late for a farewell to the only person she had trusted since parting with her maidslave Aysha.

The stiffness of the body had begun to pass off. Something gleamed in the relaxed fingers of the hand laid on the breastbone. Gently she pried them loose. It was a silvery-grey freshwater pearl, irregular in form, about the size of a date, bound with silver wire.

Should she leave it? Or had he died with it in his hand for a purpose? The nerveless fingers held the pearl so lightly that now it rolled down the deep channel between ribs and dropped at Alina's feet. Clearly it was a going-away present. She picked it up and put it in her bag.

"I shall keep this, Lula, in memory of the Hermit of the Painted Rocks."

Then, for the day wore on, she rolled as many large stones as she could over the entrance to the grotto and piled smaller stones on top of them before she set off.

In spite of the hermit's mocking advice, she saw only one possible destination: the mountains. There lived her kinfolk, lords of the Barak-Shar. Although they did not bear a good name, when they realized who she was they must receive her, and could not be indifferent to her news.

She started on the path through the Painted Rocks, her short shadow before her and Lula trotting behind. She passed the ledge where the thorn-dragon had healed her shoulder; the nook where the blue flower, nameless, clung to its sandy bit of soil; the hyenas' rock.

Walking with a long, unhurried all-day stride, she saw and understood a hundred things around her. That hole belonged to a whipsnake, shiny black as a Horseman's mustaches, longer than she was tall but no thicker than her two thumbs.

Around the blue bowl of the sky circled three vultures; so far from thinking them birds of ill-omen, she knew now they were as necessary as the slaves that swept out the Palace and more dignified, going about their business without giggling and fooling.

Those ugly thick plants, opening yellow cups to the sun between spines as long as a tailor's bodkin, were juicy and delicious if the spines were singed off.

In the tumbled scree on the far side of the Painted Rocks lived a colony of short-tailed rats—yes, there was the look-out rat on his hind legs, looking extraordinarily like Meerkat Lobum. He whistled the alarm; pebbles rattled under dozens of scurrying rat-feet hurrying to holes. Lula whined, but stayed beside her mistress.

Alina planned to keep the setting sun in her left eye in order to reach a creek tributary of Hath at the end of a day's march; but she had started late, and her legs were not as long as the hermit's. She caught herself hurrying; reminded herself that only with a regular pace could she hope to arrive.

To shorten the journey, she summoned up thoughts to march in time with her step. His Benign Supremacy, universal lord of the world, was dead. Dead like a mouse in a trap, like a runaway slave impaled, like an incompetent vizier beheaded. The godking dead, and perhaps the vultures keeping vigil above her knew it; while she was alive and on foot in the desert, although no one knew that but herself. Bearing, furthermore, a whole future dynasty.

She was at liberty, perfectly free to do anything at all, provided she avoided the obvious dangers of death by misadventure. What might she do? What might she not do?

She recited her horoscope as she walked, in the heavy silence under the wind's everlasting whistle. It seemed to her that the Dragon Throne was not immovable, but rocked like a thistlehead in a thunderstorm, gripped by many hands. Korab Khan had dropped his corner; the hermit declined to take up his at all. She, Alina, youngest and most valiant of princesses, held up the entire weight of it. This thought was colder comfort than she expected, but sustaining in a thin and bitter sort of way.

She said aloud to Lula, who cocked her ears: "It is told that in the beginning of things, the world was a jumble of rock everywhere to the shores of the sea contained in the crystal sphere of heaven. His Benign Supremacy found the sea and heaven very well as they were, but the earth in great disorder. He commanded the rocks to arrange themselves into mountains and withdraw into ranges, and the rocks did as they were told; all but one mountain sitting at the junction of the three rivers Ca, Hath and Bel, where his Benign Supremacy was minded to construct a city.

"Three times he besought the mountain to remove to a proper place, and three times the mountain refused. Whereupon his Benign Supremacy blasted the mountain into a million million grains of sand that fled screaming over the whole earth like a sandstorm," (here Lula's ears flattened) "making deserts where they fell. But Calabrinia was builded of the gold, copper, iron, jade, opal, turquoise, beryl and marble that was left.

"It is told also that one day as the godking was carried in his litter, a kitten chasing a butterfly frisked across his path and stopped to stare round-eyed at the golden litter flashing with gems. The bearers (all underkings themselves) would have trodden it under foot, but his Benign Supremacy strictly commanded them to halt, for the kitten acted correctly according to the nature of cats, and a godking could do no more and no less."

Comforted with these and other exalted thoughts, the princess walked the sun down the sky; she trod the hot sand with hard-soled bare feet and endured the burning rays on her thin brown body covered with a shift no longer white but all the colors of the earth, and ragged as a December leaf.

By dark she came to the sandy tributary of Hath; it was dry, but there was a fugitive dampness under the north bank. With her hands and the lip of the gourd, Lula helping with eager forepaws, she dug until water began to seep into the bottom of the hole. When there was enough to reflect the new-risen moon, she scooped up a gourdful, ate her chia seeds, and slept on the creek bank under a holm oak. She curled up in the leaves like a fox.

Five

...*the sable throne behold*
Of Night primaeval and of Chaos old!
—Alexander Pope

The springs of Hath rose cold and sparkling from the Blue Mountains, ran merrily down into broken low hills, and lost themselves for ten months of the year under desert sands. Waterless, this channel was the easiest approach to the mountains: a spillway of round boulders overgrown with creeping sedges and dwarf junipers. Above it, ranks of aspen and spruce swelled up to the first range of peaks.

By paths his grandsires trod before him, Morphelius Pashan, styled Lord of the Barak-Shar, conducted his ragtaggle troop laden with booty. He did not lead, but rode last to round up stragglers and avoid a possible knife in the back. His tall sorrel thoroughbred never ceased dancing, tossing its red-nostriled head and biting the jeweled shanks of the bit.

Morphelius Pashan himself was as tall and red-haired as the horse; his features were aristocratically aquiline, his eyes dark and flashing. He wore a nine-foot red silk sash around his exaggeratedly slender waist, gold hoops in his ears, heavy gold and ruby rings on his fingers, gold buttons and lace on his rather dirty black velvet jacket, and a codpiece of gilded leather.

His troop of fifty or so was well-mounted, the horses

rough-groomed and ill-mannered, but with a look of breeding about them somewhere.

The same could not be said of the men, a haphazard lot of jack puddings swept up from the four corners of the world, as different as pigs from hens; yet Alina, from the undergrowth in which she lay hidden, saw a strangely similar stamp to them, like an invisible brand that marked them out. Those that rode with helmet at saddle-bow had shaved and tattooed heads; all let their vari-colored beards straggle over rusty iron breastplates.

At the head of the troop rode Pantasilea; a lady of such royal habit that she owned no surname. She was a tall, full-bodied woman, with hair of midnight-black inclining to purple, great rolling black eyes and wide full-lipped mouth. Her robes of crimson satin were gorgeous with gold embroidery picked out with beads of jet, pearl and marcasite at the bodice, but somewhat tattered at the hem where they fell over the flanks of her horse nearly to the ground.

Her hair was braided up for riding with strings of pearls, and tassels of pearls knotted with bullion swung from each earlobe. She ostensibly carried no weapons, but as the occasion demanded she was more than likely to pull an extraordinary collection of knives, daggers, poniards and *miséricordes* from different hiding places about her voluminous person.

The men would follow her anywhere: she was their totem, mascot, leader and *belle idéale*. For visibility she rode a cream-colored horse with flowing white mane and tail (a stout gelding up to her weight), ornamented with knots of crimson ribbons and silver bells. Her reins she held high in gloved hands as she sat sideways on a sort of howdah covered with red leather; from this position she could see both forward and back.

The motley troop made a fine racket singing, shouting, swearing by uncouth godlings and insulting each other unto the fifth generation. They rode through hazelbrakes and birch clumps four and five abreast, trampling a swath a blind bearcub could have followed; they took no precautions, being in their own territory.

Alina had heard them long before they came in view, and prepared her appearance. Beside the banks of the brook that would become young Hath, she popped up with dramatic suddenness, rosewood box in hand.

Pantasilea's long-sighted eyes with stiff black lashes blinked twice as they picked her out. The Lady pulled her gelding up on his haunches as she let out a squawk like a bluejay. "A woodsprite! A salamander! Enchantments! Avaunt!" She whipped a bezoar set in gold out of her ample bosom and held it up to avert the evil gaze.

The men-at-arms fell back in some disorder as Morphelius Pashan thrust between them on his big restive horse. He reined in at the side of his consort. "What's that?" he asked. "So skinny, ragged and black as it is?"

Alina, furious, was about to apprise him of her exact rank and privileges, when she caught the eye of someone sitting in a tree over the heads of the Barak-Shar. It was the slim girl with smooth gold hair and wide beryl-green eyes. She put her finger to her lips in warning, and nodded to Alina.

Meanwhile the Lady waved her bezoar a couple of times more and said "Avaunt!" again.

"It doesn't go away," observed Morphelius Pashan in a dissatisfied tone. "Can it be human, do you think?"

"Perhaps so. Perhaps...perhaps it is a poor orphan," said Pantasilea, the enormous sloe eyes filling with immense tears which affected the band like white brandy. "We shall adopt the poor thing and take it home!"

"Yes, yes, we shall!" cried the men sentimentally. "Here, Pannicart's got a saddle with pillion, take the thing up!"

"And besides," the Lady added, "Perth is always complaining that he doesn't have enough help in the kitchen—here, creature, we won't hurt you."

Still the strange beautiful girl held her finger to her lips and smiled. Alina was ready to burst with fury, but the Barak-Shar, even their captain, were not after all quite what she had pictured to herself in the long walk over the desert. Perhaps it would be better to go slowly, pretend to be a beggarly orphan just for a while.

So she allowed herself to be swung up to the croup of Pannicart's horse and set on the pillion.

"Hup, then!" bellowed Pantasilea. "Excelsior! Onward! Grown roots to match your wooden heads, have you? March!" She struck the stout gelding with the gold-knotted rein-ends and he swung off at a side-wheeling pacing gait.

The rest trotted or cantered behind, except Morphelius; his excitable horse bounded like a rubber ball from side to side, making more height than distance with every stride.

Alina did her best to size him up, from her jouncing perch on the rump of Pannicart's nag, but it was hard to come to any firm conclusions. Her cousin, was he? In what degree?

Meanwhile the troop struck up a song, the melody and words of which were uncertain but the chorus stirring enough:

> *Hola, hola ho!*
> *Gola, gola, wo!*
> *Zora lora, tecufora,*
> *Hola, hola, ho!*

Alina wondered where the girl with green eyes came from and where she was going to—but from her place crushed against the greasy leather back of the purple-bearded Pannicart (he at least was surely no relation), her field of vision was limited. For all she knew the girl rode with the band.

At the rattling good pace set by the Lady Pantasilea, the Barak-Shar arrived by mid-afternoon at their double front gates in a fanfare of bugles.

The home base was a stockade twice the height of a tall man, made of pine logs with sharpened ends. The gates opened on a quadrangle of packed dirt, several hundred paces square. It was by no means empty. Hogs snuffled in piles of this and that, and chickens scratched after the hogs. Some ragged children raised a hoarse cheer on the entrance of the war-band, which was acknowledged with a few copper coins flung by Morphelius Pashan.

Bruised and breathless, Alina slipped off the rump of Pannicart's horse and rubbed her numb legs. Slaves in iron collars came running to take horses and packs, help the Lady to dismount, unbuckle Morphelius Pashan's cartwheel spurs, and conduct Alina to the kitchens in the back of the main cavern of the Barak-Shar.

From there she could appreciate the full luxury and squalor, pomp and chaos ruled by the exiled son of Calabrinia. The Barak-Shar had built nothing, it seemed, but the rough stockade. All else was the work of Hath in past ages: a network of natural caves, with chambers and corridors, a stream with pools and waterfalls running through them, rock chimneys open to the sky here and there, deep sinkholes to throw garbage in or use for dungeons—even the kitchens were fortuitous, making use of a natural escape of gas which burned bluely in a large rock depression.

Here a scuffle of slaves held skewers to the flame and jostled each other's stewpots. Greasy smoke curled out through a crack in the ceiling of the cavern.

"Here, you, asleep with your eyes open? Take this— and this—and this!"

Alina found her arms full of an assortment of drinking vessels, from rough pottery to gilded bronze, including a brass-bound oxhorn and a porcelain cup. Clutching them, she was propelled into the great hall, shoved from behind by a majordomo bent sideways under the full wineskin on his shoulder.

This hall was a natural cavern long and echoing, with an uneven roof of red stalactites, and a roughly smoothed sloping floor. The upper end of it was a sort of dais, set with two elkhorn chairs; on the back of one perched a large vulture with a fluffy white neck-ruff from which its long naked red neck craned in all direction. Below the dais were trestle tables wherever they could be set level.

The hall had no outlet but the low mouth of the cave, across which stretched a shallow iron trough of hot coals. The wind blew the smoke in or sucked it out as it pleased.

The hall was full of Barak-Shar of both sexes and various nations, boisterously greeting the return of the war-band. Alina glanced quickly around to see whose rank merited the first serving, but already hands were grabbing at her collection, and the wine-bearer splashed thick red wine into all the vessels without ceremony. "More!" he said, pointing with his chin toward a niche in the rocky wall behind her.

This turned out to be a sort of plate-deposit, with trenchers and goblets, mugs and plates piled every which way, not all of them washed. By the time she had made a selection, the roasted meats in great platters were smoking on the boards, and copper ewers slopped over with wine from the now-flaccid skin. Eye-stinging fumes rose from the dishes of violently pickled hot peppers, and the acrid miasma of horseradish made her sneeze helplessly.

"Here, put those down," said the majordomo irritably. "They'll serve themselves fast enough, and throw bones at you if you stay in the hall. Come back to the kitchen."

Dazed with the noise, the stink, and the billowing smoke, Alina followed. She saw then that his lop-sided gait was not due to the weight of the full wineskin: his right leg in a leather gaiter was bowed out like the abutment of a bridge and he walked with a staff.

She stumbled along the rough passage, and felt a warm, trembling lean body press against her—Lula had crept into the caverns unremarked among the lurchers and mastiffs and bulldogs.

In the kitchen upper servants and slaves drank the same thick red wine and tore gobbets of pork dripping from the spits. Kitchen terriers fought for their share among the ankles.

The majordomo's staff was mounted with a brass ball, with which he laid about him, clearing a way to the fire. With his belt-knife he cut a two- or three-pound chunk of the loin and held it up on the point.

"I'm Perth," he said. "Mine is the heaviest hand in the kitchens, as it was in the war-band before my leg got broke. Come with me and I will tell you what to think of

76

everything."

There was a pile of sacking and hides in a corner, and he maneuvered his stiff leg down onto it. "Now." He hacked off a generous strip of the meat and handed it to Alina. "Wine!" he bawled, and a small leather boot hurtled through the air to his hand. Perth did not pour it into a cup but directly down his throat.

Alina stared in wonder at the broad red face of the lame majordomo, remarkable more for coarse sandy whiskers and pug nose than intelligence. She nibbled the bloody meat (passing most of it to Lula at her feet) and sipped the sticky wine, since there was nothing else offered.

While they ate, Perth talked. He was not curious as to who she was or where she came from or how she had fallen into their power; he only wanted to make clear the importance of Perth in the Free Company of the Barak-Shar. But long before he had finished sketching the main outlines of his career, she ran away to be excruciatingly sick in the farthest corner she could reach.

When she made her way back to the kitchens, she saw no one but a few scullions dicing in a corner, who paid no attention to her. The kitchen smelled vile, and the dogs snarled at her, so she wandered into the great hall. The elkhorn high seats on the dias were empty—but the rest of the Barak-Shar had gone on from wine to clear white maize brandy and were settled for the night where they fell. A whiff of raw opium made her wrinkle her nose.

The servants had only partly cleared the long trestles, then apparently given it up and joined their betters on the floor. Three draggled women in blue veils scattered handfuls of aromatic herbs around the sleepers, layering over rather than purifying the heavy reek. They paid no attention to Alina, and disappeared through the sculleries.

Alina picked her way daintily between the bodies, fastidious as a stray cat in a littered alley. Lula leaped silently onto one of the long tables and trotted along it, snatching a mouthful of broken meats here and another there. Alina picked up a nearly full cup of the white spirit and washed her mouth with it, spitting it out again.

Suddenly a sweaty cold palm clamped around her ankle. Alina immediately stooped and drove her nails into the back of the hand, but they were too short to be authoritative. Lula dropped her bone and growled, but Alina made a hasty gesture of no, no. She was afraid of waking the whole pack. She went for her knife then, but a hand stopped her wrist and a bleary-eyed bandit reared up in frowzy menace.

It was Pannicart, by the purple geometric tattoos on his bare crown. He drew her down under the table by ankle and wrist, saying nothing, tongue protruding with the effort to focus.

"Filth." said Alina in a venomous whisper, "let go or I'll...bespell you!"

"Hah," answered Pannicart.

"I'll turn your blood to fire in your veins!"

"Hah."

For a moment it was all gasping breath and pulling back and forth. But fuddled as the man was, whenever his equilibrium was equal to his weight, he was the stronger. Alina was unable to break the grip however she writhed, and she feared to make a noise. Her hand clutching for purchase on the trestle-board touched glass—a magnificent dish of pickled hot peppers, especial delight of Morphelius Pashan!

To perceive was to act. Without mercy Alina smashed the dish on Pannicart's head. The heavy glass had little effect, but the gush of potent pepper-juice running down into eyes and mouth was instantly successful.

Free, Alina leaped onto the table and fled while behind her the roar changed to a howl and rose to a scream. The boards bucked as slumbering drunkards convulsed into semiconsciousness, but she jumped wildly over a bench and gained the relative security of the dark maze of passages behind the kitchens before anyone was able to find out what the ruckus was about.

Blundering in the dark, she saw a glimmer ahead and stopped. The glimmer came nearer, and proved to be a palm-sized horn lantern, glowing in the hand of the girl with green eyes called Anthea.

"Princess Alina," said she, smiling her white-toothed smile, "I beg you do not waste the good material here. Because the time is not yet to stand forth as who you are and proclaim what you know."

"How dare he offer me such an insult! In Calabrinia he'd be gelded in the act!"

"Insult? Look at yourself!" The girl held up a crystal mirror mounted in tortoiseshell, wide as two outspread hands; the tortoiseshell was carved in the form of a manta ray.

Alina had not seen a mirror since her last night in the Courtyard of Princesses. Although she knew that her hardships must have left a mark, she almost wept when she saw the image that the crystal gave back.

It was a gaunt, sun-blackened monkey-face, the eyes deeply sunk in livid hollows above cheekbones like knobs; dry colorless lips; a pipestem neck and arms emerging from a browny-grey rag that seemed to have no whole thread in it. Scaly raw ankles and feet with callused pads like a dog completed the picture. Well might Pantasilea wonder if she were a woodsprite or worse!

Anthea laughed a golden laugh. "You must rest and eat the rich fare of the Barak-Shar, but a little at a time lest you be sick again. For now, steal away to the village of the Hopgangers and cozen them out of apples and cabbages to stay your unaccustomed stomach!"

"Who are you?" asked Alina sharply. "Or what are you? Am I dreaming again, as I think I have before?"

"How shall I answer that, unless I dream the same, you know? As to the rest—you may be certain that I am your friend, and will give you aid and counsel!" Anthea stopped to stroke Lula's head, but the dog flattened herself to the ground and slunk behind Alina's legs. Anthea laughed again, not at all offended. "You'll know me at the last, cautious beast! Alina, take this mirror if you like, as an earnest of things to come. I will show you a place you can sleep safely, from which you can come and go as you please without passing the main gates. Come!" She beckoned with graceful white hand.

Alina noticed that the nails were polished to a high gloss, as long and well-manicured as her own used to be. Feeling like a wraith of herself, she followed the glimmer of light in the twisting tunnel, until suddenly it vanished. There was a narrow crack in the wall, through which she could just wriggle sideways.

Beyond, a passage wound upwards. At the end of it she found herself in a little round cave like a jug on its side; a triangular hole let in a cool draught of moonlight. Almost all of the chamber was taken up with a pile of high, sweet-smelling bracken; and on the bracken a clean green linsy-woolsy dress gathered at the neck, a shawl woven in silver-green and rose stripes, and a pair of soft grey boots.

"Oh!" said Alina. "I don't know how I can thank you!"

"The time will come," returned the girl with a little smile. "For now, I regret, I cannot offer you all the comforts your lineage deserves. For the wholesome food you need, you will have to give yourself the trouble of crawling out the hole behind you and walking down the goatpath to the village of the Hopgangers. But it is a great deal shorter than the main road."

"Will you come?" asked Alina, the green frock half over her head, suddenly anxious for companionship.

"No, no!" dropped the golden notes of Anthea's laughter. "The villagers are an ignorant lot. They might stone me! Until then!"

She must have left quickly by the passage, because when Alina's head emerged from the dress, she was alone with Lula.

She pulled on the deliciously soft boots and wrapped the striped shawl around her shoulders. Through the triangular window she saw the narrow goatpath gleaming palely—it was early evening still. Should she try the Hopgangers tonight or wait? But her empty stomach decided her. She crawled out the hole and dropped to the heathery slope outside. If the goats had been grazing there, she might have tried to milk one—but they must have gone home to shed and milk pail. The shiny black droppings on the path were as plain as raisins on a cake.

Briskly she set out to walk to the village, hoping it was indeed not far—nor was it very long, although longer than she like, before she saw the firefly lights of the village, and the pointed roofs and tall chimneys dark against the lighter sky. By then she had decided on her role: even with a new dress she must look like a tinker's drab, and that was what she would be.

The path she was following turned into a rutted lane, with byres and pens on either side. Pigs grunted as she passed, and shaggy crescent-horned cattle eyed her from under burr-matted forelocks, not kindly; but stout timbers confined them.

Some geese slid hissing under the rails and ran at her with outstretched necks and flapping wings; but she sent the lead gander end-over-end with a kick from her booted foot, and the rest desisted.

The house beyond was built of wood, tall and sturdy, with sharply pitched roof and many gables. The half-door was open and over it spilled warm yellow lamp-light, a smell of cabbage and frying bacon and sour beer, and a baby's voice squalling bloody murder.

Alina knocked, but could hardly hear her own rat-tat. She put her hand on the latch and walked in, not without a catch of breath—but she had acted a part before a hundred thousand in the Temple, surely she could improvise for the four pairs of round blue eyes that swiveled towards her now.

"I'll quiet the baby, shall I?" she said into the racket. She picked up the child, solid as a young pig, and dandled him upside down for a few moments as Soleba did with her grandchild. Just like Raisa's brat, the squalls stopped miraculously, and the baby grinned.

Alina turned him rightside up and bounced him. Playing up like a trouper, he gurgled and laughed.

"Thank'ee," said a hefty woman, chestnut braids on her shoulders and a frypan the size of a cartwheel in her hands, "whoever you may be. But generally we like to invite our guests before they walk in."

"So we do, and mostly we know their names beforehand," added the man with frowning brows seated at the deal table.

"My name is Alina," she said, smiling back at him in return for the frown, "and I wouldn't for the world put such ill-luck on you as to pass your door hungry!"

"What, hungry are you?" barked the old man in the chimney-corner. "Why are you hungry, eh? Don't you know how to work?"

"Yes, sir, but I have come from far away and lost all my money. I don't ask for meat or wine, only an apple or so—or a bit of yesterday's loaf—or some carrots or lentils?" As she spoke, the baby screwed up his face again, but she quickly lowered him to Lula's level so she could lick his face.

A little girl with flaxen braids effectively declared herself an ally by plumping down on the clean floor to play with the pretty dog.

"That's a change," grumbled the man. "Usually they ask for jugged hare in port wine. When they don't steal it first."

"I certainly don't," said Alina, whose stomach turned at the mere mention, "only whatever you might have to spare."

"There's always plenty in *this* house," said the woman, who had turned back to the fire with her pan. "Gerda, fetch apples from the cellar. Pa, if you'll find the end of the loaf in the crock beside you..."

"Got a look of his thieving Lordship about you, you have," grunted the man, "but I will say your manners are pleasanter."

Alina held her breath.

"Shush, Terchol," said the woman. "You're no model. It's not my brother who's hand-in-glove with'm, butler or the like, is it? If you'll wait a moment—Alina, is it?— and keep the baby quiet, I'll fetch some peas."

Terchol stared distrustfully from under his forelock like the cattle, but picked up the knife he had laid down and continued shaving thin curls of pale wood off a chock in his hand.

His wife plunked a steaming bowl of cabbage before him, topped with a thick slab of bacon, and he put down

82

the wood with another grunt. The old man got his bowl in the warm corner as the little girl came back with an apronful of apples.

"I picked the reddest for you," she whispered to Alina as she carried her bowl of cabbage to the hearth.

"Thank you," Alina whispered back, touched by the unexpected kindness. She had almost no previous acquaintance with free working people.

The woman came back from her pantry with a double handful of long emerald-green pods, still turgid with the evening dew from the garden. She carried a brown egg in her pocket as well. "Here," she said. "You're a poor little bit of a creature, aren't you? I'd hate to think of our Gerda alone in the world with no more on her bones than you have." She took the baby and put beans, apples, half a brown loaf and the egg into the lap of Alina's shawl.

"Wait a minute," she added, as Alina rose.

From a tall crock she dipped a mug of milk for Gerda and another for Alina before she settled at the table with her own bacon and cabbage and the baby at her breast.

Alina sipped the milk slowly, to the crackle of the fire and the sucking of the baby, the slurping of the cabbage and crunching of bacon.

"Sing for your supper, can you?" shrilled the old man. "Something we've not heard before."

The patronizing words carried more comfort than sting, she realized, addressed to a supposed beggar. But what might she sing? Unbidden leaped to mind the ancient lay of an anonymous poet. She lifted her voice, ever so slightly husky like the amber tone of a brook bearing autumn leaves, and sang:

> *Come, fill the Cup, and in the Fire of Spring*
> *Your Winter-garment of Repentance fling:*
> *The Bird of Time has but a little way*
> *To flutter—and the Bird is on the Wing.*

> *Whether at Naishápúr or Babylon,*
> *Whether the Cup with sweet or bitter run,*
> *The Wine of Life keeps oozing drop by drop,*

The Leaves of Life keep falling one by one.

Each Morn a thousand Roses brings, you say;
Yes, but where leaves the Rose of Yesterday?
And this first Summer month that brings the Rose
Shall take Jamshyd and Kaikobád away.

When she had finished, a candlespark gleamed through tears in each bovine blue eye, and there was a little silence.

She wrapped the rest of the food carefully in the end of her shawl, and took out the mirror. She gave it to Gerda as she rose. "Good people, I thank you kindly for your hospitality. It is not absolutely out of my power to make some return—perhaps you can use or sell this mirror. I stole it from the Barak-Shar when I begged there."

The old man laughed first, the cackling crow of an old rooster. "There's one for you, Terchol!"

"Who robs a thief has a hundred years of pardon," grunted Terchol, pleased. "From those who work for a living. If you ever need a chair, Missy, Terchol the Chairmaker at your service. Red poplar, sweet gum and chestnut splats a specialty."

"You're welcome back whenever you've a mind to come, remember," said the stout woman, wiping her eyes with the tail of a braid. "Nor to worry about payment, either, if you'll sing some more like that."

"I shall remember," said Alina gravely.

She crept back to her hideaway, thoughtful of what she had seen and heard.

In the morning she discovered that Pannicart was ill, his head swathed to the beard in cloths dampened with baking soda. The slaves were all agog over the story of the dragon that had appeared to him in the middle of the night, rebuked him for blasphemy, and vanished in a terrible burning flash. No one else had seen it, but then no one was in case to see anything at that hour.

This wonder had to give place to chores, because there

was a great deal to do. News came, of a particularly succulent caravan making its way down the mountain road three days' ride to the south. The Barak-Shar shook off their excesses to ride out after it, leaving the lairs to the women, a few squalid brats, sick and injured ruffians, and slaves; all under the authority of Perth.

This by no means guaranteed any measure of peace. The slaves squabbled, a constant background of yammering and mewling; the Barak-Shar left behind roared and yelled, the women screamed back at them, and at any moment one might snatch his cup-fellow's gold chain from his neck or his drab from his knee, and the rest would gather around to bet on the fight. If the outcome was fatal, the body was thrown into the kennels—as Perth explained (he had taken an inexplicable fancy to Alina), it was good to weed out weaklings, and mastiffs needed human flesh from time to time to make them keen. Dead dogs went to the vulture, a tidy system that saved trouble.

The women quarreled too, seldom to the death, fortunately, as there were never enough women to go around. The Barak-Shar, Alina gathered, were slavers in order to survive, as well as turn a profit.

It just went to show, said Perth sententiously. The superb Pantasilea herself had begun her career as a captive from no one knew where; in fact, Perth intimated, there was no telling what a likely young woman with influential friends might not aspire to. Provided she selected her friends carefully.

Alina pretended to hear them calling in the kitchen, and disappeared by her secret fissure in the wall; but otherwise she nodded submissively at all that was said, and kept safe in her hideaway the rosewood box full of camphor and orrisroot in which reposed the dried and salted heart of the godking of Calabrinia.

There was a knife-edge to be walked, and Alina did not for a moment forget it. She was brought up to the petty back-biting, secret treacheries and private vengeances of the Palace—knew to a hair how far one could go at one time and not at another. She succeeded, never knowing if her low and sneaking profile protected her, or if there were more to it than that.

But thinking and unthinking, she moved like a house-cat through the foul smelly caves. The fleas and ticks were frightful. It was easy to understand why the Barak-Shar preferred, by and large, to shave their heads, although beards seemed to be required by some edict of Morphelius Pashan's father. Alina missed the white-throated, flicker-tongued blue lizards that lived everywhere in the Palace and kept it free of insect vermin. She had herself often coaxed one with crumbs onto her hand. Perhaps there had been lizards, but Pantasilea's vulture had pecked them up?

For relief she visited the Hopganger family now and then, singing them songs of the great world and olden times, waiting and biding her time. Occasionally she saw Anthea, whom no one else seemed to be able to see.

Once or twice the thought crossed her mind that perhaps the Dragon Throne was not worth the price of embracing Morphelius Pashan and the Lady Pantasilea as cousins, and wondered again if there might have been some way to convince the Prince-turned-hermit, of the Isles. What of his younger brother, indeed? Was he dead, too? She wondered, but reminded herself that alliance with the Barak-Shar had been the linch-pin of Korab Khan's strategy.

She clung meanwhile to Lula, her only true friend.

As the summer passed, she gained flesh and some of her bloom came back: her cheeks and temples filled out, and her lips were carmine again against a skin more like apricots than shoe leather. Her hair grew in glossy. At the same time her breasts and belly swelled, delicately ripe like the contours of fertile hills under the silvery-green gown. Perth gave her a pair of heavy gold earrings, and became intolerable with his attentions.

Thus stood matters when the lord Morphelius Pashan and his best-beloved Pantasilea returned very merry indeed from reiving almost to the seacoast, with booty, slaves and recruits.

Six

They say the Lion and the Lizard keep
The Courts where Jamshyd gloried and
drank deep...
—Omar Khayyam

"Tara-ra-ra-ra-rah!" brayed the horns, and the Autumn Feast began in earnest. First came the traditional mutton broth, hot as bathwater, gobbets of yellow fat floating on the surface and interminable pale noodles coiled underneath. A garnish of pepper, red and black and green and white, served in snail-shells, accompanied the soup.

Afterwards came lampreys in mustard-sauce with leeks and wild garlic; transparent river-crayfish laid out on biers of watercress; mussels in the shell, their orange flesh quivering. A turtle baked whole was served, with pearl onions for eyes and an artichoke in its beak.

Then spit after spit of birds, well-basted and done to a turn: larks, ortolans, quails, orioles and pheasants. The crowning dish of the course was a roasted swan, revested in its feathers, wings spread and neck arched to strike. The Barak-Shar applauded it, beating the handles of their knives on the board and cheering (some hissed as well).

By the meat course, so much wine had been drunk that when four slaves staggered in with the wild boar on a platter wreathed in juniper and wild celery, some of the livelier young bravos got up an impromptu boar-hunt; several knives were thrown in lieu of boar-spears proper, any of which might have accounted for the boar, as Perth ruled. It was a pity they accounted for one of the slaves also. Sheer bad aim; Perth said he hoped to see some intensive practice before they left home on the next expedition.

"Home! Home to Calabrinia! Calabrinia is our home!" he was shouted down.

"A mere slip of the tongue," said Morphelius Pashan smoothly. He was more gorgeous than usual in scarlet damask slashed with purple and tied with love-knots of gold cord. At the high table on the dais he wore a hat of black velvet, its sweeping plume, pinned with a walnut-sized diamond, touching his shoulder. His fox-colored beard was curled, and ruby earrings challenged the auburn locks that hung over them.

"Of course our real home is Calabrinia, for which we celebrate the Autumn Feast—this camp is a mere stopping-place for the nonce. Seeing about me the fellowship and cheer—her Ladyship's gentle presence—" here he made a half-bow to Pantasilea, who was particularly dramatic in black silk, jet beads and black pearls. Her superb creamy bosom showed like a snowdrift at midnight. She did not return the bow, only knitted her brows. "—and this noble company assembled, I almost think I dine in the splendid halls of our forebears (barring the panthers, of course, owing to her Ladyship's catarrh), but may it please the gods to..."

"Next year in Calabrinia!" roared the company, anticipating him and stamping their feet.

The musicians struck up the tune of "Hola, Hola, Ho" and there was no hearing anything else until the dessert of flaming frumenty and candied violets was brought.

Alina, modestly setting plates with other females, wondered how the delicate filigreed ceilings of the dining salon in the Palace would look, if dishes like the huge blue-flaming suet pudding spouting greasy smoke were served often. But in that salon Meerkat Lobum had pledged fealty and friendship to Korab Khan in a goblet of wine; since the filigree ceilings had not then fallen on Meerkat Lobum's sleek head, let them suffer their fate.

The Barak-Shar were not...Alina admitted to herself that she liked the Horsemen a great deal better, barbarians as they were. But she had need of an instrument, and none is too coarse if it will cut at need. The Barak-Shar were a pack of vicious mongrels, with neither the fidelity of the hound nor the nobility of the wolf—but they had teeth and could bite.

Alina set her teeth in her lip and wiped her hands on a towel. She would step forth at last, she would speak, she would set on this cur-pack since she had nothing better.

Beside her, Anthea, in white tunic and gold belt, said coolly, "Now is the time. At the Autumn Feast they always talk of going to Calabrinia. But if you wait too long, they will take brandy and opium and conquer the world in their dreams only."

The words echoed Alina's thought so perfectly that she didn't ask herself where Anthea came from, or how it was that no one but herself seemed to notice her.

"Get their attention first," she prompted.

Alina approached the foot of the dais. The jesters who escaped heavy work by clowning at feasts were juggling oranges and pretending to lose them down bodices. Half the company laughed, the other half quarreled. She picked up a heavy crystal knife-rest, and took careful aim. She shied it underhand across the table, shattering Morphelius's goblet as he was about to pledge his lady. The vulture, startled, mantled and regurgitated its meal.

The fox-colored lord leaped up hand on sword, looking for the source of the outrage. Alina curtseyed in the high and swooping style of the royal court and said, "Hail, yesterday Lord of the Barak-Shar!"

"Hah? Ho! Yesterday? And today and tomorrow too, froward wench! Who gave you leave to play at cock-shies with the table furniture, eh?" His narrowed black eyes registered with astonishment the transformation of the sun-blackened skinny imp. She wore her long-hidden rubies, and looked very well.

Pantasilea turned beside him, swelling like a wave about to overwhelm a sea-wall.

"Today I name you First Vizier and Lord Lieutenant of

Calabrinia." Alina's voice carried shrilly in the sudden silence of the smoky cavern.

"So it is a fey sprite," murmured Morphelius, fingering his beard with beringed and besmeared fingers. "Say on."

"And who are you to tell us, the rulers-in-exile of Calabrinia..." growled her ladyship, but Alina's higher voice cut across hers.

"You may now be rulers in fact, since his Benign Supremacy is dead," she continued clearly.

"What? Silence," cried Morphelius, although a thick shocked hush paralyzed even the oranges of the jugglers. "How do you know this?"

Into the waiting silence Alina dropped her words each distinct, like silver coins new-minted. "I saw him dead, in the snow-cellars under the Palace. I have here his heart, salted, to prove it." She brought the rosewood box out from under her shawl and slid it open. "Behold the mortal heart of the late godking!"

Anthea stood behind her. Alina could smell her scent of green, bitter herbs. But the remarkable thing was the mummified heart: it looked the same, inert and mildly repulsive, like a dried fruit, but from it emanated, as if it were an odor, a tide of power and frenzy that filled the room.

The Barak-Shar stared with starting eyes; Pantasilea stretched jeweled talons across the table, upsetting a cruet of vinegar. Perth righted it quickly and the vulture pecked at him.

Alina held up the box for all to see. "Behold the doom of Calabrinia, the breaking of bondage, the mortal remains of the godking! The king is dead, long live..."

"And who are *you?*" asked Pantasilea in a low snarl.

"I am the Princess Alina," said Alina, looking it; although she did not quite know where her words came from, they came readily. "Last and youngest daughter of the same godking, named true heir in my birth-horoscope; which is so, because Korab Khan, the youngest son, is now dead also. Who will wrest the city from the bloated eunuchs that rule there?" She paused for effect. "Who will walk at ease on the marble pavements under the shade of the Moloquat trees? Those who aid me to my inheritance! Do you dare to doubt my claim?"

She yanked down the sleeve of the linsy-woolsy dress to the black four-lobed Moloquat mark with its three tap-roots of obedience, virtue and prosperity, inked on her cinnamon-and cream shoulder. Shrugging the sleeve back on, she flung out her arm towards the head of the table.

The silence was so thick that the bubbling of pots and the hissing of gas flames could be heard from the kitchen.

"How fascinating," drawled the lady Pantasilea at last. "Do tell us more." She passed a candied violet over her shoulder to the vulture.

Under the table a child and a dog squabbled over a bone, but Perth gave both a savage kick. The dog slunk to the far end of the cavern, but the child continued to snivel, out of reach. Alina maintained her arm out-stretched in challenge and supplication and symbol of inexorable destiny as long as she could.

The gesture turned all eyes to Morphelius Pashan. He rose to his feet, looking more as though he had heard his death sentence rather than the words the Barak-Shar had waited various generations to hear.

"Your long exile is over." Alina told him encouraging-ingly, lowering her arm. "Your Barak-Shar shall return to the city with me!"

She might have said more, flushed with the occasion and with the power of the salted heart, but the unpent howl of triumph that filled the hall forestalled her. Rough hands raised her to the tabletop and she curtseyed right and left. Slaves and servants crowded into the cavern, all asking at once what was happening. Morphelius himself seized the opportunity to fill a goblet for her.

Anthea was nowhere to be seen in the clamorous throng, among which only Pantasilea sat silently, toying with her rings and bending an opaque black look first on her consort, then on the metamorphosed goblin she had harbored in her kitchens.

Perth called for more wine, and Alina drank to the Barak-Shar, to victory, to Calabrinia, to death, to Mor-phelius, to Pantasilea (who responded with a slight inclination of her magnificent torso), to all the toasts that were called for. Her head spun by the time Morphelius Pashan rapped on the table before him with the hilt of his sheathed sword.

The racket continued, whereupon he dealt three or four shrewd blows with the scabbard, until he had the attention of most of the crowd.

"Honorable free swordsmen, ladies of whatever degree, diligent dependents all: The gods have vouchsafed us justice at last and my destiny is about to be fulfilled. This lady" (he bowed in Alina's direction) "has kindly brought us the news that we have so long awaited. But now we must not spoil all with precipitation. I shall undertake to study with fresh and recent reports the state of the defenses and fortifications, the current strength of the Guard; the condition of our horseflesh and the season of the year, which advances, must also be taken into account."

Alina stared at him with the scimitar-curve of her brows so pronounced as to stretch her amber eyes wide. Thus spoke the outlaw offshoot of a royal house? This the dauntless warrior, scourge of the Horsemen? Was it possible that he *feared* the city even in its headless decadence?

Morphelius continued. "Prudence counsels that before undertaking a trans-desert campaign we consolidate our flanks, reaffirm our base, establish our legitimacy—in a word, fall upon the Hopgangers and make them our vassals."

"Very good, my lord," broke in Perth. "Just what I would have advised your worthy father (may the gods entertain him the other side of UnderCa). Calabrinia wasn't built in a day, as they say."

"Yes, yes!" chorused the troop. "Take the Hopgangers! Bread and beer! Bacon and wenches! Goosefeather beds and buttered parsnips!" cried one and another at once.

"What!" broke in Alina in a shrill screech that topped every other voice. "I offer you on a platter the empress of the cities, the hub of the world's wheel, the treasure-house of the universe! You turn aside to seize a heap of turnips, a wattle cowshed, a few porkers! Is it that peasants resist only with slings and pitchforks, not the poisoned arrows of the Guard? Be careful! A sow enraged is a fearsome creature. Perhaps you had better raid a rabbit-warren instead, braving the brambles! Pah! I spit on such men. No, stay, I'll recruit the kitchen wenches and perhaps a turnspit or two for my army!"

All elbows through the cavern she dodged into the kitchen and ran.

Morphelius shook his head sadly and the diamond-buttoned plume nodded in agreement. "She—the princess—seems overwrought. We must excuse her, hey? The heady draughts of wine may be...that is, I blame myself for not...that is" (carefully avoiding Pantasilea's black and rolling eye as a happy thought struck him) "...when I have made her my wife, there will be no further problem with policy disputes."

A pause followed, which threatened to become awkward.

"Naturally not," said Pantasilea in a very low purr. "The poor thing is, as you say, overwrought. I'll make up a—sedative for her, with my own hands." She dragged the sniveling child out from under the table by the scruff. "A salver, Ichabod, at once."

"And meanwhile, said Perth, "we'll get on with the plans for conquering the Hopgangers. How if we send a herald around the seven cantons, proclaiming our overlordship and demanding that they submit at once? While they're still considering that, we fall upon them one by one with the edge of the sword."

"But why bother with a herald?" argued Morphelius. "That is..."

Pantasilea, her jeweled rings glinting, delicately mixed the contents of a golden goblet. The vulture leaned over her shoulder, cocking its bald red head sideways to see better.

Alina flung herself down on the pile of bracken in her den, burying her face in Lula's warm white flank.

"Cowards, cowards!" she wept. "Rat people on their barges would be ashamed to turn so craven after such boasting! The Horsemen are worth a hundred of them! They shall never return to Calabrinia when I am queen, no, not as slaves even!"

The tinkle-ding-ding of goat bells in the heather sounded through the triangular window-hole. The Hopgangers' goats were grazing the mountainside over the bandits' caverns. Alina jumped up, deciding she preferred peasants, however, grudging, to illegitimate aristocrats. She eased her still-supple although somewhat bulging body through the hole and dropped to the ground. With luck the goatherd might be little Gerda, by whom she could send a message warning the Hopganger village.

As soon as she sent Gerda scampering down the path with her goats, fat blond plaits and skimpy blue smock flying in the wind of her going, Alina kilted up her skirts and crawled back into her den. She almost stepped on Lula cowering against the wall, because Anthea sat cross-legged on the bed bracken.

Before she could say anything, Lula yipped, and a boy pattered through the low door on bandy legs, carrying a goblet on a tray daintily set with napkin and dish of pickled artichokes. He was a meagre and unwholesome-looking child, perpetually runny-nosed, with untrimmed bangs over his eyes.

He bowed, letting the goblet slop over, and said, "Please, y'r S'renity, this is for you, compliments of the Lady, and she hopes you feel better."

"Ask what it is," interposed Anthea in her cool way.

The boy turned toward her with the tray (in the distraction of the moment Alina saw nothing odd in that) and said, "Please *you,* y'r S'renity—it's the hot broth from the mutton, with a little brandy, and the dose from her ring my Lady mixed in after."

Anthea stretched out an ophidianly graceful hand, dipped her finger in the spilled liquid on the tray, and tasted. "Hmmm. A delightful potion. Yes, this will cure headache, lassitude and incipient hysteria. Permanently. Try it on the dog there."

"Is it unwholesome?" said Alina indignantly. "I certainly won't!"

"Give it to the boy if you'd rather—if the cup goes back full they may come after you."

"No. Thank you for your timely warning, but I do not care for your advice."

"Which is quite practical. You've started the Barak-Shar dreaming again of empire, something they'd quite given up except as a sentimental exercise; but naturally they need direction. Now what you must do is..."

Alina took the tray and set it down. She surveyed the bearer, who seemed somehow familiar. "What's your name?"

"Ichabod, so please you, y'r S'renity."

"Do you think I should drink this cup?"

"I don't think nothing, y'r S'renity. You knows best does the Lady wish you good or bad. I wouldn't take nothing from her myself if she wished me bad."

"Why would you think the lady wants to poison me?"

"Dunno, y'r S'renity. She does that a lot. Funny she'd take against you, y'r S'renity, though—you look so much like her all of a sudden."

"I look like her!" Alina's hands went to her knife, but she clasped them behind her.

"Yes, y'r S'renity. Just now in the hall, could've been own daughter to the Lady, you could. Maybe," he said with a sudden brightening, "that's it. You're going to take her place?"

"Why not?" put in Anthea silkily. "A practical suggestion."

"I would rather drink the goblet! Again I thank you. I have decided the Barak-Shar are not fit for the role I had planned for them."

Anthea rose, graceful as a camas lily in her white and gold. "A curious reaction! I had though the privations of the desert and the society of sunstruck fools would have the opposite effect. Never mind. I shall return when you are more settled in mind." She left, although it was hard to say whether by the door or the window.

So many new ideas, and old ones turned on their

heads, made her feel sick and dizzy for the moment. To the child she said, "Run along to your mistress now."

The urchin shook his frowzy head. "No, y'r S'renity."

"What do you mean? Hop!" Alina raised a threatening palm.

"No, y'r S'renity, if you don't want the drink, I'd better not go back to my Lady. For the same reason, if you take my meaning," he explained, peering up from under the hanging fringe.

Alina lowered her hand. "What about your mother?" She assumed that the child must belong to one or another of the slatternly veiled women.

"No mother. Don't know what happened to her."

This struck a chord. Alina didn't know what happened to her mother, either.

"Very well," she said to Ichabod, "If you'd prefer to help me rather than poison me, scoot back to the great hall and listen under the table. I want to know exactly what those great pot-valiant swaggerers propose. You had better get some plain bread from the storeroom, if there is any. And—do you know where the horses are stabled?"

"Ho, yes, y'r S'renity," cried the ragamuffin, wiping his nose with enthusiasm. "I knows! I knows more'n anybody thinks, so I does! I'll get you a horse!"

"If you really can do that, take the horse around by the bluffs, to the hillside out here—look through this hole. And..."

But the urchin snatched the hem of her gown and kissed it before she could recoil, scuttling down the passage to the main caverns as though Perth were after him.

Alina began to pace restlessly up and down. Now what should she do? Where could she go? Perhaps she could join a caravan of merchants for the moment. They would expect to be paid, of course, but she had her jewels; also the dusky pearl of the hermit, in its silver bindings, but she was unwilling to part with that.

Blast the Barak-Shar like the mountain of Calabrinia. May the gods send them ten plagues and four pestilences, and rockslides after. She heard a distant sound of breaking stone, like an echo of her thoughts.

In the lowness of her spirits she wondered whether Korab Khan had known how difficult it was to give away an empire. Perhaps she could merely let it ride on, like a river-barge with the helmsman dead, until it foundered or the ocean swallowed it. But in any case she must leave this den of two-legged hyenas—no wonder honest hyenas, four-legged ones, followed the Barak-Shar on their forays into the desert—like knows like!

Her bitterness tinged blue the little cave. Lula crept to her feet and laid her chin on them, comfortingly.

Alina almost regretted speaking so angrily to Anthea. She was strange and uncomfortable company, but she seemed to know many things.

Like bad news made flesh, Perth limped into the chamber, ducking under the low lintel, a pickax at his side.

"So this is the vixen's den," he observed. "Followed the brat—had to get the pick to widen the crack—and here I am! You don't look very pleased, Princess!"

"I'm not. Be good enough to take yourself off for the present," she answered shortly.

"Quite high and mighty, aren't we, missy? But maybe old Perth knows a thing or two, like to suggest that you don't try Madame's posset-cup there..."

"I haven't," returned Alina more shortly still. "Now, out!"

"As I said," (leaning on the pickax) "maybe old Perth does know a thing or two. And maybe not, ho! Maybe he didn't arrange a stray hunting arrow, so Morphelius Pashan could succeed his father—and maybe he doesn't know how the wind sets now!"

"What is the meaning of this farrago?"

"Just this, missy. Morphelius Pashan thinks to ride the train of your skirts to the Dragon Throne, and stay on it as a widower Prince Consort..."

"Indeed?"

"...but the red one isn't where to put your money. He's a bag of wind. He's small, that's what, a backwoods outlaw and that's it. The Lady heads him by the nose—

now she *is* one, she is—but old Perth knows a few tricks himself, he does, and..."

"Come to the point at once, if you please!"

"Well, since you're such a hasty one, I will, then—now if you was to give *me* that heart and let me act for you, why you'd see yourself Empress of the Sun in half a year!" Perth made a descriptive gesture with the pickax.

Alina stared at him, her amber eyes turning black as the pupils like a cat's. "So you are willing to betray your master?" she asked in a dry and crackling tone the color of dead leaves.

"Let's just say I follows the dictates of destiny, missy!"

"And if I refuse your kind offer?"

"Why, then it'll be my painful duty—no hard feelings, I'm sure—to stove in your head and take it. But it needn't come to that, now, need it?"

"No," said Alina in the same tone, "It needn't. His Benign Supremacy's heart? Certainly. It's here somewhere." She turned in the small space with a sweep of her shawl. Ichabod's tray stood still on the stony window-ledge. Pretending to rummage in her bag, Alina substituted the preserved heart for a pickled artichoke, and vice-versa.

With another swirl of shawl, she turned back to Perth and presented him with the rosewood box. "Take it," she said, "and may the fortune you deserve accompany it. There is more to discuss. But for now, leave me, I have a dreadful headache."

Perth gimped spryly out, a shark-like grin widening his jaws. "Right," he said. "They're just now for taking off after the Hopgangers, you won't feel like coming down to wave goodbye?"

Alina turned her back. She hoped Ichabod had done as he promised, but on foot or on horseback, she would leave as she had come, with her faithful dog.

But oh! Unmerciful gods, too late! Lula, poor bitch, lay limp and unmoving as a doormat. Lady Pantasilea's poisoned goblet stood empty, beside the delicately whiskered muzzle with protruding tongue! Alina saw it all in a moment: the hot greasy broth, unattended while she chaffered with Perth, trespass terribly retributed.

But this—this must be paid for. What harm had the poor dog done them? Alina snatched up her worn and dirty bag, and ran down the passage through the hole so recently widened by Perth's pickax.

Winglike shawl-ends flapping, she ran like a harpy through the women's quarters, kitchens, sculleries and reeking slave dormitories, screeching, "Doom, doom, doom! Death by fire and death by water, death by earth and death by air! Doom to the Barak-Shar!"

She had a fine panic going in the caverns almost before the warband sallied out the stout wooden gates. Before Perth and the guards on the stockade fairly understood there was a mutiny deep in the caverns, Alina harried the remaining ragtag and bobtail out through the window-hole of her den into the heather.

Like a bagful of foxes set loose, they vanished; Alina herself yelled, "For your sake, Lula!" as she burst out of the hole and plumped into the crushed heather and goat berries. She picked herself up and bounded downhill like a hunted doe.

Seven

...as it runs Time's deer is slain.

—Edwin Muir

I N a beech copse Ichabod waited, wiping his nose. He held the reins of Pantasilea's stout cream-colored gelding.

"That horse?" Alina gasped. "Oh, Ichabod!"

"Handsome Tam's better than he looks, y'r Serenity, anyway he's the only horse they'd let me have, for my Lady as usual, y'r Serenity. He's a better 'un than you think."

"He'll have to be," replied Alina. She took the reins, wide swags of silk-fringed cord, and put one foot on the footboard to vault onto the wide padded seat. "Jump up, Ichabod. We've got to go faster than you can run."

"Yes, y'r Serenity, what has you done, y'r Serenity?" His eyes shone under the lank bangs and he forgot to sniffle.

"Smothered the kitchen fire and left a candle burning the great hall."

"Is that all?" he said, clearly disappointed.

"Is that *all?*" she answered, putting the horse to a racking good downhill pace. "With the fire out, the gas will spread through the caverns. When there's enough in the great hall, it will explode. They deserve it for poisoning my poor dog. But we don't want to be nearby...where does this road go?" The old gelding had directed himself into a narrow beaten track between high banks.

"Hopgangers' village, y'r S'renity."

"Oh!" said Alina, drawing rein. "Will the Barak-Shar come this way?"

The horse's ears flickered, forward, back, right. He raised his big head. Alina sighted along the line of his nose and caught a shadow of movement in the brush along the top of the bank.

"I hope that's a lookout," she muttered. "When the valiant Barak-Shar break down the barn doors, may they find nothing but goose-shit to their knees. And slip in it."

Tinny in the distance, a bugle sounded.

Alina clucked to the old horse, and he picked up his rolling amble at a faster clip, one-and-two-and-three-and-four, iron shoes clicking, head nodding to his own rhythm. It was a good ground-covering pace, but—"We'd better not stay on the road," she said, scanning the banks on either side for a way up. But they were rocky and steep as a wall, crowned with dark holm-oaks that leaned out to meet overhead.

Again they heard the bugle. From ahead, a squadron of crows came flying low over the trees—"Caw! Caw! Caw!"—as though disturbed. It was already dark in the lane and the horse stumbled in a rut. Alina pulled him up and stopped to listen. She heard nothing but the uneasy sighing of the wind in the branches; but the ground vibrated, a mute powerful drumming. They hurried on.

At last! There was a gap in the bank where a tree had fallen. Winter rains had poured down, cutting a rough stair. Alina put the horse at it. "Come up, Tam, tchk, tchk!" she begged.

"Ooh, hold on, y'r S'renity, he's a-gonna!" squeaked Ichabod as the old horse settled back on his broad haunches, paused a moment, and leaped to the top of the rain-gully. A moment's scrabbling with his shod fore-hooves, and they were up. "Told you he's a good 'un," began the child.

"Hush!" said Alina. From the bank she could hear something like muffled thunder. She dismounted and led the horse under a huge holm-oak that bent its dark foliage to the ground like a tent. The century's worth of leaf mold was soft and warm under her knees as she knelt where she could see the road, framed between a twining vine of brilliant scarlet and brake of yellow aspen; she did not think she would be seen in her soft greeny-gray dress like a downy owl.

The muted thunder rose to a roar, and around the bend ahead poured a packed mass of cattle, back-swept horns crossing and clashing as they jostled shoulders, rolling eyes, damp muzzles raised to bawl over the shaggy rumps of the rank before. Alina recognized the red cattle of the Hopgangers, heavy of neck, deep of dewlap, evil of temper. A great many stampeded down the narrow road, heavy cloven hoofs making the ground shake and the dust rise in a cloud above them. Behind ran herdsmen with flails, goading them on towards the caverns of the Barak-Shar.

Clearly the Hopgangers had heeded the warning Alina sent, but not to flee—she forgot her surprise in the trumpet-blast, much nearer, blowing the charge, as the Barak-Shar swept into view.

The flashing of steel through the dust in the last level rays of sun, the bellowing of furious cattle and squealing of warhorses, the dull blare of cowhorns and screaming of trumpets were snuffled out by the cataclysmic roar as the caverns of the Barak-Shar blew sky-high like the primeval mountain of Calabrinia. Dirt and rock blotted out the sun and a silent sheet of orange flame rose into the sky like a curtain, torn instantly to shreds in the blast.

The earth heaved beneath them. In the perfect ringing deafness which followed, debris fell like dark hail, and the banks above the road crumbled slowly onto the petrified battle-scene. Last of all, three downy white feathers from a vulture's neck ruff wafted down.

Then Alina, huddling under the branches of the oak, felt a hard kick in the belly, under her green dress dark with sweat; it reminded her forcibly that there were three of them.

After traveling all night west and south down a narrow gorge between saw-toothed ridges, the gelding was lame. Ichabod whimpered and Alina would have too, if pride had let her.

"You might better have escaped with the slaves," she told him. "Their luck is better than mine."

The night had been sharp, and she now noticed how many of the leaves were chrome yellow, viridian, crimson lake and sienna, like a paintbox. On the high ridge to the north was a sprinkling of snow—the year was drawing in. The grass under the horse's halting feet was pale gold and delicately headed with the whiskered husks of grain.

As the dawn widened, birds sang urgently and answered each other, from boxwood to birch and chestnut to elderberry. Alina looked about for anything edible, and a place to rest, but Ichabod stopped crying and listened to the birds.

Presently he poked her in the back.

"Oh! Don't do that, you startled me!"

"Beg pardon, y'r S'renity, but the bluejay says the old ladies have put the breakfast porridge on."

"The what?"

"The porridge. We'd better hurry, it'll be done when we get there," Ichabod explained.

"Where? What do you mean? Do you know someone who lives here?"

"I don't know nothing. The bluejay knows the old ladies."

"Bluejay?"

Ichabod pointed. There was an intense flash of blue as the jay vanished into the foliage.

"Do you mean you think the bird talks?" Alina asked incredulously. Last-born of the Court of Princesses, she had had very little experience with children, but Ichabod seemed too old for such games.

"To me, he does. The old ladies with the porridge live that way." He pointed. There was an opening in the trees, perhaps even a path under the drifts of fallen leaves.

As Alina turned to look, the old horse swung around to her movement and went for the clearing. She was dizzy with fatigue; she brushed stiff, dusty strands of hair off her forehead, leaving a streak of dirt, and considered briefly. It seemed as though she had done this already, a long time ago.

"All right," she said, as Handsome Tam hobbled purposefully forward, following his pointing nose.

Behind the lighter hardwoods was a thicket of pines. Alina eyed it nervously. She knew what pines were, from exotic specimens in the palace gardens, but she had never seen them leaning together and whispering with the wind in their stiff, drooping branches. It was dark under them, as though night lingered, and the iron horseshoes fell silently on the cushion of needles.

In the middle of the pines was a clearing with a stream running through it, a brook that played like an otter among its boulders. On the bank of the stream was a house from which floated the smell of porridge cooking. Ichabod sniffed audibly, and Tam planted his large sore feet on the doorstep and halted. Alina climbed stiffly to the ground.

It was a strange dwelling, very unlike the tall flat-roofed stone houses of the city trailing off into slave quarters behind; nor was it like the caverns of the Barak-Shar, the painted wagons of the Horsemen, nor yet the gabled cottages of the Hopganger villages.

It was long, and low, and rambling, with a doorway but no door; a curtain made of wooden beads on knotted strings hung there instead. The house itself was built partly of uncut rocks piled dry, partly of logs with the bark clinging to them still, and partly of mud brick very indifferently modeled. A sort of second story of wattle-and-daub, on a level with Tam's ears, supported a thatched roof. Clumps of leggy bright yellow flowers grew in the eaves.

Chickens scratched on the roof; an orange-striped cat contemplated them from a lopsided window under the thatch; to one side of the doorstep was coiled a black snake with a narrow yellow stripe down each side, very still but fixing a lively glittering eye on them. Three large goats, yellow as butter with brown ears and legs, stood on their hind legs nipping leaves off the brambles that sprawled along the walls.

Unsure how to announce herself, or to whom, Alina ran a finger down the blade of her knife. She decided at last to rattle the bead curtain.

Immediately there came a shriek from inside, a bustle and a scuffle, and a half a dozen strings were flipped aside.

"Ah! There you are! What are you?" exclaimed, declaimed and demanded a very tall and gaunt old lady with the milky white eyes of old age. Without waiting for an answer she shrieked, "Dorcas! Someone's here! Dorcas! DOOOOR-cas!"

"I wish you a fortunate morning," Alina began, not a little disconcerted by the reception, when another tall old lady, a little more stooped and a little less gaunt, threw aside the remaining strands of curtain and stood peering at them with bright black eyes like jet beads.

"I beg..." Alina began again, but the first old lady broke in.

"Of *course* you do, so does everyone, it's either one thing or another, when I heard the commotion yesterday afternoon I *said* to Dorcas, I said, *someone's* bound to fetch up on the doorstep and probably more than one, so she's put more porridge on. Come in and wash your hands and faces too if you *don't* mind, the water-jars are full I filled them myself this morning but perhaps the horse would rather take a mash with the goats."

Without slackening speech in the slightest she yanked Ichabod off the saddle and marched him into the house. Alina followed, as the bright-eyed Dorcas clucked wordlessly to Handsome and led him around to the back.

Inside it was a warren of little odd-shaped rooms with haphazard windows, furniture of willow-withes, and woolen rugs on plank floors. There were pots and pans, spindles and spinning wheels and hanks of wool, here a basket of tabby kittens, there another of young weasels. In a hat nestled a clutch of brown eggs; a cheese-press stood in the middle of a hall. An enormous loom took up a whole room to itself, except for a shelf full of small stoneware crocks running all around the walls just under the ceiling. Everything was cobwebby at the corners and edges, with a more or less clear passage through the middle from room to room.

The blind old woman led them through the house (larger than it looked from outside, and the rooms all higgledy-piggledy) to the kitchen, talking all the while.

"You may call me Hermione, though of course I've other names as well, it doesn't signify, does it? The little boy must be Pauli, he looks like that or will when he's washed, which we can do right after breakfast, and you can be Lucia, can't you dear? Ah! Here's Dorcas back, and fortunately there's cream for the porridge, I said, we'd better *save* some, whenever there's trouble there'll be guests, won't there?"

Meanwhile, in the cluttered, flagged kitchen Alina and Ichabod gobbled hot porridge with cream and honey until they were full. Ichabod's skinny little belly mimicked the more pronounced contours of Alina's and they both sighed.

Dorcas never spoke, but kept up a kind of slow bustle around the kitchen, turning a row of cheeses on a shelf, stirring something in a crock and adding a fistful of dried herbs to it, pouring a saucer of milk for the orange cat and accepting a mouse from him, punching down a ball of dough in a wooden trough. Pauli's eyes followed her as if they were on strings.

An owl sitting on the chimney-breast rose suddenly and flew out the window, startling Alina very much; she had thought it was stuffed.

"Now, then," said Hermione, breaking off what she was saying and picking up a fresh thread of conversation, "Let's have Pauli bathe *first*, he needs it the most, don't you think so, Dorcas? And the young lady and I can have a nice chat, particularly if she means to stay the winter, though of course you can't *live* here, you know, nobody can, I told the lad that years ago, you know who I mean?"

"Not quite, please, mistress Hermione," said Alina with unaccustomed meekness. Being fed gruel and slated for a bath took years off her age.

"Why, of course you do, that lad (it was years ago now) who took and become godking of that city (what's its name?) that we hear about so much these days—you have something of a look of him, but didn't the packman say he was dead, the last time he came? Yes, that was it of course, *he* wanted to stay, Johnny, that is, not the packman, forever, but of course he couldn't, you know—"

Alina swallowed, the smooth thick porridge suddenly making a lump in her throat. "You don't mean his Benign Supremacy?"

"Yes, it was something like that. *We* called him Johnny. Now, Lucia, do you want anything else to eat? Because if Dorcas is nearly finished, then..."

"I am the youngest child of the godking," said Alina with less than her usual intonation, baring the tattooed shoulder. "Can you feel the Moloquat?"

"Well, well, a small world, as I've always said, and whenever there's trouble people end up here one way or another. That *is* a nasty place. I wonder if it'll come off in the bath? Probably not without a good stiff brush and sea sand, and I don't know if we've got a grain left but I'll go and see..."

Still talking she trotted away to "look" with her glaucous white eyes, leaving Alina again disconcerted with no company but the marmalade cat.

No—there was more company. A strange creature came stumping across the kitchen from what must be the direction of the back door. It trundled along on four stubby legs, trailing a fat brushy tail, sniffing busily with its blunt black nose. It stopped and looked up at Alina with shoe-button eyes (not unlike Dorcas) and sniffed. Its body seemed to be made of crewel needles.

Alina palmed her knife, but the creature was so small—hardly bigger than the tranquil cat beside her—that she was ashamed to fear it.

Hermione returned, and seemed to sense the new presence in the air. "Oh, that's just Quill, don't mind her, don't pat her either, she prickles. She doesn't care for strangers usually, I can't think why she came in to see you—come, Quill, that's rude, don't stand there sniffing like that, we'll bathe her as soon as possible."

With another sniff the queer animal waddled past Alina and out through a hole in the kitchen wall, behind the woodbasket.

"Are you ready now? Dorcas is all set." Hermione drove Alina before her with shooing motions as though she were a strayed chicken.

In the yard behind the kitchen there were onion sets and clumps of herbs, a clothesline and poles, and a large round cauldron of dull silvery metal set up on stones over a small fire of fir-cones. It steamed lavishly. A wooden bucket half full of soft, pine-scented soap stood before it, and to one side a towel horse held a vast fluffy towel, white and voluminous as a cloud.

Alina had not seen, let alone enjoyed, such a bath since she left the walls of the Palace. It beckoned to her with wreaths of steam. She itched. She dropped her bag and her hands went to the neck of the dress.

At that moment she saw Ichabod among the clothes-poles. She did not recognize him for a full minute. He was a slender, upright boy with a clean, lightly freckled, well-favored face, dry nose, hair combed back from his brow, and the bearing of a young prince. He wore a clean, pale blue tunic.

"Ichabod?" she said.

"Pauli now, if you please," Hermione corrected her. "Not Ichabod. He washed up quite well, as you see. A nice boy. We might be able to keep him quite a while."

"Ichabod, don't you know me?" Alina asked sharply.

"I should be delighted to have the honor, madam," he said, with a courtly little bow to conceal his confusion. "But I fear that I..."

"That's enough Pauli, go along with Dorcas now," broke in the old woman. "Now it's *your* turn, Lucia dear."

"Wait! What have you done to him?"

"Washed him, of course. He certainly needed it. Now come this way..."

"But he doesn't remember who he is!" Alina resisted the strong old arm.

"Nonsense. He's just remembered who he ought to be,

that's what. And if you'll just do the same, dear, it will be better all around, believe me."

The scented bathwater steamed up into the pines whispering overhead, the morning sun shone with a pearly light on the soap in the bucket. Alina could almost feel the grime and sweat of the night journey washing away; not only dirt, but also the memory of Korab Khan's decomposing body, night escapes, loss of Braseli and Lula; her ingratitude to the Horsemen, the grotto and the desert, the filthy caverns of the Barak-Shar: all poured out with the bathwater.

But then she thought (with unusual clarity, like the piercing early light), "But who am I already, except who I am and who I ought to be? It's all very well for Ichabod to become Pauli, I daresay, but not for me. I'm not a child, I'm nearly sixteen, too old to start again from the beginning. And," (a flutter-kick recalled the fact to her) "there's a twice-royal child to consider. Although peddlers may carry the news of his Benign Supremacy's death like any piece of cheap goods, I, I the heiress, carry the dried heart, the real one. What if I forgot which was which?"

The old lady called Hermione was still speaking, although Alina had lost the thread. She broke in. "No, thank you. I would like a bath, very much, but I can't afford your kind."

There was a silence. Disconcertingly, Hermione's blank eyes stared past Alina as though they saw other things that were not there, things that had been or would be. The minutes dragged on and the blatting of goats could be heard distinctly.

Dorcas returned alone, and fixed her bright black eyes on the princess.

"Well then," said Hermione with sudden briskness, "It'll have to be the brook for you, ashes from the hearth and a handful of sisal. There's a place downstream with some flat rocks. Dorcas can take you there when the sun is high enough to dry you."

The old ladies seemed to take it for granted that Alina and Ichabod—or Pauli—would spend the winter with them. And Alina, taking into consideration both her waxing belly and the waning year, could see no better course, particularly as her horse was dead lame.

It would have been cozy enough with the eccentric sisters in their tumble-up house full of creatures and chance passers-by on the mountain-road, except that at first Alina suffered from dreadful nightmares. Anthea appeared in them, her white kitten-teeth lengthened to fangs and her polished fingernails grown to talons, angrily mouthing words that Alina could not remember when she woke in a cold sweat.

But after she offered to pay for her and Pauli's keep with the baroque black pearl of the hermit, Hermione had some advice for her. "Keep your pearl," she said, after rolling it in her lined dry palm and trying it on her teeth. "Around your neck on a cord, for luck. We don't need it. And while you're here, you won't have to worry about *her*—you know who I mean—"

"But I don't—"

"Well, never mind then, just ask Dorcas for a bit of string."

Alina did so, and the nightmares stopped. Fortunately, because she needed the sleep. The days were almost too short for the work to be done: the last cabbages and parsnips in the garden pulled; storage-apples to be culled; goats milked, chickens fed, bread kneaded, firewood split, water fetched, wool spun and dyed and woven. All the guests in the old ladies' house earned their keep, princes and peddlers.

Alina remarked that they actually worked harder than as slaves in the caverns of the Barak-Shar, and Pauli said daintily he wouldn't know about that. Alina wanted to slap him, but didn't because it wasn't really his fault.

Fall gusted into winter; the stream froze every night and hardly thawed at midday. The trees lashed bare black branches against a pewter sky; the colored leaves turned to crinkled brown flakes crushed underfoot.

The old ladies (who were certainly not what they

seemed) took great care to store provisions, although Alina observed that they had curious charms and cantrips that seemed to hold up better than more impressive enchantments. They could understand all animals (as Pauli, it seemed, could understand birds), clabber milk with a look, make people forget what they shouldn't remember, and shuffle years like a pack of cards: their respective ages seem to vary considerably from one day to the next, as did the number and arrangement of the rooms in their house.

"They never do anything dramatic," Alina said to herself, "like turning lead into gold or old men young again—but they do seem to be able to make things do quicker what they'd do anyway, like Tam's sore feet healing."

Hopefully she repeated her horoscope to them, one cozy evening by the fire:

> *Earth, Air, Water, Fire:*
> *One shall hold my heart's desire.*
> *Air, Water, Fire, Earth:*
> *One be foredoomed from my birth.*
> *Water, Fire, Earth, Air:*
> *Two be foul, yet two be fair.*
> *Fire, Earth, Air, Water:*
> *'Ware the bane of godking's daughter.*

Dorcas only nodded doubtfully, like a spinning top come to the end of its movement.

Hermione said, "Sounds silly to me. Why don't you make it any one of them you want? If it's raining, water is your heart's desire—if you're cooking porridge, then it would be fire—and speaking of that, Lucia dear, I smell something scorching now."

Alina jumped up to stir the pot, which had not yet scorched but was on the point of doing so, and moved it off the lizard-tongues of flame licking up the sides of it. She felt heavy, in mind and body, the kicking stranger (who seemed to be less and less to do with her long-ago lover) weighing like a clod of earth.

And then snow came, stealthily in the night, so Alina woke in her thick quilted wool mantle in her cot under the dormer and almost screamed to see the pines bowing under the load of glistening white, and wind-swirled drifts mounting halfway up the door.

Dorcas rejoiced in it; she and Pauli stamped a path to the goatshed with glee, flinging themselves into drifts and throwing handfuls of it about. Dorcas scooped up a bucketful of snow and brought it into the kitchen where Hermione was entertaining a passing packman and nursing a lapful of weasels.

"What is that for?" asked Alina.

Dorcas only shook a spoon at her, and plunged it into a pot she hung over the fire. Presently she stopped stirring and dripped syrup from the spoon on the snow in the bucket, long amber trails of it—again and again.

Then Pauli pulled out a chewy taffy and broke it in pieces for them.

"Eh, thanks, lad," said the little old packman, pulling his chair around. "Haven't had snow taffy in a long time, I haven't—belike people'll have to make do themselves, with the roads so bad, and dangerous as they are these days. No apricot jams from the City this year anyway, the crop failed altogether, I hear..."

"Hardly to be wondered at," Hermione put in comfortably. "The amaranth, too, I've heard...?"

"Like as not—and these here recruiting-sergeants are as bad as the bandits, hauling off lads for the City Guard from as far as Lake Tal..."

"Much trouble with brigandage, now?"

"Well, to tell you the truth, those Barak-Shar seem to have gone crazy, fighting among themselves. And when thieves fall out, honest men prosper," he added piously.

"Of course when they settle their differences one way or the other...?"

"Ah! Then we'll all have to watch out. That Perth, he's a long-headed fellow. Who knows how it'll end?" He munched taffy with a judicious air.

Alina, who was not much given to foreboding,

felt none.

But close onto the longest night of the year, she was coming up from the goatshed with two pails of milk when Hermione in house-slippers rushed out upon her.

"No, no, back to the shed, *they* are here, you can't be seen like this. Pauli is all right, I can pass him off as our nephew, but not you with your shoulder all marked up like that, not if it were ever so, get back into the goatshed and I'll send Dorcas down with a wrap..." all the while pushing Alina's unwieldy body backwards down the slushy path to the shed. "There's clean straw, you put it down yourself and have a drink of nice milk until Dorcas comes."

In the warm odorous shed, along with the shaggy yellow goats chewing their cuds companionably, Alina felt put out in more ways than one. Must she spend the night here? Who were these guests, to turn her out of her cot under the eaves?

But then came Dorcas with a candle, her list slippers slopping through the snow. The goats regarded her with slitted pupils. She was somewhat out of breath, and carried a folded piece of fabric over her arm, a large handkerchief, loose-woven, cobwebby, with no more color than a fly's wing.

Alina looked curiously at it, and found she couldn't see it until she turned her gaze to the side—and there it was again as Dorcas shook it out: larger than it had seemed, with uncertain edges. Alina could not even say if it was knitted or woven.

Dorcas draped it over Alina's head before she could say anything. Suddenly the warm candle-lit shed full of goats and milk and straw went grey and blurry. Alina put up her hands to lift the edge of the veil, but couldn't find it. And her hands! They were knotted and stringy like thick gloves, spotted, with ridged chalky nails.

Dorcus pushed her out the door and up the path. It was no good asking her for explanations.

In the kitchen Pauli was turning sausages on a spit. He

jumped up and said politely, "Will you have a seat by the fire, aged beldame?"

But Dorcas shook her head and a look of comprehension spread over Pauli's fair face. Alina was so astonished she let Dorcas lead her on.

Now she could hear voices, other voices: a tenor, one that made her think instantly of a fox-colored beard neatly trimmed, a red sash, a diamond pin and a plume.

"As I have mentioned: we have suffered some reverses. That does not affect the legitimacy of our claim, nor the necessity of recovering the —ah, person and the proof of it. We are prepared to take measures..."

What a pity Morphelius Pashan had survived the Hopgangers' oxen.

A contralto feminine counterpoint chimed in: "...which may be the worse for you, do you understand?" This voice Alina painted with snaky black locks, rolling black eyes, and a bosom like a white bolster pinned with rubies.

Dorcas opened the door.

Hermione said warmly, *"Such* a shame we didn't know anything about it until this moment, we could easily have sent a message with our nephew Pauli, *couldn't* we, sister? But with the weather so bad and all we simply..."

"Are there three of you now?" said Morphelius loudly, looking directly at Alina.

"...*and* your poor cold troop, so sorry, I do hope the mulled ale Dorcas took them will help fend off the cold, such a bad year, *isn't* it, here's old mother Eelwife came to visit and got snowed in..." Hermione's voice flowed on as she included Alina in a wide gesture. *"As* I was about to tell you, the poor thing went off on her own, as mother Eelwife here can bear me out, oh, *months* ago it was, yes, we couldn't persuade her at *all,* a very willful girl we thought her and so you'll undoubtedly find her yourselves if you do find her."

It seemed like a long visit, but at last the Barak-Shar were convinced that their errant princess—so they called her—and her stolen mount were nowhere to be found. Pantasilea looked thoughtfully at the old crone spinning bent-backed by the fire, and also at the shaggy cream-colored mule in the old ladies' lean-to next the goat-shed—even tapped the mule's nose with her jeweled fingers—but that was all.

At last they left, with no few veiled threats, but without what they had come for.

Hermione bustled back in from seeing them off. "My goodness, Dorcas, I hardly *thought*—but then you never know, do you? Alina, your relations will certainly be back, and that Pantasilea looked as though she smelled a rat. You've a cool hand with the butter, and a light one with the pastry, but I'm afraid you'll have to go just the same. It's that nasty heart that draws them, just as it does Quill (she wants to eat it, I'm afraid). We could have given it to her, of course—would have, if you'd taken a bath in our cauldron. But perhaps you know your own business best, and now it's too late in the year for baths…"

"Couldn't I," Alina interrupted, "just stay here disguised?"

"No, no, you aren't disguised! All Dorcas did was throw fifty years or so over you—your own years, you understand—so naturally anyone looking for a princess in her prime would be out in their reckoning. But you can't just leave them or they'll stick."

"Does that mean," asked Alina, "I'll live another fifty years?"

"No, not at all. They're your years as a flock of geese is yours—look after them or lose them."

"I don't understand."

"Never *mind,*" said Hermione crossly, "who asked you to? Now, Dorcas, where's that bag?"

It was Pauli who brought it, showing her it was stuffed to its shabby seams with bread and cheese, a packet of rosehip tea, and a lump of snow-taffy. Alina felt for the new tin soap box (marked with Quill's tooth-scratches) in which she kept the heart: a little shrunken, drier and dustier than before.

Handsome Tam, no longer a mule, followed Dorcas up from the lean-to wearing his caparisons.

In a strange access of emotion Alina flung her arms

around both the old women and then Pauli, crying, "Thank you, I'll miss you so!"

Dorcas deftly flipped the cobwebby veil over Alina's head and wadded it up small.

"I'll come back and visit, I promise, when everything is settled," she said as she mounted.

Pauli passed her up the bag, with tears in his eyes. Dorcas only shook her head. But Hermione's voice sounded already far away as she said, "You can't come *back,* don't you know that? You can only go on now, it's too late. Too late! Good luck!"

Alina set her teeth in her lower lip so as not to disgrace herself crying like Pauli, picked up Tam's reins, and turned his head down-valley to the distant sea.

Through the longest night of the year into the shortest day rode the princess. The bit rings rang, the thick harness creaked, Tam's big feet went pad-pad-pad on the packed snow. The sun was brilliant but cold on the ermine snowfields above the path to the right—to the left the bank fell steeply to the narrow rocky gorge of Sa, fretting in his icy and boulder-bound bed. The black willow-twigs were encased in glittering ice, breaking the light into spots of rainbow. The sky became the pale sweet blue of little birds' eggs or turquoises from the mines of Lake Tal, where Sa was born.

Wearily Alina shifted position, for the cold numbed her even through the thick woolen mantle. She was grateful for the easy rolling gait of the old pacer and for the broad sidesaddle she had previously scorned; for long journeys in a gravid condition, they were comfortable.

When she had hummed all the ballads she could think of, counted the number of hawks in the sky, and decided exactly what she would do if she met with the Barak-Shar (provided they played their part as they ought), she reviewed in memory the delicately tinted drawings in the Hall of Maps of the Palace. The Sa that she was following was a noisy, unnavigable stream that was Lake Tal's outlet to the sea. He ran along the feet of the mountains, falling

116

in a series of cataracts to a narrow rocky mouth far to the north of Ca's marshy delta.

There was a town on the narrow harbor at the mouth of Sa, Firstport; there were three more fishing-villages along the coast that made up the Four Ports, but she know very little more of them than that. Still, she thought crisply to herself, the Porters were not yet tried and might prove useful. However, this time she intended to be cautious and feel her way with one foot instead of jumping in with both.

Short as the winter day was, Tam couldn't go on without a rest. Alina began to be anxious for a place to stop. No village, traveler's inn, nor even solitary shepherd's hut did she see, although she passed more than once what might have been burnt ruins.

It was a little past noon, but already the sun was red and swollen as a blood orange and the slush where it had melted had again a fine glaze of ice like thin glass. She heard something like the tinkle of broken ice-sheets under her horse's feet—but it was the sound of mule-bells ahead, on the keen breeze.

She glanced around, but saw only barren snowfields to her right, and to the left the gorge at the bottom of which Sa muttered and brawled under his ice. It would be best to face it out boldly, but first she untied the cord of the great grey pearl that hung around her neck and slipped it into her bag. No—the first place a thief would look. Her fingers turned stiff and cold as soon as she took her hands out of the mantle, but she managed to braid the cord into Tam's thick mane on the underside of the fall of taffy hair.

The distinguished chief merchants Musa and Dara, very fine in turbans and curly-toed slippers at the head of their forty-mule packtrain, were surprised to find a gentle lady on a palfrey all alone.

Alina, with a falsely candid eye, explained that she was a lady on pilgrimage to the Temple at Calabrinia, but had lost her escort, waylaid by bandits—on the inspiration of the moment, she gave an exact description of Morphelius Pashan's band.

The rough and capable-looking muleteers loosened sabres in sheath and looked about alertly.

Alina accepted the merchants' offer—they were most solicitous, even pressing—of the hospitality of their tents for the night. She promised to remember them most kindly to her husband, a prominent vintner with a country villa on Lake Tal.

"You must be meaning to take ship at Secondport, this time of year," said Musa with the authority of a splendid grey beard. "The north road is very bad. You'll want to get a barge up-river before the spring floods, for it looks like a bad year."

"Indeed?" said Alina, with false surprise.

"They do say it's all because of his Benign Supremacy, being dead, you know," remarked Dara, younger and with an azure cast to his black whiskers. "One doesn't want to speak of it before the servants, but this may be the last load of astrolabes and clocks we get. Something is certainly wrong in the City."

"Indeed!" Alina repeated.

He shook his head, turban wagging. "I hardly know what profit we'll gain on the circular route this time, now the contumacious Hopgangers are charging tolls every few leagues on the road—before, they kept up the highways as their duty to his Benign Supremacy."

"Now they make us pay toll of one-fourteenth part of a gold *excellente* per head, cut with a chisel as they can't do arithmetic," stated Musa.

"Is it not sacrilege to deface the image of the godking?" said Alina, affecting to be shocked.

"Ah, but they claim to know for a fact he's dead," explained Dara. "There are strange stories about—why, in the City, they say the youngest of the royal princesses gave birth to a three-headed dog and hanged herself on a Moloquat tree!"

"How interesting," murmured Alina, both to say something and to dissimulate the enormous kick that thumped her mantle from inside. "As it is now quite dark, may I take the liberty of retiring to whatever tent your liberality has put at my disposal? I see your men have already attended to my mount, and by his godship, I'm more tired than the horse!"

Musa and Dara made each an airy gesture of assent, and conducted her one on each side to a tidy red and yellow canvas tent fitted with a handsome clock in the form of an exact replica of the golden statue of his Benign Supremacy, holding a clockface instead of the globe of the world in his right hand.

The two merchants, with sidelong distrustful looks at each other, bade her elaborate goodnights, and set each his own guard at her tent-flap.

Munching dried fruits and sweet oatcakes and pale wine left for her on a tray (those of the merchant caste do not eat in company), Alina congratulated herself on her good fortune and rolled herself up in the rabbit-fur comforter on the scissor-legged cot. The clock chimed a mellow nineteen, and she slept at once.

Slept dreamlessly and deep, until at some hour unmarked by the clock, a hand shook her: a white strong hand with shiny nails. Anthea in her white tunic and gold belt shimmered in the dark of the tent. A steaming golden cup, from which the scent of all spices rose in enticing waves, she held out to Alina, fresh-wakened in the chilly night.

"What a time I've had finding you," Anthea snapped. "And what a fine salad you've made of it! It was weeks before I could be sure you weren't blown to bits or stamped into paste, then I couldn't go where you'd gone when I found it out—really," she said nastily, "the question is hardly which of the elements is the 'bane of godking's daughter,' when godking's daughter herself seems to be the bane of all rational arrangements. The false heart is quite as effective as the real one for the moment—you have confused the issue considerably, and you'll have to pay for it."

Sitting up in a huddle of fur and wool, Alina blurted, "How do you know my horoscope? *Who are you?*"

"I've already told you I'm Anthea, the one who doesn't pay, and we'll get along a great deal better when you've taken this cordial. I know your horoscope for a very good reason which is not to the point just now. Drink it while it's hot."

Alina drank the steaming goblet at her lips, and fell asleep again at once—nor did she think it anything but a dream, when the bells and drums of the muleteers woke her in the morning.

Dara, particularly, did not like to let her go on alone. "It isn't the distance," he kept saying, "and there's hardly any snow the other side of the pass. But the roads aren't what they were, and..."

But Alina reassumed her manner and assured him her husband's servants awaited her in Firstport, and she should do very well. It was not to be thought of that she should turn back and accompany them—no, no, it was a question of a curse to be lifted, she must go on. She only hoped her bad luck might not affect them, as it surely would if she spent more time in their company.

The packtrain of forty mules with bells on their green housings looked prosperous and safe and comfortable, hung with rugs and bundles of firewood and hams. But there was Tam as well, saddled and waiting; he had still the pearl braided to the underside of his mane. Alina mounted the footboard and settled herself, waving cheerfully to the polite merchantmen, "Oh, yes, I'll write, certainly, on to the sea!"

But by midday she was terribly, terribly sick. Was it the oatcakes of the merchants, fried in butter that was no doubt fresh when they packed it? The altitude? But the cakes had tasted quite good, and she was already much lower, the snow no more than a powdering on the north sides of the trees. Whatever it was, she must go on.

But then she was sicker still, until she thought she must have vomited up her very entrails, and the unborn princeling besides. For hours she lay like a sick animal in the thin sunlight, while her horse cropped the frost-bitten grass. Waves of nausea coursed through her as regularly as the rhythmic figures of a Temple dance.

She thought of dying. It would take very little effort.

With detachment she considered the possibilities. She could lie back, let go, allow her wrung spirit to pass freely to the bank of UnderCa. Let the current carry her, as the hermit said—ride the runaway horse in the direction he gallops, as the Horsemen put it. Let the Barak-Shar have all the hearts they wanted to fight over.

No. Instead she pulled herself to her knees, and with her knife scraped pine bark and dried grass into a heap. She called Tam, and pulled down the saddlebags when he came and stood by her. In a very long time she contrived to make a little fire, and brew a draft of rosehip tea, hips of the pink roses that grew over the old sisters' clothes-poles.

In another while she felt able, although weak, to mount the old horse and continue.

So it was that at dusk she rode slowly down the steep zig-zag road to where the winking lights showed Firstport, perched like a gull's nest on the rocky shore of a bay. Her first sight of the sea was with the winter sun setting into it and turning all the water of the bay to blood.

Eight

Oh, what can ail thee, knight-at-arms,
Alone, and palely loitering?

–Keats

To Brev the Fisherman, the bay was not a sea of blood but a quiet grey harbor with the lights of Firstport winking him home. But to get there from the open sea he had to round the shark-toothed rocks of Narwhal Reef with wind and tide against him.

He rowed, therefore; sturdily, being a sturdy man of middle height with broad back and shoulders under a blue jersey knitted in intricate chains and cables. He had an open, wind-burned, broad-jawed face, clean-shaven as a razor clam, with deep-set grey eyes. His curly brown hair was damp with salt water, and dried salt crusted his brows.

The small gaff-rigged boat was of the sort used by the poor but proud fisher-folk of the Four Ports; by the painted eyes and gills on the prow it could be seen that she was a Firstporter and no other.

She rode high in the water, bouncing like a cork on the cross-chop and making more leeway than was safe in shoal waters. Brev laid into the oargrips like a galley slave keeping to the safe channel.

Though poor, he was not an unskillful fisherman. That winter day he had sailed far out to sea to find a school of silver mackerel that wanted nothing so much as to fill his purse seine full of flashing finny bodies. But through sheer ill-luck, a rainbow dolphin (which is itself a fisherman and akin to those of the Four Ports), was also after mackerel and foolishly fouled the net.

So Brev, being of the Dolphin Clan, had to strip to his brown skin and dive in the chilly water with his broadbladed knife to free the dolphin before it drowned. He succeeded, and the dolphin flipped its tail in farewell among the whitecaps as Brev, shivering violently, dried himself with fish sacks and pulled his jersey over his wet head.

By then the mackerel were tired of waiting; they trailed away through the slashed seine and were seen no more that day, such were always the fickle ways of fish.

Brev said no word critical of the Lords of the Deep, or dolphins, or even the inconstancy of mackerel. He set himself to mending the net with his hard clever sailor's hands while the boat rocked on the restless winter sea. While he worked, he cast a line off the stern with his lunch of salty bread and herring for bait; at last he caught on it a small, evil-eyed shark that flopped on the floorboards trying to work the worst spell it could think of.

The short winter's day was nearly done, and promising ugly weather for the morrow, before the net was made whole. Brev reluctantly decided against another cast. He hauled his sea anchor and set a course for home. The way this tide boiled over the rocks at the harbor mouth, he'd be lucky to see home at all, late or otherwise—on just such a squally winter afternoon some three years gone, his father and two brothers were lost at sea. Their bodies had never washed up, so it was certain that since then they played dice at the bottom of the ocean for pearls and fishes' eyes, and forgetting the dry land.

The sail bellied out like the front of Clytie, his pregnant wife; she would be nervous. And his mother would have set loaves to bake in the ashes; if he were very late they would be either cold or burned, depending on what the women decided to do.

Only a thin rind of sun showed above the horizon when he clawed the boat all unwilling into slack water in the lee of Narwhal Reef and dropped the sail. He shipped the oars, and rested a moment; the failing daylight over his shoulder danced on the choppy swell, and made it look as though the glassy dark water reflected a person.

It must be a trick of the light. He rowed on, and rounded the point. Raising his far-sighted grey eyes to the razorback reef where no boat could land, he thought he saw someone. He passed his sleeve over his eyes, and stood in the rocking boat, but still he saw it: a girl, slim, mother-naked, with a short shining helmet of hair, who waved and beckoned to him.

In his haste, Brev dropped an oar, and had to scull after it, lean out and grab it from the water; as he did so, the little shark saw its chance and fastened tiny triangular saw-teeth into his toe. Brev whooped, and settled the shark with the boathook.

But meanwhile the boat slipped leewards as the tide took it, and when the fisherman looked up, the reef loomed over him: graveyard of bigger boats than his cockleshell, the hissing swell swirling over the ship-killing fangs of the rocks. Then a dolphin struck the boat a hard shove towards open water, and another, as Brev bent again his weary back to the oars and pulled clear. He did not see the dolphin, streaking for the open ocean pursued by some invisible fury, nor did he see anything when he looked back but some bedraggled cormorants on the spine of the reef. He shook his head.

When he had moored the boat, secured the gear and rigging, stowed the oars, and taken his paltry catch (carefully) by the gills, it was full dark and cold as a dragon's bosom.

The village of Firstport straggled uphill from its harbor, all cobbles and brooks and low cottages of fieldstone and thatch. Next to the cottages lived sheep, and dun ponies a little larger and hardly less shaggy than the sheep, and curly-tailed little dogs with no bark.

Weary and limping, Brev climbed the steep fishy-smelling street to his cottage, twelfth from the quay, with its apple tree behind the garden wall and the mare putting her nose out of the stable and the little black dog jumping

124

up on the wall. The small-paned bright windows were fogged on the inside—he hoped it meant a good fire and bread hot but not burnt; and womenfolk sufficiently anxious to let him take his seaboots off by the fire but not so anxious as to be in a taking.

Brev was a simple man, and mostly wanted peace. Once he had longed for other things, but now he would settle for peace. He felt doubtful of having it; for the weather was breaking up, he was late home, with only a dogfish for a couple of days' chowder and poor chowder at that.

But Myrrha, his mother, and Clytie gave him a welcome, although Myrrha did just mention in passing that the men of the Sea Turtle clan had come in hours before with such a catch of cod you couldn't imagine. Clytie clucked at the tale of the dolphin in the net (Brev said nothing about seeing a siren) and set before him a plate of toast piping hot and not a bit burned, the jar of pickled herring, and a foaming jack of cider.

While he ate she knitted baby things and told him what she had decided about the crochet edgings.

Afterwards he said he might just stop in at the Common House, to hear anything good that might be going; for the Porters were all bards and poets (some better and some worse, but all proud), and Brev was a fine singer of his own compositions.

Myrrha shrugged eloquently, but Clytie said, "That's right, love, you won't be long, will you?"

The Common House served cider and kelp ale on tables made of bits of old deck planking. It might go as far as a bit of salt fish if pressed, but was by no means an inn. The Firstporters were independent people, and saw no reason to encourage people to lollygag about by furnishing beds for those so improvident as not to have their own. The Common House was maintained by donations and kept by anyone who liked company; it was a peculiar institution and not to everyone's taste.

When Brev entered with a good evening to you all, he was surprised to see a stranger in violent altercation with Jebjelly the host. A foreign-looking boy with thin sharp features and amber eyes, muffled in a wooly mantle the worse for wear; he looked like a moulting hawk, and had (evidently) a temper to match.

Jebjelly said loudly, "No, you can not have a room. For charity's sake I'll give you supper if you can eat herring, and a feed for your great bag of bones, 'cos I hate to see a beast ill-treated—but as for seeing our overlord, I'll have you know, missy, the whoreson isn't born can tell any man of the Four Ports what to do, no, nor will be!"

"We've got wives for that," observed a codger with pipe and ale-tankard.

"So we do, saving cholera and childbed fever and sharks in the rivermouth—but overlords be damned!" snorted Jebjelly, slamming a dried codfish on the counter as though it were tyranny itself.

"Nonsense," spat the girl. (Brev realized it was a girl, though as ugly a one as he'd seen lately.) "Who takes your taxes, makes your laws and leads your militia?"

"Missy, we don't pay no taxes, and that's a fact. Never did. River-tolls, that's fair, we use the Ca and pay the toll. But among ourselves, we live according to our own customs or our neighbors make us, that's all!"

"Give her some hot milk punch, Jebjelly," interposed the codger. "Arguing's dry work. Now you drink that, missy, and it'll give you a second wind, like."

Alina, haggard and drawn, sipped the foaming mug while she pondered this.

Brev poured himself some ale and listened.

"So you see it ain't a bit of use coming here with your Calabrinian airs and graces," Jebjelly went on. "No use at all. So have your supper and set a while by the fire, I won't say you mayn't, and then you can just turn around and go back where you came from."

The dilated black eyes looked such daggers that had Jebjelly not been busy chopping herring he would have reeled back from the glare. This was the second peculiar thing Brev had seen that day, and he wanted to inquire into it.

"Wait a moment, Jeb," he said. "The missy needn't take her business away with her for lack of a lord in Firstport, does she? She can tell us all, if she likes. I'd rather listen to something new than Cob's comic ballads. And, missy," he added kindly, "there's no inn, but that's not to say there's no such thing as a dry bed for you in Firstport, and my wife and mother glad to show you to it. What business brings you out by your lonesome in a black frost?"

Alina, looking very ill, made a gesture of weary desperation. "I bring news, in case you have not already heard it, that in the city of Calabrinia his Benign Supremacy is dead. The city hangs like a rotten fruit that waits to fall. I, princess Alina of the blood, have hawked the throne about almost full circle and got naught but saddle-galls for my pains."

Jebjelly put a trencher of herring in front of her and spat deliberately to one side. "We've no truck with his Whatfership, you're right on that."

"What may interest you is that this news has changed the old stasis of powers. I do not know what the Horsemen will do, if anything—but the Barak-Shar have gone mad and are swarming like wasps. They are at war—they have pursued me—I do not know how far."

"Them Barkers!" sniffed the codger, who appeared to answer to the name of Cob, and be put out about something. "We're not afraid of a few bandits. They steal a box of herring or a sheep once in a while—shiftless thieves. Seasick as soon as they look at a boat, they are, though mayhap one or two of the worthless lads of Secondport'll have joined them"

"More than one or two, from all over, have joined them," Alina snapped at him, her eyes black in the lamplight and huge, with purple shadows around them. "They have fallen on the Hopgangers already with the edge of the sword, and if they were not quarreling among themselves about—quarreling, they would have been upon you before now, crazed with I dare not tell you what ambition!"

"Th' spaewives'll magick 'em," muttered a fishwife hugging her hot cider at a center table. "Hang 'em up on the fish-drying racks."

"Will they?" said Alina. "Have you powerful enchanters? I have seen none in my travels that could turn the edge of even one sword, let alone many!"

"It's true the cantrips don't work like they used to," remarked another. "Said or sung, they go sour on you these days."

"Don't they say it's because the godking is dead and the Dragon Throne is empty?" said Alina in a flat voice. "Everywhere I have been it is the same."

But the Firstporters were more concerned with arguing than with the underlying harmonies of the universe, and Alina lost their ear.

Brev saw it was not a night for ballads and catches. He finished his ale. "Missy," he said, pulling gently on the hem of the mantle, "best come along with me. You look mortal tired."

"Yes," she said, "yes, this is the world's end, and I am very tired. I will go anywhere, it does not matter." She put her hand to the grey pearl set in silver hanging at her throat, and let Brev lead her over the ice-rimmed cobbles to his home.

"Oh, now, really, this is too much. I've said it time and again, your father (may he roll double sixes against the Lords of the Deep) would always let you do it, bringing home that otter cub that stole eggs, and the time you..."

"Mother, this is Alina, a princess of Calabrinia. She will stay the night."

"Oh," cried Clytie, "she's pregnant too, just like me! Alina? What a pretty name. Let me help you with your shawl. When are you due? Where is your husband? Of course you shall stay as long as you like with us, and when you feel better you must tell us stories of Calabrinia and the lands you have seen."

"You are very kind," replied Alina between her teeth. She allowed her shawl to be taken and her cold hands chafed. She cast a pitiless eye around the poor clean room with nothing in it but what was humbly useful.

The two women had dropped their knitting on benches by the fire; they wore coarse heavy brown homespun skirts and shawls, and their hair screwed up in a knot. The old woman, with hair the color of iron and face crumpled like paper, had a cold eye and a knitting-needle stuck through the bib of her apron. But the younger one was hardly older than Alina, round-faced, with clear blue eyes and a halo of fine, light-brown curls that captured the light of the fire. She smiled encouragingly.

Alina began to thaw, in body and in spirit. These rough fisherfolk were hardly to blame for being rough fisherfolk—and she could not travel farther even if there were any place else to go. She essayed a wan smile, which Clytie and Brev returned, as though she were a weakly lamb that had made it up on its legs.

"I thank you for your hospitality, good people," she said. "I am ill—I have travelled far and lost my baggage. I cannot pay you now, but..."

"Nor we aren't so poor as all that," broke in Myrrha with every sign of irritation. "My son's the best fisherman in the Dolphin clan, that's the same as to say in all Firstport and we..."

"Have a spare bedchamber for a traveler dead on her feet, if Mother will take her to it now. Goodnight!" Brev hauled his unwieldy spouse to her feet, kissed his mother goodnight and made to treat Alina the same, but that she drew back like a snail's horns.

When the women had gone to bed, Brev locked and barred the cottage door, not something he usually bothered to do: but the curly-tailed dog that slept in the byre whimpered and whined, and Brev himself, although he went to the gate and looked into the empty street, had the curious impression that there was someone or something outside.

The storm he had foreseen arrived at midnight. The next morning the sky dawned pewter-grey, with the sun streaming horizontally under the edge of the lid of clouds for a few moments before it was lost to sight. The cottage windows rattled in their frames and smoke blew down the chimney; the sea sucked and roared around Narwhal Reef, sending up spray like a whale spouting. Brev went

129

out to feed the animals and check his mooring. When he returned, he let in a blast of damp air that blew the kitchen-smoke back up the chimney for a moment of clarity.

Alina, heavy-eyed, was minding a panful of kippers and coughing, while Clytie fetched eggs from the hencoop. Myrrha was here, there and everywhere, like a bumblebee in a rather smoky and fishy foxglove blossom.

Brev wiped his boots on the mat. "Too rough," he explained. "Thought so. None of the boats will put out today."

"So I suppose you've had to go by the Common House for that important bit of news," snapped Myrrha, "leaving the three of us to struggle along as best we might."

Brev was slightly taken aback by Alina's presence—although he had not actually forgotten taking in the exotic waif the night before. "Royalty all over the place," he muttered. "Mare'll like as not foal in this storm," he offered as a change of subject. "It's near time."

Myrrha dished him up a plate of kippers and fried eggs. "What else did you find out? You were gone long enough."

"A boy came in on a donkey last night. He said that the Barak-Shar are mustering in unusual numbers, and will be a threat to the Ports when the snow melts. Like what you were saying last night. The odd thing is…that is, the boy, he…"

"Eat your eggs," said Myrrha. "The Barkers, did you say? Ohhh! Never mind boys!"

"Those Barkers—is it true you can't hurt them?" asked Clytie. "I've never seen any." She motioned Alina to sit at the round table in the middle of the kitchen and help herself to kippers.

"They can be wounded and killed, but they take a white powder that makes them feel no wound, cold, or weariness—there are many of them and their only trade is arms." Alina stopped, but everyone looked expectant. "They study nothing else and do no useful work. Now they are no longer content to be only bandits—united and determined, they will be a formidable foe in front of their leader, Morphelius Pashan."

"Whereas we have no leader, even for choral singing," said Brev, unexpectedly quick to understand her. "Most of us can swing a boathook at need, but not a sword. Although with a poem or ballad, or even arm-wrestling I could best..."

"Any other blowhard at the Common House," snapped Myrrha. "I saw those Barkers, before you were born, and I don't want to see them again. I think you men'd better do something, and I don't mean sing roundelays."

Alina didn't try the kippers, only drank a little milk. She rose from the table. "Everywhere I go it is the same," she said. "Enchantments will not hold, strife blows up like storms in winter, everyone says, 'I cannot, I dare not, I will not,' and bows his head to the wind like an ox in pasture."

Brev across the table choked on a fishbone and turned slowly a deep mahogany red. When he could speak, he said, "Is that what you think, missy? I'll be drowned if I let a pack of uppity Barkers interfere with me and mine. I'll make them sorry if they try it, I will. And I'll turn out the others. Every fisherman in the Four Ports better look out or be ashamed to drink with an honest man again!"

Alina stared astonished, Myrrha dropped an egg, Clytie cried out, "Oh do be careful, Brev!"

"I'm going to the Common House and tell them that, and ride to Secondport after."

Alina looked skeptically at him. A good sort, no doubt. A likely man for a day's work and an evening's song, apple of his mother's eye and his wife's clearly—perhaps even a possible captain for the City Guard when she came into her own. Or no. She felt a curious reluctance to recruit him for palace service, considering the indispensable requirement. Yet what other use might he be? He did not look royal, or noble, or even (in his oilskins) kempt. A fisherman redeem the Dragon Throne? But he was the closest to a volunteer she had found yet.

"Shall I give *you* the dried heart of his Benign Supremacy?" she said, cautiously.

"What, whose heart? No, my own will do for me. Can I

131

take your big horse, though? Our mare's too close on foaling to run up and down the coast road in a storm."

In a few minutes he was gone. The women looked rather blankly at each other, until Clytie burst into tears.

"There, there," said Alina, for the first time she could remember a little ashamed of herself. "I shall see that you are all rewarded richly when I come into my own."

Brev, rain beating almost horizontally in his face, drew rein so sharply that Tam almost sat on his haunches in the road. Before them stood a yellow-haired girl in a short white tunic and gold belt, gleaming as if the sun were shining. She had beryl green eyes, and when she smiled as she raised a hand for him to stop, she had teeth like a kitten's.

"Such a hurry for nothing," she said in a friendly way. "Stop a bit, some to my lodging for a little refreshment, and I'll tell you some good news."

Brev gaped with astonishment. It was a lonely stretch of road, and the girl seemed to have stepped dryshod from nowhere. "I'd be well please to hear good news, missy, but I've no time to stop and less to leave the road."

"Not even if my news makes a foolish joke of your journey?" asked the girl as pleasantly as if they two were out picking mayflowers of a morning. "I'll gladly tell you, even so, and ask nothing in return but the dolphin you wear around your neck."

Brev put his hand to the smooth bit of silver. It seemed a small price to pay—he could always get another. And if the strange lady offered as it were a chart to unfamiliar waters, he needed one.

"What would you want with my dolphin, now?" he temporized, since a Porter never agrees to anything at first—too much like subservience. "And what sort of news have you in mind to tell?"

"Oh," said the lady, still dry in the rain and always smiling, "I could tell you whether you'll father a boy or a girl, and what will be its fate. I could tell you how it was the sea swallowed up three good sailors like your father and brothers. And I could tell you the mind of Morphelius Pashan so far as it concerns the Four Ports! Wouldn't that be worth a little delay to learn?"

The cream-colored gelding sidled and pawed the road. Brev wrinkled his broad brow in thought.

In the cottage of Firstport, Alina dropped a trayful of jelly pots and screamed. Clytie and Myrrha rushed to her.

"I'm bleeding," she cried, surrounded by shards of stoneware and gouts of blackberry jam.

"It's the jam," Clytie began.

"No, you soft silly, it's her time! Help me get her to bed at once," snapped Myrrha.

The cold rain still fell heavily, although the wind had dropped. Brev's jersey was sodden with it. His mind was filled with Barak-Shar, whom he visualized as shiny black creatures like huge beetles—chitinous, with pincers—and it was hard to connect them with Anthea, whose girlish breasts outlined in white seemed like a confectioner's creation. There seemed to be no harm and perhaps much profit in the bargain she offered—and yet (the horse threw up his head, setting all the silver bells on the head-stall a-jingle) it was a lonely road, and a strange bargain, and his business was to take a message to Secondport.

The rain came down more heavily, in grey spears of icy water. Anthea, dry and smiling, waited. "Do you think I cannot do as I promise? Let me show you a wonder. Have you never wished to see the great city, Calabrinia? You may—it is a small thing, for me!"

Brev came to the conclusion that the matter could not be left so, it was his duty to find out what passed on the rainy road to Secondport. He dismounted, bowed and said, "As you will be so kind, missy!"

Anthea's pink tongue flickered between her teeth and the green eyes turned dark as emeralds with gardens in their depths. "With your consent."

In the flick of a lizard's tongue the rain blotting the

rocky coast, the coast itself, the muddy track, all vanished. Brev Fisherman, still holding the nervous horse, found himself in the midst of a great city.

It was Calabrinia, navel of the world, built of cut stone, polished marble, mosaic and plasterwork like petrified lace, and washed by the spray of fountains breaking the sunlight into myriad rainbows trembling in the orange-blossom scented air. He seemed to see narrow ways between house-walls where vines hung crimson flowers over the heads of passers-by, and vast squares filled with color and noise in which multitudes of people bought, sold, lounged, hurried, shouted, laughed, cried, whispered, made assignations and carried out assassinations. He saw slaves and merchants and fortune tellers, guards stalking after their leashed panthers, ladies riding in litters with purple silk curtains, noble youths on exquisite palfreys, brown-robed priests two by two, idle young wastrels gathered under the invigorating Moloquat trees telling lies.

He saw the Palace, like an open jewel-box; the Temple with its gilded dome and the great golden statue; the rich alluvial fields with new crops just showing their tiny green sprigs, the orchards and vineyards and the store of art and science and luxury: all the long dream of empire under the sun beside the slow green Ca.

"Are you dazzled?" inquired Anthea in a low purring voice. "Well you may be. It is the desire of this city that drives the Barak-Shar mad, and the fear of the empty throne that sends them frothing and biting their neighbors like mad dogs."

Brev passed his broad hand over his brow, brushing away icy rain or cold sweat, he did not know which. He said nothing.

"Yet someone must rule the city and the empire," said Anthea sweetly. "Why not you? Is not one sturdy free Porter worth ten ragtag aristocrats?"

"Who are you?" Brev asked, and his hand on the bridle trembled so that the silver bells rang again.

"Leave the beast to go where he will, and throw your dolphin amulet after him—then I will tell you that and many things more besides."

The city vanished, and it seemed to Brev as though they were in a chamber of crystal and mirrors like a hollow diamond, in which burned a leaping green flame in a glass brazier. Around it were cushions of deep emerald-colored velvet sewn with gold sequins like stars and before it, reflected in all the mirrors a hundred hundred times, was Anthea; without the tunic, and whiter than cream cheese and strawberries.

Brev dropped the reins, and the jingle of silver bells faded from his ears.

The cool voice of Anthea murmured, "Take off the amulet. I do not care for silver. Then come here and change your wet clothes."

Brev took one stumbling step, hardly more forward than backward; the fresh gash from the teeth of yesterday's dogfish opened and the pain startled him like one of Myrrha's sawtoothed comments. It didn't seem altogether likely that he was cut out for a sorceress's lover, even if he was the best fisherman in Firstport. And if that wasn't it, there must be something else in it.

He took a decided step back. "Thanking you kindly, missy, but I don't like to wade where I don't know the depth nor how the currents set. No offense intended, but I'll just be on my way." He put his hand under the soaked jersey and took the warm smooth silver dolphin charm into his palm.

And found himself in an instant in the pouring rain, alone in the middle of a muddy road, with no horse and many leagues to go.

As he slogged (a touch lame-footed) towards Secondport, he wondered whether he was a mooncalf-fool, or well out of it, and whether he'd ever know which.

At the cottage, Alina was well into labor, panting in the short shallow gasps between pains, and cursing his Benign Supremacy, Korab Khan, Meerkat Lobum, Morphelius Pashan, all men, rain, the sea, Calabrinia, and her own luck. More reasonably she might have cursed the draught that she-who-pays-no-price had dosed her with in the luxurious tent of Musa and Dara, but she had forgotten about it.

Myrrha gave her a thick towel twisted around the bedpost to pull on. Clytie trotted back and forth with cold cloths for her forehead and kept saying, "Shall we not try to get word to your husband? He will be so anxious! I can't bear to think of it!"

Alina, with gritted teeth, replied, "What husband?"

"But you're a princess, not a—well."

"Princesses have consorts, if the dynasty requires it, not husbands."

"Oh! But..."

"A lover —ummph! —is a hawk you wear on your glove to fly at game. Ummmph —ahhhh! The greater the quarry, the greater bird to carry, and the harder he gripes. For royalty —ahhhh! —only an eagle will do..."

Myrrha, scandalized, sent Clytie to borrow arrowroot from a neighbor. Otherwise Alina made an excellent subject for childbirth, being young and strong, and the princeling seemed to be coming along excellently.

By early dusk he took his first breath—but shortly after it, his last.

"Too bad," said Myrrha. "A pretty babe, though a trifle darkling. Next time, take my word for it, these long journeys in the last three months won't do."

Clytie wept so hard she had to be sent to the kitchen to make camomile tea.

But Alina, furiously dry-eyed, refused to believe that so much trouble could go for nothing—she threw the tea at Clytie, and hugged the tiny corpse to her as if she could force it to life again. Even when she was convinced that her son was truly dead, she refused to give him up; refused so violently that even Myrrha was afraid to persevere, and left her to herself.

Nine

...all trouble seems
Dead winds' and spent waves' riot
In doubtful dreams of dreams.
—Swinburne

S o matters stood, a night and a day after, when Brev
returned from Secondport on a borrowed pony. He
had achieved nothing like a concerted front against
the Barak-Shar, although there had been a great deal of
argument and a messenger sent on to Thirdport.

On the doorstep Myrrha met him, wringing her hands
and twisting her apron into a rope. "Brev, what have you
been doing? That great tapioca-colored beast came back
yesterday with his reins dragging in the mud...we were
all of a tizzy...can't you pay some mind to your own
business, here's the cupboard bare with two next-to-use-
less girls in the house and I had to practically beg on my
knees for that Jebjelly to trust me for a bit of fish, he's all
taken up with that bird-boy...and there's your princess,
not a whit better than she should be, lost the little byblow
but sitting up there with the body, I call it indecent..."

Wearily Brev edged past her and took off his sodden
jersey. It wasn't raining at the moment, but nothing dried
in the seafog.

"Clytie?"

"Poorly, thank you, with the shock and the worry. I
sent her to order the coffin, not liking to leave the house
in this sorry state of affairs..."

She followed him to the door of the room Alina occupied, making knots in the apron, but let him go in alone.

Alina was in bed but sitting up. Her breasts were bound up with cotton rags soaked in sharp-smelling cider vinegar; her eyes were sunk in dark-stained circles; her mouth was set in a rectangle of fury. The knife-hilt was visible in a fold of the blanket.

Brev closed the door, pulled up a stool and sat down, just out of reach. The blanket was grey, her face was grey, the window was a solid block of grey fog a little lighter than the walls. Brev struck a spark from his flint and steel and lit the clay lamp. "Alina," he said.

She glared.

"I'm sorry," he added, looking only at the wall on which the lamp-flame cast leaping shadows. He bent over and hauled off his muddy boots, then leaned back on the stool and propped his back against the opposite wall. He said nothing else.

After a long while, he scooted the stool along the wall a few inches, then a little more. Her hand went to the knife-hilt and he hunched his shoulders in anticipation, but she did not throw it. Finally he put his big square hand over her clenched fist and held it.

A while later the stumpy bedposts trembled and he heard dry sobs. "Alina," he said again, "I really am sorry. Clytie's sick about it, and..." It seemed safe to move closer. He put his arm around the shoulders to hold in the sobbing. "If you'll let me have the...baby, I'll take as good care of him as if he were my son."

There was another long shuddering silence, but at last she straightened up and reached under the bolster. She had the body hidden there, wrapped in a towel; it made a pathetically small bundle. Alina herself seemed greatly diminished, hardly a noticeable bulk under the thick blanket, but as he closed the door, a tin box struck it and rebounded.

As Myrrha said, to neighbors and anyone who chanced to be within earshot, it just goes to show that when things

138

begin to go wrong there's no holding them at all, and when bad luck comes to stay you might as well move out yourself.

For Clytie returned from her errand with the pains upon her, and being but a poor slip of a thing (as her mother-in-law had said from the beginning, hadn't she), gave birth to a great lump of a boy and died of it three days later.

Brev was struck dumb. But the thought grew in his mind that things were going wrong not altogether of their own accord. He took the silver bells off Tam's harness and parcelled them out: two on the cradle of his orphan son, where the wide blue eyes could see them; one around the neck of his pony mare, one on her new filly-foal, and the three remaining on his best ewes; he remembered the strange lady he met on the road to Secondport did not care for silver.

He cut a strong piece of fishing-line to hang his silver dolphin on, and told his mother that her silver and jet earrings were the most becoming she owned.

Apart from these matters, he had to fish—in the sullen intervals between winter storms howling out of the west, he took the boat out. Splitting and gutting the catch, hauling it to the salting vats, mucking out the sheep and horses and fowl, catching a bite of supper before going to the Common House, where it was confidently predicted that the heavy snows in the mountain would keep the Barkers where they belonged—was plenty to do. His son, named Corwin, he left to the women, although he could hear (as could anyone between the harbor and the Common House) that the boy had a fine pair of lungs. His wife he deeply regretted, but that he could do nothing about—and so days passed, in which the rain continued sluicing down the slate roof of the cottage as if to make tears superfluous. Another stranger, reputed to be a prince of some sort, settled himself in the Common House, but Brev had no time to worry about it, or even mention the subject at home.

Alina got up and about, in a temper like a vixen with colic. Myrrha was equal to it; she rose to the challenge, growing stouter and relishing her tea as she hadn't since the loss of her husband and sons.

"Why, in the name of all devils in earth and air and undersea, can't that child keep quiet for the space of ten heartbeats?" screamed Alina one morning.

"*Your Highness* must excuse the inconvenience—lacking your aristocratic advantages, sheep's milk disagrees with him!"

"Is that all?" sniffed Alina, stalking barefoot into the kitchen.

"Slut," muttered the old woman.

"Then you might have told me, instead of passing out these cheese rags—" Alina said, pulling out of her bodice wads of milk-stained cloths pungent with vinegar. "Give the brat here."

"Now I've seen everything," Myrrha snorted, but handed over the roaring baby.

Alina took him awkwardly and held his face to her swollen breast. She winced as the sharp-gummed little mouth closed like a shark's on her nipple—but at least there was silence. And presently the placid relief of flowing milk, so that she settled into a chair with a little contented sign.

Peace crept into the kitchen as cautiously as a stray cat not sure of a welcome.

When Brev came in under the risen half-moon he saw no baby in the cradle by the chimney-corner. The silence in the house was as thick as fog. Horror in his blue eyes, he interrogated his mother with a look.

"No, no, Corwin's fine as silk thread. You'll never believe this, but her Highness took a notion to give him her breast, when oysters dance polkas, *I*'d've said, but..."

Brev took the narrow stair four treads at a time, then paused and rapped gently with one knuckle.

"Pass," said a sleepy voice.

He did. By the moonlight he saw Alina curled around a fuzzy head, a comforter over them both. Her coil of black hair like spilled ink flowed around her, and her eyes were great calm dark pools. She no longer looked ugly to him, not even plain.

"I also take care of your son as if he were mine," she said.

Brev made no answer, only closed the door slowly and very, very softly.

The winter ceded inch by inch to spring forcing its way up from the south. The high snows melted and Sa ran like a millrace; even the brooks that tumbled down the gutters of the streets of Firstport ceased their playfulness and rose over the doorsteps.

The sheep lambed, and overnight thousands of yellow crocus dotted the hill pastures—Myrrha went out with a close-woven basket to pick the orange stamens for seasoning, leaving the baby with Alina.

Alina ate like a horse: hard rye bread and winter apples, fresh salt fish, and mussels she gathered herself from the rocks at the harbormouth: she went lightfooted as a goat, with the baby on her hip and her hair braided out of his reach, her amber eyes shining with life and restlessness and malice. But although the dark-plum bloom on her cheek was the same as the spring before, a certain tendency to reflection was noticeable—not only the baby she carried everywhere weighed her mind. She even troubled to pry loose enough fresh bearded mussels to carry home for Brev, in return (she told herself) for his hospitality, nothing else.

But there was no great rejoicing in the coming of spring for the town as a whole: with the opening of the passes, the Barak-Shar might sweep down at any time. Even Jebjelly, with time, had digested the situation and admitted the need for defense.

There were first-class shots with sling and stone among the Firstporters, and even the most left-fisted could pick a thieving gull off a basket of fish at thirty paces; so a comforting theory got about that a file of slingmen standing their ground could do great damage to cavalry soldiers in leather helmets, if they all fired at once and kept firing in the right direction.

"And there's no lack of stones to throw, free for the

picking," observed Jebjelly thriftily.

However, no amount of theory could make an army out of the Firstporters. Even as a rabble they would not coalesce into a unified mob. Brev lost weight, and two deeply chiseled worry-marks appeared between his sun-bleached eyebrows.

One evening just at dusk he came from the Salt Meadow where the Porters had been essaying their skill. He rode his pony mare with the foal frisking at heel, the only cheerful one of them.

Myrrha met him at the gate with a tonic of tea and wormwood.

"Later, Mother," he said. "The mare's all in a lather. Kicked blazes out of Willwin's roan—the beasts are as bad as the men. I've got to rub her down and give her a branmash."

"Why shouldn't the lazy vixen do it, she's little enough to occupy herself—come in and drink this while it's hot."

"The chickens are shut up and the sheep in the fold, and I've left a mash for your mare," remarked Alina with crisp precision, entering the fray with Corwin on her hip. "There's chopped comfrey in it, she'll like it."

She followed to the stable and perched on the manger while Brev rubbed the mare down, letting Corwin make friends with the foal. Presently both insisted on nursing.

"The bells sound pretty," remarked Alina presently. "Is that one of your customs, like never agreeing with each other?"

"Not until lately, Princess."

"Why lately?"

Brev straightened up from picking out the mare's feet. The warmth and animality of the stable made him unknit his brows and the worry-marks softened somewhat. "I was thinking on asking you about that, Princess. For it was the day you came I first saw the—whatever she is, the one that doesn't fancy silver near her. She's as fair as you are dark, but there's a certain likeness..."

"What nonsense are you talking? Do you mean poor Clytie?"

"Not a bit of it! This one has short hair golden as an

142

excellente and eyes like the insides of the sea-anemones on Narwhal Reef. It was on the reef I first saw her."

Corwin wailed briefly, cut off as Alina hastily switched him to the other breast, already leaking milk down her shift. "Nobody can land on the reef."

"That's what I thought," agreed Brev, "even at the time. It seemed strange."

"I do know someone with such eyes...not to know, exactly. She wears a dress of white samite, with a gold belt."

"Now, then, mare, shift over...where do you know this person, not to know, from?"

"A good many places," said Alina, "and betimes I was glad to see her. But not here," she finished thoughtfully. "Not here."

"Haven't seen her or weren't glad to?"

"Neither—are you finished?"

"Just about. Well. Isn't that a silver setting to your pearl? The lady doesn't like silver. That's why I took the bells."

"You're welcome to them," said Alina absently, thinking when she had been wearing the pearl, when not, when she had seen Anthea. "I stole them myself."

In the parlor they drank tea with wormwood and just a drop of spirits, for Myrrha to keep up *her* spirits. They took turns rocking the baby to sleep, and Myrrha knitted when it wasn't her turn. The sea-coal fire was hot, blue at its heart and yellow at the tips of the flames, and the wind whined on an envious note at the windowpanes.

The curly-tailed dog had followed them in, and now lay at Brev's feet, gazing into the fire with half-closed eyes. The bells on the cradle rang their tiny note, like silver beads sewn on the blanket of peace over the cozy little room. Brev heaved a deep breath of contentment. Myrrha dozed over her teacup.

"I'm so bored I could spit starfish," remarked Alina. "Is there nothing to do but sit by the fire like a smoked kipper? Don't you ever do anything, dance or hunt or something lively?"

Myrrha sputtered in her tea. "Hunt? Hunt? Your crack-brain Highness, the Barkers are following on your tracks, to hunt us all into the sea so we can roll cogged dice with the lords of Undersea like my departed!"

"Is that what happens?" asked Alina. "All the peoples I have met expect a different afterlife, perfectly logical I suppose, given the different ways they live—the merchant-caste carry a sort of eight-sided coin, pierced in the middle, called the *vademecum,* eight sides for the eight signposts along the way, and the hole for clear sight to them—"

"Along what way?" asked Brev, interested.

"The way across the Desert of Death, to the east of Calabrinia and Ca—the way is led by a great black mule with nostrils of flame. The more a merchant wants to take with him, such as wives, slaves, horses, the more coins he must keep by him...everyone knows exactly what to expect, except my friend the hermit, who was unsure. Now that he is dead I cannot imagine what the keepers of the afterlife will do about him."

"What the Barkers will do about us is more to the point," muttered the old woman as she picked up the stitches she had dropped. "Why do they want to come, anyway? No, don't talk about it, it gives me the colliewobbles. Sing something, why don't you? Sing the ballad about...about..."

"Cor and Old Dolphin?" suggested Brev, and without waiting on the answer, raised his strong sweet baritone in the ballad all the Portfolk knew, whether of the Dolphin clan or not. He rocked the cradle in time, with his foot.

That ballad tells of Cor the boldest fisherman of all the Ports, who sails farther out to sea than any man goes, to ask news of his sweetheart Evangeline whom the sirens took away to dress their hair for them.

Cor calls on Old Dolphin, ten spans long and older than the town of Firstport, and asks about Evangeline. No, says Old Dolphin, forget her. She's gone to the bottom, and the Kraken guards the way.

Cor promises to catch ten thousand mackerel for Old Dolphin, every day of his life, if he can have Evangeline back. No, says Old Dolphin, she's gone far away and only the sharks know where she's gone.

Cor will be a son to Old Dolphin and serve him forever, if he can only see Evangeline once to tell her one word he forgot to. Well, says Old Dolphin, get on my back and hold tight and we'll see how far we can get.

Cor says that's saying as fair as can be, and on he gets.

After a long time drifting with the tide, Cor's boat opens its painted eyes and spreads its blue sails, and comes home to harbor without him.

And from that day to this no one has seen Cor, nor yet a dolphin half as big as Old Dolphin, nor heard any news of them dead or alive.

It was a tuneful ballad, though in a wailing minor key, and Brev trailed off to the whispered last stanza:

> *Seek the sands where sirens sleep,*
> *Chart the course the Kraken keeps,*
> *Ask the sharks, from what dark deeps,*
> *Shall Cor come home no more, oh!*
> *Cor come home no more.*

A bright drop shimmered in each of Alina's amber-dark eyes, as she gathered up the baby to go to bed. Myrrha was already asleep in her chair with the dog curled beside her.

Brev stayed to bank the fire, still humming the melancholy refrain.

Alina lugged Corwin's dead weight (he grew like a whale calf) up the narrow stairs and tucked him in. She was melancholy also, with a waterish, gentle lassitude like low notes on a flute; dissolving, unraveling, unknitting her will from her bones, so that she wandered to the window silvered over with moonlight.

She hardly knew herself in this mood. The sun of Calabrinia hatches hot tempers, choleric and easily ignited—red murderous rage, black depression or sun-bright manic enthusiasm were the only three points of Alina's compass that she knew. What was this strange miasma of the spirit, something that stole out of the far salt reaches of the sea to envelop her as the sea mist curled around the houses of the town?

Below she heard a heavy step on the planking. Brev must be looking in on the animals and taking a quiet piss in the yard. No, she thought. It really wouldn't do at all. Resolutely she turned her marked shoulder, until Brev's square blue back disappeared around the corner of the house. Like all the Firstporters he had a lubberly seat on a horse, no sense of what was proper, and spoke his mind with appalling freedom.

She pulled the darned linsy-woolsy dress over her head and put on the white cotton bed-gown Myrrha had (for decency's sake) given her. Still she did not feel like sleeping. The mist rose only to the first story of the house; above it the moon trailed clouds of silver across the velvety indigo sky, so much—softer—than the blazing bediamonded black enamel sky of the desert. She could hear the slap of the tide turning against the pilings of the quay, and smell the salt air.

She opened her door and crept down the stairs again, step by step, careful not to let them creak. Her bare feet were silent on the planking. She reached the larder—yes, there were some jellied eels in a crock. She helped herself to a generous portion and took it upstairs to eat, although jellied eels were not what she really wanted. But they were delicious and soporific even so, and finally she slept, dreaming of a mariner deep-drowned and long-bewailed.

The next day Alina had little time for moping; indeed, the complexion of Firstport public life changed. It became no less acrimonious—in fact, more so—but a new and strenuous element was added.

It was Brev's idea that Alina might address the assembled fisherfolk on the menace of the Barak-Shar: their habits, arms, disposition. He hoped that the women might be convinced by Alina's first-hand account, and ginger up their menfolk.

Alina had not been back to the Common House since the night she arrived. Now the first face she saw was that of a fair and freckled youth who seemed to have grown since last she had seen him. He had a merlin on his shoulder.

"Pauli! The mysterious prince is *you*?"

He bowed his princely little bow. "Since my older brother buried his name, I am Prince of the Isles."

"Of course! " cried Alina, her cheeks flaming dark red. "The Prince, the real one! You shall rally and lead the Firstporters, to turn back the..."

"My dear Alina."

"What?"

"Sit down and calm yourself—have some clam juice."

"But Pauli, this is wonderful, I had no idea! The two of us..."

"Oh, dear no. Dorcas and Hermione thought it best to send me here, but my talents lie in quite another direction. I have been able to teach the Porters a new form of part-singing which is really extraordinary. If you have a moment to listen..."

"Pauli! This is serious!"

"Art is always serious. I suppose what you have in mind is something tiresome and practical. Women are always nagging about something practical."

Alina's palm itched to slap him, but Corwin weighed down her arm. "Are you a prince or not?" she demanded.

"Yes—a prince of the Isles, madame, whose function is purely decorative, unlike your esteemed predecessors."

"I wish the Old Ladies left you as you were," she snarled. "Ichabod had some spunk, as well as a runny nose!"

Pauli bowed again, if possible more gracefully than before. His fingers strayed after the reed pipes on the table beside him. The little merlin mantled and shrieked at Brev, standing by bemused.

"But you, my dear, are of a different stripe. Did you not grow up with lion hunts, chess games, epics of war and conquests for your bedtime stories? Did you not do your embroidery overlooking the evolutions of the Guard on the training grounds?"

"Of course," said Alina.

"Well, I chiefly employed my time, before the Barak-Shar kidnapped me, in learning bird calls at my mother's knee."

Mention of mothers always irritated Alina, but when she grasped that the closest thing to a drill-sergeant with knowledge of theory in the Four Ports was herself, she accepted the challenge. She did more than lecture on the Barak-Shar, she galloped up and down the small open space adjoining the Common House, screaming for organization and discipline.

Lubberly Jebjelly responded, "There's no man born can tell a Firstporter what to do, and by the Great Sea Turtle, no man ever will!"

"Do I look like a man, fat ale-tub?" Alina yelled back. "Now do as I tell you, by the Great Frogspawn or whatever uncouth demiurge you will, but *dress that line!*" She balanced the knife on her palm, keeping it out of Corwin's reach.

"Whoof!" sputtered Jebjelly. "Don't know if I wouldn't rather the blade than the rough side of her tongue. Neighbor Brev, the next time I hear them speak ill of you and missy there, I'll ask 'em would they tickle a she-shark for pleasure and profit."

"Your throw," prompted Brev.

Between the whiplash of Alina's tongue and Brev's patient prodding, slowly the wayward ponies were schooled to work in formation and the men learned to hurl a deadly volley of stones and reload for another in unison. Pauli helpfully suggested they might think of it as a form of part-singing, with stones for notes—and some of them grew even enthusiastic.

"This close-order work—it do make a difference, don't it, Jeb?" said a grizzled boat-captain. "Like all haul t'gether and warp 'er in against wind and tide. Like to see them Barkers come, so I would!"

"About like I'd want to be dismasted on a lee shore in a williwaw," grunted Jebjelly, but he hurled his stones with precision.

Alina prided herself on the change. "Who needs a prince, after all?"—but Brev thought the arrival of some

Hopganger refugees with lurid tales of fire and sword did as much or more to stiffen the resolve of the Porters.

Or perhaps to break it: offerings of fish and offal were made to the sirens, which was right and reasonable; so many that the water between the point and Narwhal Reef boiled continually with feeding sharks.

But also, great stores of ship's biscuit moved mysteriously at night; also creek water in barrels, hard cheese and winter-storage apples and boxes of salt herring, went to the holds of certain fishing boats. Small valuables, dishes and quilts and trunks of clothes, were smuggled aboard and battened down wherever they could be stowed. Clearly a certain number of the Portfolk intended to trust to the open sea rather than the chances of a battle on land, whatever they might say at the Common House.

A side effect, however, was a buyer's market in livestock. Brev traded a spare sail and a pair of oars for a nanny goat with twin kids. Furniture, farm tools and blacksmith's forges were offered for a song—but on the other hand the price of pitch and canvas rose precipitously, particularly as the prospects of more stock from the embattled north looked poor.

By this time, with spring firmly established and the high passes showing lush green instead of snowcap, the great question was not what to do when the Barak-Shar came, but when they would come? Even the bravest found it hard to keep courage screwed up to the sticking-point day after day.

Alina was desperate for a suitable prince. It was always in the back of her mind. But of the moderate selection offered, all candidates showed a fatal flaw, such as being dead (Korab Khan), uninterested (Pauli), or utterly revolting and perverse (Morphelius Pashan). No wonder she was driven to find attractive a mere fisherman, through (what else could it be?) sheer propinquity.

She consulted in memory all the historical legends she could remember that in any way paralleled her present case—but all the low-born lovers turned out to be princes and such in disguise. She inquired of Myrrha if perhaps Brev had not been sired by a mysterious stranger, and Myrrha threw a jar of buttermilk at her. And in truth Brev's square brown torso bore no cryptic marks, or indeed anything but a good deal of curly brown hair. He was, further, muscled like a fisherman, his nose was straight and blunt, he had straight burnt-blond brows over frank grey eyes—not at all the sort of face to look well on the *excellentes* she meant to have minted with her own sideface foremost.

But she did ask him to teach her the making of eel-traps, to pass the time, and Brev taught her as patiently as he taught the stubborn mare drill. At last the trap was finished, and they took it and Corwin down to the end of the jetty to see if it would work. Brev carried the baited trap and a line for flounders. It was a crisp bright day, and the gulls against the blue were almost too white to look at.

"What are these ballads you set such store by?" Alina asked suddenly. She sat on the very end of the jetty, teasing eels with her toes. "They are always different, from singer to singer, and even from one time to the next with the same singer. Now the chants and dances of the Temple are exactly as they have been for a thousand years, not a word or a step missed."

"What happens if you miss one? Does the Temple dome fall?" Brev had pulled in two flounder and was cleaning them rapidly and bloodily without looking at Alina.

Corwin crawled around her, attracted equally by the drop to deep water and the deliciously colored pile of fish offal. Alina's grip on his shirttail kept him from either.

"A slight error might occur, corrected at once," she bragged. "We have great discipline. *You* just improvise to suit yourselves as you go along."

"Not everything. We remember, and we pass along what we remember, each of us—some things aren't re-membered the same, nor need to be."

Alina sniffed, and investigated her trap.

Brev added, "You can't stand outside a way of doing

and judge it."

"Why not?"

"You judge by your own customs, which you can't get out of."

"Oh, can't I?" said Alina, taking her feet out of the water and getting a firmer grip on Corwin. "I have been many places and seen many customs. I am out of the City, in more ways than one."

"And dangerous as a rogue whale away from its pod," replied Brev, shoving the fish guts off the quay.

"There's a fisherman talking! I'm not a whale. I am what I am, here or in the City or anywhere."

"What is that?" asked Brev. He rinsed his fishy hands and knife, and turned his wide sea-blue eyes full on her. "I wonder. Do you know yourself?"

He wanted an answer, very much, but—"Ayyyyy!" she cried, for a small owl had suddenly dropped out of the sky and gripped her shoulder—the one marked with the black Moloquat.

Brev struck at it as Alina ducked, but they both arrested motion as the owl cried in a metallic voice, "Alina, princess of Calabrinia!"

Deliberately she turned her head and looked into its marigold eye, high-bridged nose to hooked beak. "Do you call me, bird?"

"Alina, princess of Calabrinia," repeated the keening cry.

Brev reached out but she batted his hand away. Corwin clung unnoticed to her shirt. "I am she. What do you want? Who sent you?"

For the third time, "Alina, princess of Calabrinia!" Half-folding its wings, beak wide as if panting, the bird cried, "Earth, Air, Water, Fire, Haste to claim your heart's desire! Elyse calls you to the Isles!" Loosening its grip on her shoulder, the bird tumbled end-over-end to the planks, eyes glazed over in death.

Corwin wailed in earnest. Alina picked him up and handed him to his father. She turned away.

"What? Where are you going? Here, your shoulder's bleeding!" Brev, baby under his arm, pulled a bandanna out of his breeks and tried to apply it to the gouges the bird's talons had made.

"Didn't you hear?" Alina rounded on him. "I must go!"

"Where? What?"

"The owl spoke." She picked up the limp bird by one wing, and turned toward the cottage carrying it. Brev followed with his crying son.

"Spoke to you? I heard it squawk—"

"It summoned me to the Isles. It is my destiny that speaks." She was over the threshold of the cottage, with Brev almost treading on her heels.

"The Isles! But that's—more than a week's journey! Much more, if the winds set contrary around the cape. And taking a boat upriver at the—you'll be a month at least!"

"I shall ride across the desert. I shall find a way."

"But—" Brev was angry, but kept his temper reefed like a spritsail in a blow. The dead owl lay on the floor between them, and she pushed it out of the way as she moved about, putting things in her old bag. "What about the militia? They will say you fear defeat—more of them will desert, set sail between dusk and dawn in their boats crammed full of provisions."

"Will they!" she cried. "Tell them from me that all those who put to sea now shall never land again! They shall become the nomads of the ocean, dwindling to a few half-mad eaters of raw fish and drinkers of brackish water, never daring to hear the scrape of keel on shore! If the Firstporters will not hold without me, with me you shall not!"

"How do you know this?" he demanded.

Alina paused, uncertain for a moment. "It is a fey message that came to me," she said. "But I think what I say is true." She was shod and dressed, her bag over her shoulder.

"You have an eel-trap set, the first you ever made."

"And the last, no doubt," she snapped. "Will you move aside?"

Brev moved. "The first I ever had dealings with princesses," he said bitterly, "and I hope the last." But she was already over the doorstep. Corwin cried.

"What of Corwin?" he called.

"You have a goat."

"Don't you have any of a mother's feelings?"

"How should I, who never had a mother?" her voice came back from the street. "There is Pauli on a pony, leading Tam already saddled—it was a true calling! Good-bye, good-bye!"

Much of the village was gathered, Myrrha came panting from the watercress-brook in the meadow, and First-port congratulated itself on being well-rid of bad luck with the two foreigners gone off again on their own queer business.

Ten

...rivers at their source,
And disembodied bones.

　　　　　　　　　—Elinor Wylie

A ND yet, says the imperial dragon, hurry as they might, the story must move backwards in order to move forwards, as does the sagacious lobster in the ocean bed.

Some days previous to the events chronicled, the hot bronze bell of the Calabrinian sky resounded to the stroke of the rising sun. The distant echoes penetrated to a shadowed chamber of lath and honeysuckle, with bird-bespattered fountain and sprays of violet orchids hiding from the sun, where mad Queen Elyse of the Isles talked to her multitude of birds.

The moon no longer called her blood; day and night were all one to her, each passing year unheeded as the demise of a mayfly—but now the equinox dragged her sluggish lymph to an unwonted neap tide. She rose from her couch and clapped her hands for her slave; a tall woman, bony and gaunt, with wild white hair and swags of blue-veined flesh, finely crumpled like linen hung out to air. Her eyes were pale transparent blue. She wore a chamber-robe yellow with age, the unraveled hem a trailing cat's cradle; under it her ankles were like spindles the flock has been spun off.

"Bring me clothing," she said haughtily to a goldfinch,

"and send my two sons to attend on me."

The maidslave bowed her forehead to the floor, for mad Queen Elyse was not a bad sort as queens went, and hurried to the Wardrobe.

This was a large suite of rooms, very untidy, in the charge of a large eunuch with a blue hat and brass-and-ebony staff of office.

"Clothes for Queen Elyse," said the maidslave as pertly as she dared. What did eunuchs care for spring?

"What? Are you sure? She hasn't wanted clothes these ten years!"

"She does now. It's spring—even you must notice."

The eunuch bent a black-browed look on her, but did not bestir himself. As well try to discipline a sparrow with his ponderous staff. "Very well then. Forty-third pole on the left. Hurry up now."

With a saucy hitch of the buttocks (not only was it spring, but an ingenious stableboy had loosened a stone in the back wall of the baths that gave on the horse yard), the girl tripped down the long corridor between rows and rows of gowns.

Some were of silk satin and silk velvet; some of shot silk and slubbed silk; there were damask and dimity, sarsenet and cambric, trimmed with pine marten, stone marten, ermine and moleskin and otter, feathers of ostrich, peacock, and pheasant, all caught up with lace and bullion, ruching and piping and smocking and faggoting.

The maidslave, who wore only a blue all-purpose smock rather too short behind, felt no stirring of envy trotting between the gorgeous garments like flayed pelts of queens. The round buttocks that hiked up her smock behind were fetching enough, without finery, to move stones—and her mind was divided between her errand and the absolute necessity she would make the matron feel for having the baths scrubbed very thoroughly indeed. It would take most of the afternoon, mildew being what it was.

She passed the forty-third pole and had to go back. Speaking of mildew—! She ran her hard little hands quickly through the decayed robes. This one would have to do.

Shaking out the wrinkles as she went, she took the mad queen a cowslip-yellow gown with point-lace at neck and sleeves, and a grass-green cloak the mice had nested in.

Queen Elyse was speaking to a rock-dove on her finger, but turned her head and said to the girl, "That's right, dear, now dress me."

Which was quite extraordinary, because in the whole time the little maidslave had served mad Queen Elyse, she had never known her to address anyone who was not a bird. So when she had arrayed the old queen in her lackluster finery, she summoned the majordomo.

But the majordomo wouldn't believe her until Elyse screamed for him like a parrot from her bird-filled apartments—which set the peacock yelling and the smaller birds twittering and squawking according to their habit, and then the lapdogs of Vanessa the Barbarian Queen began to yap, which made Lindora the Lovely's monkeys chatter.

"I will have an audience with the First Vizier," said mad Queen Elyse when the majordomo finally appeared, half cross-gartered and wholly out of breath. "Arrange it at once, and bring me jewels suitable for the occasion."

"But, but," spluttered the majordomo, fending off pigeons and trying to tie up his garters at the same time, "But, but..."

"At once," said Elyse, and turned to a pair of mockingbirds.

The majordomo pulled himself together and attempted to explain. No one, no one at all, spoke anymore with the First Vizier, who was so exalted that he paid no attention if spoken to. She must really mean the Second Vizier Meerkat Lobum; who, unfortunately, was unavailable at that moment, owing to some insignificant disturbance involving the poorer quarters of the city, but as soon as he was at liberty would no doubt have the greatest pleasure in..."

Mad Queen Elyse was not listening. And one of the parrots, being evilly disposed, took offense and nipped his ear, so the majordomo fled.

The maidslave, greatly enjoying the excitement even before she got an opportunity to scrub the baths, scampered after him to remind him about the jewels.

"Jewels!" said the majordomo in disgust. "She can have paste ones, she won't know the difference."

"You'll be sorry," said the maidslave, whose pertness was due to having a mistress who spoke only to birds.

Queen Elyse saw at once that the parure of emeralds was false, and ground them under her bone-heeled slipper. She made such a hullabaloo, throwing seed-dishes and cuttlebones at the lattices, that the majordomo had to unlock the jewel-room and get out a set of real emeralds and moonstones, which had originally come from the Isles with the then-widowed Queen and her children as a condition of the Treaty.

The maidslave trotted back and forth in the corridors, with the gardens on one side and the lattices of the queens' private apartments on the other. She kept up a running commentary, so that the elderly queens dropped their embroidery, overturned their board games, put aside flute and lute, playing-cards and nail files.

They popped their heads out and inquired. What was the matter with Elyse? Why did she want to see Meerkat Lobum? Where was he, anyway? What sort of disturbance in the city? Oh, she was going to see the First Vizier? Was he still alive? They'd love to go too, for old times' sake.

So when Elyse emerged from her chambers, in moldy silk and magnificent emeralds and a bullfinch on her head, a gaggle of queens accompanied her, chatting and laughing and chucking the tiny pages under the chin.

"Save this one for me," exclaimed Lindora the Lovely, whose dewlaps hung like a hound's but whose great dark eyes were painted like the bows of a Firstport schooner. She shot a dramatic look at the majordomo, who blushed.

He greatly wished that Meerkat Lobum had not taken the greater part of the Guard with him; that the household eunuchs had not got quite so fat and indolent, himself included; that the breath of spring would go somewhere else instead of infecting the harem with more than usual indocility.

Their way was blocked by tall doors inlaid with ivory and mother-of-pearl and ebony, shut and locked. A cobweb stretched dusty threads from one jamb to the other.

The majordomo raised his staff and tapped on the doors.

"That's not how!" cried Vanessa the Barbarian, whose more-than-generous form overflowed her skimpy leather garb as her still-magnificent hair scorned combs and fillets. She seized the staff and beat a martial rat-tat-tat-tat-ta!

Nothing stirred.

"The First Vizier is dead! He's dead!" cried the queens. "Dead and unburied!" It was hard to say which voice started the cry, or which one first rushed at the doors—but they creaked, cracked and burst inwards.

The slavegirl scuttled in after them, hoping to see a dead vizier—and at first she thought he *was* dead, mummified in his great tall gold chair with gryphons for legs.

But then the parchment eyelids opened a bleary crack, and a reedy voice quavered, "Eh, what's that?"

"Please it your Excellency," the majordomo began, but his voice was lost.

"Elyse! Elyse!" shrieked the queens. "Elyse wants to talk to the First Vizier!"

His old bald head, mottled like a tortoise's, turned; the gold-brocaded black robe remained in place as rigid as the tortoise's shell. "Elyse. Eh, fine girl, Elyse. From the Isles, she is. What can I do for Elyse?"

The mad queen swept forward with dignity, wearing her bullfinch like a diadem. "I beg the favor to return presently to the Isles—to die, and do something I have just remembered. I request also that my two sons accompany me"

"Eh? Sons? Suns? Shawms? Shams? Shames?"

The majordomo sidled up to the gryphon chair. "Sons, Excellency. She had two—one lost in the desert, one taken by the Barak-Shar. She has forgotten."

There was a long silence, in which the queens shuffled and pinched each other. The ancient tortoise spoke. "It will be necessary to consult the soothsayers and necromancers—where is the head sorcerer?"

The majordomo whispered, "Extended leave of absence, Excellency. Overwork. Nervous exhaustion. Strangulated hernia."

"The College of Necromancers?"

"Temporarily recessed, owing to ominous auguries, Excellency."

The queens became more restive, while Elyse waited like a scarecrow on a windless day.

"Ah, well," said the First Vizier, graciously essaying to raise his palsied hand, "certainly you may. Speaking as the mouth of his Benign Supremacy, I grant you permission. For yourself and maid, one equerry. You there..." the old eyes rolled drily around to the slave girl standing with her mouth open and her elbows out. "What's your name?"

"I—I don't have one, your Excellency. Never did. Left here a baby these sixteen years ago."

"Slack. Very slack, I can see that." He closed his eyes. He had not gone to sleep however, since in a minute or two he opened them. "Prisca is your name. Attend the Lady Elyse to the Isles. The audience is terminated."

And this time he really did go to sleep, so the queens and others departed on tiptoe, making elaborate signs of silence to each other.

"When does your Highness propose to depart?" inquired the majordomo hopefully, once they were in the corridor.

"Now, at once," she returned with brittle hardihood. "Pack the ring-neck doves and half a dozen finches in traveling cages and order a litter. I shall wait in the Court of Turquoises."

And there she waited, enjoying the revivifying aroma of Moloquat, standing on a block of marble paving that had been badly stained, but sanded and scrubbed clean of the worst of it. She eyed the leashed panther of the guard at the archway, and strolled over to inspect it more closely.

"Looks wormy," she said critically. "And if your sergeant doesn't see to brushing her better than that, you'll have mange to deal with."

At that moment the litter entered, on the shoulders of six stout slaves dyed indigo blue with shaved heads; Elyse dropped the subject of mange and began shrieking for her birds. The little maidslave, new-called Prisca, came at a full trot with the brass cage full of finches and a carpet-bag, while the majordomo himself bore along the marquetry cage with the doves.

All these things were handed up into the litter after Queen Elyse, and the bearers turned smartly out the gate with Prisca scampering beside the last two. She was sorry to miss her assignation with the stableboy in the baths, but much gladder than sorry: she had never been out of the gates of the Palace in her life.

The eunuch hastily assigned as equerry came running after the litter.

"I see that my sons are unpunctual!" said the old lady to the doves. "I must speak severely to them about it. Leave open the curtains of the litter," she added. "For many years I have not been out about the city."

The broad zigzag of the Avenue of the Temple opened before them as more guards swung back the ponderous gates of gilded bronze. The litter swayed through, followed by Prisca at a trot.

Weighty odors of Moloquat, jasmine, magnolia, honeysuckle, gardenia and spikenard wafted over other smells: decay, dogs, and fried fish; and an elusive, chancy reek, now definite, now not; unidentifiable, but having some affinity to oozing mudflats laid bare by an ebbtide.

Elyse raised her long and drooping nose and sniffed. "What *is* that smell?" she asked Prisca, as if she were anyone.

"What is the smell?" Prisca asked the bearer on her left, who shrugged his blue shoulders.

"What is it?" she insisted. "My queen wants to know!"

The equerry inclined his tall body without breaking stride. "So please her Highness, no snow is brought this year from the mountains, owing to the activities of bandits and the devastation of villages that formerly supplied snow in blocks. With the melting of last year's supply, many things have come to light in the cellars. Some of them are rotting."

"It pleases me little," remarked mad Queen Elyse, "but as I shall soon go over the Falls, it is not my concern."

"Oh please ma'am, don't say that," begged Prisca. "Why should you die in the Isles?"

"Why not?" returned the queen, and Prisca had no answer.

The street was half-blocked with rubble fallen from a great gap in the curtain wall of the city, and it was ticklish to skirt it with the litter.

"Need we have windows in our walls to view the river by?" Elyse inquired.

"Ca made his own windows, and doors too; the floods were very high this year," answered the equerry without prompting.

"Hmmph!" said Elyse. She did not comment on the number of beggars in the streets, the dilapidation of gardens and squares, the many boarded-up shopfronts with refuse piled in the doorways. Perhaps she did not notice.

Prisca, her bright dark eyes in her round face darting from side to side, noticed everything but was too ignorant to draw conclusions. She did observe that when the bearers bent the knee passing under the outstretched hand of his Benign Supremacy in golden effigy, Queen Elyse irritably gathered up the train of her gown and made no reverence.

Beyond it the Temple yawned darkly; the wide steps were choked with stalls selling everything from fighting cocks to powdered horn of unicorn, and the square in front seethed with hawkers of worse and more secret commodities as well as combs and fresh gourds, drinking water, raspberry brandy and beebalm salve.

"Old scrolls? Poetry, mathematics and philosophy a specialty today, old scrolls to light your fires!" insinuated a peddler.

The guards presented their pikes butt-forward and the litter breasted the crowds like a dinghy in choppy seas, at last swaying down the ramp to the wharves.

High-prowed barges, swollen amidships like elderly

carp, bumped cropped square sterns at their moorings. A few silk-sailed pleasure-craft bobbed apart from them, some fast yellow skiffs for upriver work rose and fell in slips, but the wharves were by no means crowded. Prisca stared with wide eyes across the river and down it: the whole world seemed to open before her like break of day.

Meanwhile, Elyse passed her pale cold eyes along the row of boats. "Where are the great triremes and galeasses?" she asked.

"They say there's no longer a deep-water channel through the delta, your Highness—silted up. All the river traffic is by barge, now. With your permission."

The equerry strode rapidly down the wharf, speaking to the bargee-Rats here and there.

"That one!" cried Elyse in a carrying and imperious voice, as he came to a freshly painted apple-green barge.

Shrugging, the equerry motioned the bearers to unload the litter. Queen Elyse descended as though she passed between rows of a hundred gongmen with brass gongs, a regiment of the Guard in dress plumes, and a dozen high officials of the realm. But before she stepped over the short gangplank, she stopped to the dirty boards of the wharf and threw a handful of dust over her shoulder.

Prisca skipped over the plank after her with the bag, and snugged into the bow while the birdcages were stowed. She hugged her knees with delight, looking at the river as though it were life itself.

The bargee-Rats, both mournful-looking men of great age—forty at least—handled each a pair of long slender oars, bow and stern. A black-eyed girl of about Prisca's age snubbed down a yellow awning amidships for the queen to sit under, and moved with practiced ease to cast off.

The barge sculled slowly out to midstream to find the current; green oily water swirled under the dip-and-swing of the oars, and the square striped sail swelled gently to a following wind as the girl raised it. Queen Elyse seemed sunk in lethargy among her birdcages; no one spoke. A pair of merganser ducks of enamelled black and green took off ahead of the bow; Prisca, happier than she had ever been, forgot completely the disappointed stableboy.

Prisca was astonished at how soon the massive ramparts of the city, which had seemed the pillars that hold up the dome of the sky, vanished astern and were lost: first in the acid green of watered crops in their combed ranks, then in the interminable grey-green of the desert on either side. In the distance she saw gazelles, so fine-drawn in the heat-haze as to seem like strokes of a pen; every sand bar was littered as with drifted logs, crocodiles sunning themselves.

The Rat-girl threw them scraps from the galley, and let Prisca do it too. "Do they still speak of Princess Alina in the Palace?" the Rat asked carelessly, dropping a chicken-head equidistant between two horny snouts.

"Oh," said Prisca, "even on the river you heard of that?"

"Just the name, really, no more."

"Well," said Prisca with caution, "The official story is that she was snatched away by a celestial dragon for terrible crimes against the throne, and her name may not be mentioned. But we know..."

"Your old lady wants you," said the Rat.

"You must not be over-familiar with the bargees, Prisca," Elyse admonished her. "They are a very useful sort of people in their way, but it isn't our way, you know."

On the fourth day the prow cut into the blue lake of the Isles, four of them: Al the largest with the chiefest of the population; En, bowl-shaped and covered with apple trees, with a spring of sweet water in the center; Ere, the isle of apricots; and grassy Ure, rising only a handspan above the flood of the river, used to pasture flocks of little four-horned grey sheep. The islands, and a thousand islets, eyots and tussocks among them, were conjoined by a cat's cradle of ropewalks floored with planks, so strong the pygmy elephants native to the lake basin could pass over them.

They approached Al by the ship-channel, through the famous Water Gate of Al. Prisca almost shrieked to see it, a waterspout made tame. From high tanks water shot continually in horizontal streams, bruising as iron, cold as icicles, forming a barrier the interior of which was as opaque as a glacier's heart, but the edges a shining haze of perpetual rainbow.

The tallest of the bargees played a mournful seven-note tune on the boat whistle; unseen gatewardens threw a lever and the bars of water were deflected upward, a hundred-foot plume on either side of the channel, letting the boat glide through the rainbow mist.

Once landed, Elyse expected as a matter of course to go to her old palace; after some consultation, the equerry agreed, as it was now a caravanserai and took guests. Prisca had just time to whisper their destination to her new friend, bargee-girl Aysha, before the litter was hoisted to the backs of two pigmy elephants just the height of her head.

The elephants had twisty tusks longer than they were tall, of yellowed ivory wrapped about with blue ribbons, and Prisca kept a wary eye on them as she followed through the narrow streets of Al. There was some trouble—the equerry was not used to elephants, and the islanders seemed to find his emasculate condition a matter for mockery and public opprobrium. There was also trouble at the caravanserai, which Elyse insisted on regarding as her private palace still; but the other guests were dislodged by means of a few golden *excellentes* apiece.

Prisca settled her mad old queen in a large room over the water, furnished in white wicker and the colored cottons favored by the islanders. There was no bed but a woven hammock. Water reflections danced on the ceiling, and the jewel-colored birds of the islands flew in and out the open windows with a sough of little rapid wings.

"Now," said Elyse, "enough shilly-shallying. Let my sons be brought before me!"

And there was a brouhaha indeed, for the equerry was unable to convince her of the impossibility of it, the

164

aged servants of the caravanserai were equally unable to do so; and even the clever barge-girl (who had somehow attached herself to the party) could not alter the Queen's mind.

"Then I shall send for them myself," she remarked calmly, opening the door of the doves' cage and letting them fly out.

After that, the water reflections still played on the ceiling and the water music purled past the window, but Elyse fell into the hammock and slept like a marble queen on a sarcophagus.

At dust the cock dove returned and a made a great flutter and to-do about the room. Prisca tried to shoo him into the cage, but Elyse woke and listened, then rose from the hammock.

"Come," she whispered.

Unlike their ceremonious arrival, the departure from the caravanserai was stealth itself. Naturally Elyse knew (who better?) the back gate, private paths through the green jungles, bridges of a single footrope and handrope, through mangrove swamps and still lagoon with cypress knees poking above the black water. With Prisca behind her she trailed her musty green cloak like a creaky ghost deeper into the morass of watery land and muddy water, until Prisca had quite lost her bearings.

So she never know the whereabouts of the grassy eyot on which Elyse wept above the name-grave of her eldest son, whose unnamed corpse had dried months since in the heat of the Painted Rocks. Indeed, she could not tell what made Elyse choose the featureless hummock among a hundred others. But even so, she sniffled and wiped her nose on the hem of her frock; until at last the bats began to flit from tree to tree with little cries as if they too were distressed, and Elyse got up from her bony knees.

"Now I must do another thing," she said. With both hands at her mouth she uttered an owl-call, and kept it up until a small brown owl appeared, flying silently as a big moth. "Go," she said to the owl. "Find the lost princess— the one you know of! And tell her to come at once."

"There is more need than ever," she muttered, leaning

on Prisca's shoulder. She was so shaky and tottery that Prisca almost despaired of getting her back to the caravanserai.

Thus some days passed, while the old queen rested and received those of her former subjects who remembered her. Prisca was at liberty to make herself a flowered flowing smock such as the long-eyed islanders wore, comb out her hair and put hibiscus blossoms behind each ear.

On the fifth day, Princess Errant Alina, riding hard over the eastern horn of the desert, begged passage on the island ferry for herself and her squire, a freckled lad of courtly bearing. When at last she was ushered into the presence of mad Queen Elyse among her birds, she stumbled into her lap and said only, "I'm so terribly tired."

Then Elyse clapped her hands so the rings struck together like castanets, sent Prisca scurrying for servants, baths and robes and perfumes, hairdressers and manicurists and masseuses, cream cakes and apricot preserves and thin sweet white wine, all before the dawn chorus of birds fell silent in the heat of the day.

Pauli said apologetically, "We came as quickly as we could."

"Better late than never. You've grown. So she has the pearl, has she?"

"Yes, mother, it seems so."

"You also may rest."

When the many ministrations were exhausted, Alina fell deeply asleep and slept so soundly that Elyse's bony fingers removing the Pearl of the Isles from the cord around her neck did not disturb her. She slept until the birds woke her at the first light the next morning.

She heard in her sleep a high falling trill, liquid as water; an interrogative two-note call like towhee? to-wheeee? against a confused musical burble of background chirps and warbles. At first she mistook the swing of the hammock for a moored boat.

But the damp fresh air had no tang of salt in it, and

there was no booming of surf always at the edge of hearing. And the room was larger, lighter, and warmer.

As soon as the princess stirred definitively, Prisca slipped out the door to alert the caravanserai. She hurried back with her tea, sweet almond cakes, warm milk and honey, and huge green summer pears speckled all over with russet spots, everything on a wicker tray too big for her. Behind her Aysha beamed, her arms full of silks, camel-hair brushes and little pots.

For a moment then, except for the purling of the river under the window and the swaying of the hammock, Alina might have been waking in her own chamber off the Court of the Princesses, from a long and peculiarly vivid dream subsequent to making hempseed candy with the other princesses.

But as soon as she sat up the stretched muscles, fresh bruises and abrasions cleared her mind with astringent pains. Also her head ached with a dull pounding like the coming of thunder. "Aysha!" she said. "So you did get away!"

"Foxed them pretty well, didn't we? I ply the river now with my own barge, but I stayed to see you for old times' sake. Never thought you'd turn up here, but the old lady thought so."

"Do you still have money from the jewels?"

"Still have? Why, I've made a small fortune besides, selling cuttings of Moloquat up and down the river!"

"You stole sprigs of Moloquat? To plant outside the city? The sacred tree? How could you?"

"Easily. They've rooted quite kindly in a lot of places, like your sacred self."

Prisca put the tray down and tactfully trotted out of the room.

"Of course, you're no one's slave now. No one's answerable for you. How changeable we are—I have learned to cook. I wear shoes as often as not!"

"Imagine that—drink your tea now, and we'll get you dressed, just like old times," said Aysha fussily.

Alina stirred the green tea with a silver spoon. "And if I won't, just like old times?" she asked with a ghost of her old manner.

"I'll go and tell the head eunuch that you have female complaint," replied Aysha, straight-faced.

They both laughed, but Alina laughed too long until she doubled over and sobbed in near-hysteria, spilling the tea.

"Now, now," said Aysha, "just take the milk, slowly does it—I'll make them find some proper clothes and bring them."

"If you're quite ready?" said Prisca, poking her neat dark head like a seal into the room. "The prince has been with her Highness this half-hour." She tittered and vanished around the doorframe.

Alina shook out her skirts irritably—the billowing court dress felt awkward—and made a suitable curtsey. Elyse was seated in a large wicker chair with flaring back, like an airy and insubstantial throne. At the back of it stood Pauli like a prince on a chocolate-box, while finches fluttered around the room trilling.

Mad Queen Elyse held a dove on her hand; her face was chaotic, vague and remote, a bad color; but the pale eyes fastened on Alina like a taloned foot.

"Ah," she said. "Yes, no wonder the pearl came to you." She lifted the irregular pearl, light for its size, on a new silk cord. The dove pecked at it, but Elyse kept it between finger and thumb.

Alina said, "It is not quite mine. I took it from the hand of a dead man who was my friend, far from here."

"Yes. He went over the Falls—over the Falls some time ago. Now only Pauli will be left to speak to the birds. The rest of you must be content with speaking with men and dragons."

Alina thought the old queen was as mad as ever; could the message have been a mistake? But she maintained a respectful posture.

"You've got very plain, too, and lean as a hound."

This stung, but Alina admitted the truth of it. "There is another old woman who makes eel pies and tells me the same. I might have saved a journey if that is all you have to tell me."

"Vanity is for servant girls like Prisca, or peacocks," said the queen, not looking so vague as before. "Peacocks are curious, and stupid as well; what they investigate they never remember, so go through it all again. I trust you will be more sensible.

"You have been a *little* hard to follow," Elyse went on in a severe tone. "It was hardly to be expected you would get so far. Or, frankly, do so much harm in such a short time!"

"I? What harm have I done?"

"My dear! They tell me you have turned the world upside-down, that's all! Here's your maid strewing Molo-quats broadcast on the world—the Horsemen, poor innocent barbarians as they were, have begun to build forts in the northern grasslands and write in hieroglyphics to each other!"

"They do? If so, what have I to do with it?"

"They tell the tale like this: one day, when the Horsemen were rolling forever across the desert, by permission of the lions to drink water, by permission of the Barak-Shar to pass, by permission of the godking's gold to trade for what the desert doesn't give (and the desert gives less than a stepmother), they came upon a dragon. Only they did not know it was a dragon, for it seemed to be a young girl nearly dead of thirst with her horse and dog beside her. They took her in out of charity and she showed them great magicks: how to make stones hang in the air like hummingbirds, black marks on white cloth that turn into a person, a horse, a mountain..."

Pauli nodded judiciously and put his arm around Prisca's waist where she stood open-mouthed listening.

"Pauli!" Elyse broke off. "Leave that girl alone, she didn't even have a name a quarter of a year ago—and the dragon showed them how to bury a stalk of amaranth, and said that if they did so they would have amaranth a hundredfold the next year and nothing to pay—a shocking doctrine, incidentally—and then there came a terrible night when the dragon poisoned a hundred fanged de-

169

mons, but the Barak-Shar came upon the Horsemen anyway; at which she mounted her mare and flew into the first of the Barak-Shar, changing into a fiery winged lizard with five talons on each foot, of blue, yellow, red, green and violet, like the flames of the Fiery Mountain on whose slopes they took refuge, and they never saw her again—pim, pam, pum, the story's done!"

Alina could see a certain distorted water-reflection of the truth.

"The Hopgangers have taken to music and visions, and subverted the garrison of the Guard sent to discipline them. And as for the Barak-Shar, you've turned them from amusingly romantic banditti into a genuine scourge. But," said Elyse with a soothing gesture of the hand, "it was kind of you to take Pauli to my sisters—high time he went—you are basically a good girl and I shall let you marry him."

"What? Marry Pauli?"

"Yes, of course. You must marry a prince. Korab Khan was unsuitable, and he's dead anyway. Do you want all magick lost forever? Which reminds me: I am very close to the Falls and you must see to it all. My sisters will help you, but you must do it at once."

"Do what, please, my queen?" said Alina, seeing that it was no use to get angry.

"Why, return at once to the city and take up the reins, of course! It's a perfect disgrace. I hadn't been out for ten years and I could hardly believe such a shocking state of affairs. You are the heiress, you must see to it," replied Elyse, madness lighting her pale old eyes.

"What else have I been trying to do!" cried Alina. "But I cannot return without sufficient force to make Meerkat Lobum admit that his Benign Supremacy is in fact dead or I should be bowstringed in the first hour!"

"Things proceed according to their wont, in the city as in the lesser places—Pauli, I said leave that girl alone!— you must negotiate with Meerkat Lobum. He knows he cannot hold on much longer, with the corpses he keeps in the snow-cellars rotting under him. He will be more than glad to kiss the foot of the legitimate heiress and let bygones be bygones." Elyse lay back in the chair and her voice thinned to a thread. Alina bent forward to hear.

"It is not a unique case of rebellion—these things occur in royal families. My older son buried his name purely to spite his Benign Supremacy; and then when you turned up at the Painted Rocks—yes, yes, I know all about that—he felt obliged to die then and there."

"Because of me?"

"Exactly. Every step you have taken has been your own self-will, off the path laid before you. Naturally the consequences have been disastrous."

Alina was finding it all difficult to follow. Her head throbbed like a drum, and the light through the window was a livid stormy color. Elyse's voice was hardly more than a husky whisper, in her mind rather than her ear. "I could not do otherwise than what seemed wisest to me."

"Mad girl! Seemed to you? As well invent the dance in the Temple!"

"Why not? As well as make up a ballad," Alina muttered to herself. Aloud she added, "Tell me then, did I take the Pearl of the Isles or did it 'come to me' as you said?"

"Answer that yourself," Elyse said in the ghost of a snap.

Alina thought, and really did not know. She temporized. "It protected me from evil apparitions..."

"What? Anthea? Well—you must be careful. I wouldn't trust her altogether."

Alina leaned forward and stared with her amber eyes into the depthless aquamarine eyes of the mad old queen. "Do you know this Anthea? Is she not evil?"

"Why, I wouldn't say that. Not really." Elyse dropped her gaze to the emeralds on her bony fingers and the twisted blue veins on the backs of her hands. "She is powerful, and mischievous. The undying ones are like that. Their malice is composed of caprice and curiosity in equal parts. There is no one to bring them to account, you know."

"She said everything must be paid for—she only does not pay."

"Well. That's not quite so. She *can't* very well pay, being a dragon, can she? Of course she can't *change*, either," Elyse added thoughtfully.

"Anthea is a dragon?"

"Oh, yes, of course. Did you never see her in her proper shape?" Elyse seemed politely surprised, waving her jeweled hand airily, so that a finch dropped down to her finger.

Alina drew her silks around her and sank down onto a cushion. "No," she said.

"You can always tell by the shadow," Elyse explained. "At any rate, she is an imperial dragon and an immortal, and she likes to meddle. Most of them don't bother for long, you know. But she set up your godking centuries ago and got him to build Calabrinia to amuse her. She changes the godking as necessary when he looks like wearing thin (you can't keep a mortal going forever); you she bore for future reference, and..."

"Bore me? From where? Am I not really a princess?"

"You misunderstand. Anthea bore you as your mother, although that is not common knowledge—still, you might have guessed. Surviving the bite of a thorn dragon is *very* indicative. Anyway, they brought in a girl to suckle you (Prisca's mother, in fact) and regretted it ever since, because you have turned out so unpredictable."

Alina's olive cheeks went ashy under the dusting of cinnabar, and only the boned bodice of the court dress held her upright. She felt a stabbing pain, more tearing than the half-forgotten spasms of childbirth—it was as though some tissue tore asunder, raggedly and irrevocably. The blood pumped again through her veins after a moment, air whistled gently in and out of her lungs as before, but something was severed and gone forever. Her mother was a dragon.

Of course she had heard of such things, who had not? But one never thinks that oneself...

The birds dipped and darted around the room, and she noticed that red honeysuckle twined around the mullions of the window. There were frogs in the river below. Pauli and Prisca were invisible behind the tall wicker back of the chair. Aysha offered her a glass of the pale cool wine of the Isles, but she did not take it.

"My mother is the same dragon that gave the Moloquat seed to—to the first godking?"

"The very same. And I am sure that if you cooperate now, she will give you such gifts as will bring a second golden age to Calabrinia and found a dynasty for the next thousand years, although I personally have only an academic interest in it."

A fit of coughing took the old queen, and Aysha hastened to her with the wine, standing patiently until the coughing fit spent itself. But mad Queen Elyse's eyes were closed, her veined hands fell to the sides of the wicker throne weighted down by rings. She breathed with a faint flutter of thin-winged nostrils.

The equerry knocked thunderously on the doorjamb, and Aysha gave a faint yelp and dropped the wine. "Madame your Highness!" he bellowed. "A boat of some uncouth sort approaches the dock, ignoring all signals to desist."

Eleven

Have you built your ship of death,
oh have you?
Build then your ship of death,
for you will need it...

—D. H. Lawrence

IT was a ding-dong fight Brev had with his mother when he remarked he was going to the Isles to find Alina and bring her back.

Myrrha had said once too often that guests and fish stink after three days and how nice and quiet it was without her ladyship always underfoot and wanting this and that.

Brev dropped the tangle of line he was patiently unsnarling, and said, "No, it isn't!"

"Isn't what?" asked Myrrha. She hadn't really been listening to herself.

"Isn't nice and quiet. I liked doing things with her, hearing a different voice. Seemed like she liked me well enough too."

"Oh, as she liked her great gallumphing horse, that she's no doubt ridden to death in the desert by now? You've served her turn, now she's gone off about her business; and let her, say I."

"The business should be soon over. I'll take the boat upriver and bring her home."

"What?" shrieked Myrrha, like a gull in a gale.

"Yes," said Brev, picking his son out of the tangle of line. "Corwin will come to keep me company."

"What?" shrieked Myrrha again. "He'll starve—sicken—fall overboard!"

"Nonsense. High time he learned something about boats. And Alina fancies him, I thought." Brev was not so simple as his open face appeared.

"I won't have it! I never heard of such a thing! Why, she won't even sit on a joint-stool like a decent person, says it gives her the back-ache!"

"I believe it's all floor-cushions in the City," Brev said with intent to soothe.

"Cushions!" snorted his mother. "Well enough to give her the child to suckle—though you may yet be sorry for the after-effects of such milk!—but you can't mean to handfast that creature!"

"I can mean to," replied Brev, looping up the tangle under his other arm. "She may not consent, being a princess and all."

"Then she's more fool than wanton, and that's saying a mouthful," his mother fired at his retreating back. "She'll not find a better man in all the Four Ports, no, not if there were eight of 'em! But you can't go, you haven't any clean shirts!"

From the moss-covered steps of the old Summer Palace of Al, flanked by slaves and officials with Pauli and the old queen on the verandah above, Alina watched the sturdy, blue-eyed Firstport boat nudge between the shallops of the islanders. The breeze carried snatches of rain in squalls.

The skipper dropped the blue sail and put the helm over, so that the little craft turned up into the wind, lost way and coasted up to the landing stage. She blinked twice and thrice, but there it was. A child with a mop of brown hair, a large spotted nanny goat, and a small curly-tailed dog occupied the boat as well.

Brev dropped a line over a bollard and jumped onto the dock; silver dolphin gleaming at his throat, knitted cap in hand, he climbed the moldering marble steps as though they were barnacled ledges upon his own wild shore, not a bit abashed. He looked very square and salty, although Alina recognized his best blue shirt and least-patched breeches.

Elyse he bowed to coldly, Pauli he slapped on the shoulder, the rest he ignored. In front of gaping servants and guards, he hugged Alina, silk and whalebone and all. "All ready to leave when you are," he said.

His broad open face and deep blue-grey eyes, wide chest with the sunburned V at the neck, and big, rope-scarred capable hands, were more welcome to her than the familiar faces of the past. She said nothing, not wanting to speak until she was quite sure it would not be something she did not mean to say—whoever *she* might be, and that she wasn't sure of. Dragon's daughter, pawn in a vast game of chess, chivvied from square to square by chuckling old ladies—

"Mind your own business!" snapped Elyse. "She can't leave. What shall a princess do besides be a princess?"

"She made a very nice eel-trap," remarked Brev mildly. "There've been six eels in it—big ones—since you left, Alina!"

"Silence!" said the old queen with the flare of a dying fire. "Eel-traps! Have you no respect for the royal house of Calabrinia? No comprehension of the tragic sense of duty?"

"I guess not, ma'am. I just do what needs doing."

"With a cloddish lack of sensibility. Alina, I shall not inquire further into this matter, considering you to a certain extent a victim of circumstances beyond your control..."

"I'm not a victim," said Alina with Brev's arm still over her shoulders. "I did make an eel-trap, myself."

"And you've traipsed about in shoes, and done a great many other unsuitable things. But now you must accept your destiny."

"Why, if she doesn't like it?" inquired the fisherman.

"My dear Brev," said Pauli gently, "perhaps you aren't aware that her mother is a dragon?"

176

"A lot of us might say the same. In this case, I wonder if maybe a very large fish spear, the kind you use for hunting sharks, mightn't be useful."

"Dragons cannot be killed," said Elyse, waving him a dismissal.

"How not? If you make a hole with something pointed, the blood runs out, however much as may be, then—!" Brev made a graphic gesture.

"You have met Anthea? Did you ever touch her?"

"No."

"For good reason. All her appearances are just that— no body, neither hard and brown like a nut (like you) nor a dried leaf like myself—all bodies decay. Did you not know dragons are immortal?"

Brev chewed this over like a fishbone between the teeth. The rain fell gently and wetly—Alina put her hand to her aching head. I've reached the last row on the board. They want to queen me now, willy-nilly.

Elyse levered herself upright in the wicker chair. "And," she continued, "if in some fashion the race of dragons could be eliminated, I must tell you that it would be most unwise to do so!"

"Why so?" asked Brev foursquare. "I mean to study on it at least!"

"Because the light has no shape without shadow. Challenge and response. Were there no lions at the waterhole, the gazelle would be a stumpy lump of a creature, trundling across the desert like a pugdog in a boudoir. If there were no winds and waves, would you build your blue-eyed boat to her graceful lines? Without the punishment of the oars, would your back and shoulders swell with sinew as they do?" The ghost of a snicker fluttered the wattles at her throat. "If with a wish I could make colored silk handkerchiefs out of my dear old friend Anthea—I wouldn't do it!"

"Never asked you to," Brev muttered, but he looked thoughtfully sidelong at Alina, whose wide glowing amber eyes seemed to look not so much at as through all of them.

Elyse gasped and sank back in the chair, seeming to

177

shrink and collapse in upon herself. Pauli and Prisca stepped forward at the same time and bent over the almost-empty robe of yellow silk. The freckled prince unwound the cord of the pearl and handed it to Prisca.

Outside the verandah, the rain slackened and ceased, and the sun broke through the slate-colored clouds; a rainbow, double-arched, made a specious bridge from one island to the next.

"Is she dead?" asked Alina. No one answered, because suddenly, and from nowhere in particular, Anthea was there.

Her transparent green eyes were infused with a piercing interest, although the pink mouth displayed its pointed white teeth in the same delightful smile as ever. The sun gilded her slim straight figure as though it were the golden statue of his Benign Supremacy in the marketplace. Her long black shadow, distorted, streamed down the steps to the quay.

Alina felt dizzy and sick, and her eyes would not focus without effort. The dazzling figure was hard to see, and she dropped her gaze to the undulating, jagged shadow instead: a dark, two-dimensional dragon-form. She put her hands over her eyes, and did not see how Pauli and Prisca fell back to either side and Anthea stepped forward and picked up the form of Queen Elyse as though it were the empty casing of a silkworm, balancing it on her shoulder lightly.

"Come, Alina! On the whole I am not ill-pleased with you, although you did not always do as I would have had you. You have been wayward, but not inattentive. In the Palace you learned wiles and airish manners, and were wise enough to leave it in time; in the desert you learned to live harshly and frugally and mixed your blood with fiery venom; in the earths of the Barak-Shar you learned sense and courage from their opposites; and you have come at last to the watery Isles where the lymph of Empire is pooled—the Dragon Throne, your heart's desire, still awaits you. Come!"

Alina put her two fists to her temples to hold the pounding blood and stared at the dragon lady with eyes like two very hot pieces of copper. Everyone waited to hear what she would say.

"Ah!" she cried. "Perhaps I learned more than you know! I will have no more horoscopes flung in my face by anyone! Venom or remedy, it's all one, according to the dosage and the illness! Fire cooks the porridge or burns it depending on the skill of the cooks, water—"

"Bears up the boat or drowns the fisherman," put in Brev.

Anthea gave him a basilisk look—he dropped his eyes but did not retreat.

"I defy your idiot verses! And you, whom I think I have little cause to thank! I ask myself if the Empire is worth a pot of salt herring, and the answer is far from clear!"

"Mad girl, how dare you speak of turning your back on your own blood, on a thousand years of learning, science, government, culture!" Anthea's green eyes were icy cold. "I do not say, you cannot throw open the gates to the barbarians (you nearly did that, and barbarians might well have served our turn)—but I tell you you cannot pass out of the gates yourself and leave the whole ancient, wise, cruel artifice of civilization as if it were a vase of flowers on your dressing table!"

"Why not, if they are cut flowers, dead and stinking?" Alina flashed back. She looked so remarkably like Anthea in all but color that Brev took an involuntary step backwards and Pauli and Prisca drew together.

Only silent Aysha smiled and clasped her hands. "They should never have let her wear shoes!" she whispered.

"Flowers that fade in a day? Not so," said Anthea, settling the yellow cocoon more securely on her shoulder. "With you as godqueen the Empire shall subsist for hundreds of years yet, like a butterfly caught in amber."

"Or a rotting corpse with a magick ruby in its mouth? Perhaps you do not lie—"

"I have always told the truth," purred Anthea, "only, like the Horsemen, sometimes in my own way."

"You are wholly a dragon and I am only half. But I won't bear my part of it. Let the pieces fly loose, the slaves look to themselves, the waters and the sands rise or fall to their own level! Furthermore," she continued, "the heart of his Benign Supremacy I shall send to a creature called Quill, the only one I know likely to make good use of it—"

"Be careful," said Anthea. "Of these wild impulses of yours. It is getting more difficult to counteract them. I have held the Barak-Shar in check for this time; I took your child to punish you and fix your attention..."

"Ahhhhhh!" cried Alina, "it was *you*?" and taking the tin box she flung it full in Anthea's face. "I never want to see you again!"

The dragon lady caught it in her long-nailed left hand and stretched her lips in an uncharming grimace. "So be it! I shall have the last word on this subject—meanwhile, I see no reason why Morphelius Pashan should not attack Firstport as soon as he likes!" She vanished, leaving a sharp negative after-image, like a bolt of lightning against the sky.

For a long, long moment no one spoke or moved. Then the birds began to twitter and fuss again, and Brev said, as though nothing had happened, "As I was about to say, we can go whenever you're ready, Alina. Corwin's been missing you."

Alina held up her head very high and gathered her gold and crimson skirts about her. "Yes. My business here did not take long after all. Goodbye, Aysha, I congratulate you on doing so well for yourself. Pauli, I'm sorry to leave you like this, but Prisca can help you to manage the Isles, if you want to do that. Keep the pearl. It's really yours."

Pauli, tearstains on his fuzzless cheeks, still managed a princely little bow. "Are you quite sure?" he asked.

"Yes. A fresh heart is better than a salted one, and good will above gold. Give me some pigeons to take with me and I will send you news—you!" (This to the equerry, standing at attention like a dried codfish, with his eyes bulging.) "See to revictualling that boat. There's a horse to go in it. Brev, I am ready. There are only ghosts here."

The question remained, what would Anthea do? An offended dragon, blood relative or not, is certain to be heard from sooner or later. Brev, while he had no interest in dragons as such, had grasped that Anthea, for whatever reason, was shy of silver. He felt that they had not seen the last of her, and he held to his idea of sharp points and long poles. But for all the voyage on the water, they saw nothing of her. Meanwhile the faded blue sail was always full and tugging at the sheet, and the boat's blue eyes seemed always to spy out where lazy Ca's currents ran the briskest over shallows and rapids.

Alina sat all one afternoon in the stern of the boat, the nanny goat beside her, contemplating the sun dancing on the wake, and her own toes dabbling in the foam. Not imperial toes, inheritors of the godking's throne, just toes. Then she changed Corwin's diaper (which needed it) and said, "Brev?"

"?"

"There is no godking. And there won't be. And maybe there never really was, just Anthea—just my mother, pulling strings."

"All right, then."

"How can you take it like that?"

"How else shall I take it? Anyway, old ladies are difficult. My mother, now—"

"It's not the same. Don't you understand? Not just that I quit, I won't rule the empire, but no one will. No throne! No center, no order!"

Brev gave it some thought. He saw no reason the world shouldn't continue existing without an imperial order. In fact, he had some plans for it. "The fish won't stop biting," he said finally. "And Corwin will keep outgrowing his breeches. And—we are friends again, aren't we?"

She paused for a time. "As princess I have had servants and masters, lovers and enemies. A friend, never—but for my part, I will be your friend, whatever falls out."

Alina packed away her court dress and borrowed Brev's spare clothing to wear on the boat; so that when they beat up the coast and made harbor at Firstport, many people thought (with relief or irritation as the case might be) that Brev had failed of his intent and merely picked up a deckhand at Port of Calabrinia in the delta, or one of the other Ports.

They were soon and sorely disabused of the notion. Alina, rested and set up by the sea air, was more intolerable than before. Word had come that the Barak-Shar were united and moving fast; consequently she commanded that all the fieldstone walls of pasture and orchard be dismantled at once, loaded into every available cart, and dumped on the beach.

Then, it turned out, she wanted a causeway built out to the Narwhal Reef! It must rise to just under the surface of the water at low tide, no deeper than a tall horse's shoulder at high tide, no wider than a double plank. Public opinion was against a project both foolish and dangerous, tending to stir up trouble with the Lords of the Deep, impossible anyway, and more work than anyone wanted to do.

But Alina stamped her foot and shrieked orders and curses and threats, and Brev set an example, betting he could move more rock than, say, Jebjelly, between noon and sunset—and at last the job was done.

Then all the houses were to be boarded and shuttered, the fishing fleet to move to deep-water anchorage beyond the reef, and the children must take the ponies, sheep and goats to hidden pastures in the folds of the coast.

Only Handsome Tam was left, with his old luxurious tack cleaned and mended and laid out ready beside a magnificent cloak and banner that Alina and Myrrha made from the silk dress of the Isles.

But casting off a dragon-mother is one thing; keeping it that way is another. The preparations were hardly complete when Alina came into the parlor of the cottage and found Anthea taking camomile tea with Myrrha, pleasant as kiss-your-hand.

"Don't I believe you!" Myrrha was saying, shaking her head. "Take my son Brev, now..."

Alina had with her a fine clutch of eels and Corwin under her arm. She handed eels and baby to Myrrha (who rushed them out to the well to clean) and stared defiantly at the visitor, flinging her fat black braid hung with a silver bell over her shoulder. But Anthea was cordial.

"I thought I'd drop by and see if you've thought better of your pettish outburst. It's not quite too late."

"Tell me first, what is the true meaning of my horoscope? I suppose you must know, and may tell me if you will."

Anthea's alabaster brow creased very slightly. "None, actually. It is customary to provide the noble babe with some such device to structure character, as one provides a trellis when planting a climbing vine. Any lath or hoop will do."

Alina considered this in silence for a while. Anthea seemed quite at ease. "It wasn't a horoscope you provided for my baby," she observed, with a certain tightness at the corners of the mouth.

"A matter of pruning," said the other. "Sad, but necessary. You needn't pursue it."

"So there is no spell to break?"

"Not as far as that doggerel goes, certainly. That realization is the first step up to the throne, which you have just made. You must rule illusion, not be subject to it."

The clatter Myrrha and Corwin made on the stairs covered Brev's approach. He stopped at the door, and retreated silently like a cat from a pool of cuttlefish ink.

"No," Alina was saying. "I appreciate your visit in this friendly spirit. But I think I will neither be under illusions nor rule over them. If without the Dragon Throne the center will not hold, let it go—let the magick run out of the bottles as it will. Let people do as they like and take the consequences—myself included."

"Do you realize what the consequences will actually be?" Anthea inquired, finishing her tea. "You will toil through the years and the years will punish you; you will become bent, wrinkled and weatherbeaten, like the Mother Eelwife Dorcas showed you; before long you will die. Shall you not rather live a thousand years, as beautiful as the morning star, with a hundred thousand slaves to serve you from noon to night and night to noon!"

"Thank you," said Alina, sweet and cold like Dorcas' snow-taffy. "My tastes have changed."

Brev, eavesdropping in the chicken-yard, did a little dance in the litter, and stuffed his bandanna in his mouth to keep from chortling.

Anthea rose, the beryl eyes hardening. "Why is that?"

"To you it wouldn't signify."

"Don't you realize, whatever uncouth philosophies—or whatever else—you embrace, you bear the Moloquat mark?"

"Be drowned to it and you! Look!" Alina pulled down the sleeve of her smock. On her left shoulder was a reddish abrasion, irregular in shape and half-healed. "Myrrha got it off me with sea sand and cuttlefish ink."

Anthea turned pale, white as paper; the clear green eyes blazed up like a gas flame. The gown of white samite went fttt! and burned to ash in an instant, as the erstwhile smiling girl became an imperial dragon in seeming as in truth.

Upstairs, Myrrha shrieked as the twenty-foot spiked tail shattered the beams and the humped back of green and blue and violet scales buckled the floors above. A beautiful dragon, with crimson wings (of necessity folded in the confines of the cottage) and delicately articulated belly-plates of the palest lavender-green, but a very angry one; already the nets hanging by the chimney were alight, little flames dancing along the meshes.

"Brev!" Alina cried, and he came ready with the tool he had been making: a ten-foot narwhal tusk tipped with a hammered leaf-shaped blade of silver.

The dragon gave back before the point, hissing dreadfully, as Myrrha scuttled out with Corwin and the curly-tailed dog. Back, and back, out of the cottage afire in several places, down the narrow lane, and at last to the open beach; there, between highwater and lowwater she took wing.

"Beware! Your doom is even now upon you!" she cried.

Following the high whistling of the dragon's flight overhead, Alina saw a blurred darkness, punctuated with flashes of polished steel, flowing like lava down the mountain.

Summer had risen as high as the pastures in the Blue Mountains. Wild flowers bloomed in their thousands, uneaten by the Hopgangers' sullen kine. "Kee, Kee, Kee!" cried the gryfalcon, and meadow voles hid in the massed poppies. Wobbly young of the mountain sheep found their balance and ran up vertical slopes for the pleasure of doing it.

But all creatures scattered before the largest band of Barak-Shar ever to set out upon reiving. Swelled by strayed horsemen and recalcitrant plowboys, miners, fishermen, disgruntled younger sons and whosoever preferred stealing to working, they trampled the meadows four and six abreast, trolling out "Hola, hola ho" so that the dark pines quaked like aspens. Before them rode Pantasilea, more than ever magnificent: with white flesh and purple velvet slashed with black satin, she resembled a summer thunderhead pushing above the horizon. She had a new mount, a black mule eighteen hands at the shoulder, with toes instead of hooves, of which she was inordinately proud; although she had neither forgotten nor forgiven the theft of Tam.

In her jeweled hand she held a baton of gold and diamanté, with which she directed the army.

For army it now was. Morphelius Pashan, in gilded armor with his chestnut beard oiled until it shone like polished wood, commanding from the rear on his tall, nervous thoroughbred, admired the regular ranks of pelf-hungry, glory-bedazzled ruffians, as quick with a sword as a crossbow, with an oath as an "aye aye, sir!" Since his new friend, or protégé, or double-gaited doxy, had come among them, it seemed to him that his flowering ambition had brought forth the iron fruit of war.

No ill auguries shadowed their march in golden summer. Crows, when seen, were decidedly upon the right hand; no black cats, talking cows, headless horses or other natural presagers of disaster crossed their path. Morphelius Pashan, perhaps more than Pantasilea, wished their new friend (who did not ride, although she had given Pantasilea the black mule), was with them. This person, coin-golden and slim as a knife, with beryl-green eyes, came and went at her own will, unexpectedly. Ill-speakers said she had promised the Dragon Throne to Morphelius and Pantasilea, also to Perth, and perhaps a couple more—but there is no end to an envious tongue, as everyone knows.

The troops were better armed and schooled than ever before. They bore for a standard the imperial Calabrinian swallowtail with the five-clawed dragon above the Molo-quat emblem, following it over the villages of the Hop-gangers, through the camps of the Horsemen, even to the mines of Lake Tal—now they would overrun the Four Ports!

Some rumors of fortifications had reached him—let the crabcatchers pile stones as high as they liked! They could never stand against the Barak-Shar. And then...and then...even in his thoughts Morphelius hardly dared name Calabrinia, city of cities. But it floated in his mind's eye: the golden city, its walls higher and thicker than igno-rance, its towers stronger than despair, its riches greater than avarice, power beyond imagining.

The chestnut horse leaped a filbert brake, scattering a covey of mountain quail under it, and nearly unseated his rider with frantic plunging.

"Hola, hola, ho, at the Dragon's Tail we go!" bawled the men, cutting a hoof-pocked swath through the mead-ows, striking sparks from the flints in rock passes where they rode single file, sending pebbles rattling down steep canyons and muddying the brooks so that the speckled trout in them choked.

Before evening they saw the sea sparkling afar, and then the steep-pitched roofs of Firstport like a sandcastle awaiting the tide. The tale of fortifications was a lie, Morphelius was pleased to note. In fact, the crabcatchers seemed careless of danger: the town and harbor were still, with warm afternoon light poured over them like honey, and the evening mists drifting off shore.

Pantasilea halted and made every man check his girths, draw sword, and form for the attack.

Suddenly below appeared a horse and rider at the head of the cobbled main street. The rider wore a crimson silk cape that billowed from his—no, *her* shoulders. She was armed with a thickish lance—no, a banner unfurled from the staff and flew free, a crimson banner with the three-lobed Moloquat! The great cream-colored horse, richly caparisoned, executed a stately capriole so that the banner streamed in the breeze.

"My horse!" cried Pantasilea in blind fury, and spurred forward.

"To the King's Heart! To the Moloquat! To me, Princess Alina!" screamed the rider, thin and shrill; the bugle blew "advance" without orders, and with a rolling howl from a thousand bearded throats, the Barak-Shar threw themselves down the mountain road.

Just then, out of the looming bank of mist on the water, the celestial dragon appeared, shimmering as she reached a middle height and was lit by the low sun like a huge jewel: a bright enamel mosaic, a creature of burning bronze and gold and mercury, a heraldic device, a figure of dream and nightmare. It was preternaturally appropriate.

With the dragon-madness on them, men and horses galloped at breakneck speed down the slope, through the narrow street, faster and faster—they could hardly have halted if they would. Their shaven heads shone, the tattoos blurred.

Before them flew the crimson banner. Alina sighted on the highest point of Narwhal Reef as she had practiced, and drove Tam into the surf exactly where the hidden causeway stretched straight and narrow under the surface. Through the water she galloped, rooster-tails of spray fanning around her, Tam slipping on the stones but catching himself, for they must not fall, the Barak-Shar were gaining.

They reached the line of surf eight and nine abreast and plunged in; all but the huge black mule. He balked, rearing against the vicious cuts of Pantasilea's whip and spur; but the massed men and horses behind forced him into the salt water. The sun dropped into the bank of sea-mist, and the Firstporters hidden behind their barred doors did not have a clear view; but it was said afterward that the beast took a great leap clear out of the water, and turned into a coal-black chimera that flew away into the deepening dark of the west—with or without the bandit queen, no one was sure.

Perth spurred after the cream-colored horse that seemed to skim the waves like a seagull, confident of having at last his desserts. But the beach shelved off under the hooves of his stout bay gelding, and Perth went under, his mouth full of cold salt water and the beginning of wisdom.

Pannicart hauled on his hard-mouthed nag and tried to turn back to land, but the column behind bore him inexorably to drowning; thus dying more cleanly than he had been accustomed to living.

And now even if they had all drawn rein, it was no use. The famous riptide of Narwhal Reef took them like the jaws of a shark, and drew them down into the boiling cauldron of the Sea Lords, onion-bald heads and shaggy mounts and all.

Alina, meanwhile, leaned over the wet neck of her old horse, and asked for one great effort more. Tam's sides were heaving like a bellows, but he obeyed gallantly: clawing up the stone ramp to the reef and running straight off the sheer drop to seaward with such momentum that he flew clear over the pointed ship-killer rocks and splashed into deep green water beyond.

Here Brev waiting with his boat picked up Alina and got a body rope on the horse, whereupon he sculled off the rocks as fast as possible.

Morphelius Pashan, being last, did not perish in the sea. His nervous thoroughbred took fright and refused the water, throwing him among the empty clamshells and seawrack at the tideline. However, five Firstporters of brawny arms and no chivalrous instincts rushed out and settled him.

Night fell fast, deep and velvety-black; the rising tide

brought in flotsam and jetsam, and the Firstporters combed the beach with dark-lanterns in hand for anything useful that might turn up. A few exhausted horses shivering on the sands they lured with apples, and the odd survivor or two of the army was pressed into service to rebuild the walls with new stones—but that was later. At the moment they were well content with the defeat of the Barak-Shar, and thriftily pleased at the manner of it: for as Jebjelly pointed out, instead of all those bodies to bury, the Lords of the Deep had them; and with luck, would be so surfeited with man-flesh that the leakiest and crankest boat could put out to sea in safety for weeks to come.

Twelve

Cut is the branch that might have grown full straight,
and burned is Apollo's laurel-bough.
— Christopher Marlowe

W HILE the last ripples of the great drowning were spreading yet across the Western ocean, Alina the next morning took herself to the chicken house. The humble cottage of Brev and his mother was uninhabitable at present with the coming and going of well-wishers and people helping to rebuild the damaged house.

She had supplied herself with a pen, a piece of plank, some squares of oiled silk cut from her cloak, and a scallop shell full of cuttlefish ink. Laboriously she inked tiny characters on the bits of silk; as she finished each, she twisted it into a cord and tied it around the leg of a pigeon, which she then released into the bright morning air.

Be it known by these presents, said each square in the highly condensed court script, *that Hr. Rl Hnesse Princesse Alina, Heiress Presumptive, hereby irrevocably revoketh and abdicateth sovereygnty and Imperial sway over whomsoever it may concern. Be it further known and promulgated that the said Princesse cedeth her Right to NO ONE, whereby may all bonds of Empire be dissolved, nulle, voide and defaulted. All slaves and bondservants in whatsoever degree do be henceforth free whether it liketh them or not, and each must order his own affairs as best he mayest. (signed) Alina.*

There was a sudden commotion among the fowls, and she turned, flexing her cramped fingers. "Brev."

"Yes. Are you finished?"

"Almost. Pauli must send messages on to..."

"Now that you have unraveled everything to your satisfaction, what do you mean to do yourself? Fly away hissing?"

Alina looked at him, a half-frown between her brows. Brev seemed queer and nervy, now that it was all over. The company of dragons is unsettling, and even though he brought her back from the Isles knowing she was a dragon-daughter, and said they were friends, he might have thought better of it. "I hadn't made definite plans. Why do you ask?"

"In case you wanted to go anywhere by boat. The Isles, say."

"No," she said slowly, still frowning. "Pauli is Prince of the Isles, and will remain so if he is sensible. He will no doubt marry Prisca, and there is a certain sentiment that attaches to a long-lost prince and a clever slavegirl."

"Yes," said Brev, beginning to pace up and down in a distracting way, "these sentimental attachments. Like Corwin, who is crying right now because I wouldn't let him into the chicken run. I explained you were busy, and would soon be gone."

Alina continued to gaze at him with opaque amber eye, narrowing somewhat.

"I think you should stay here in Firstport," said Brev over-loudly, with a captainish intonation.

"I am a princess of Calabrinia still," she reminded him haughtily. "Even when Calabrinia is no more. I go and stay at my own will!"

Brev retreated. "Oh, as you please of course. If your Highness will inform me on what terms I may have my chicken house back—I'll inform you on what terms you may remain for now!"

Alina dropped her quill and drew herself up. "You, a fisherman, to make terms with me!"

"Calabrinia, then, or points north?"

"I have still the mark of the Moloquat. It cannot be wholly erased," Alina replied obliquely, in a tone more of regret than hauteur.

"A pity," remarked Brev, moving a little closer to lean against the door of the chicken house. "The other shoulder is so smooth, creamy-tan, like a duck's egg."

"No doubt," Alina pursued, "I would be prettier without the mark."

"Actually," said Brev with a certain armed easiness, "I think I'd miss it. Anything of yours, even your temper and your aim with sharp objects."

Alina made a great matter of finding her dropped quill and mending the point with icy hands. "Would you miss me, if I went to the City?"

Brev took his time replying, as long as it might be to knot a line and sinker and bait the hook. "I wonder why you'd want to be the nine hundred and eighty-second unemployed princess in the City."

"Why is neither here nor there. What I asked was, would you miss me?"

"Not really, providing you take another salted heart with you when you go. Mine."

Alina moved the ink-shell out of danger. "I've had enough of that sort of thing. If I did stay in this backwater on the edge of the world—it would be just as well, to teach Corwin something besides fish—what sort of terms did you have in mind?"

Brev took her inky right hand and spread the fingers lightly against his hard palm. His hands were warm, pulsing with heat that passed to her.

"There is a ceremony—nothing very elaborate—called handfasting. The Herring Festival is a traditional time for it."

"Are you asking me?"

"Yes."

"My pedigree is far more distinguished than yours."

"Right," Brev agreed, keeping the hand, which was not trying to escape.

"But—as Myrrha will point out—not, perhaps, above

192

reproach. Not altogether desirable."

"Well, as to that—your father is dead as a dried haddock, isn't he?"

"Oh, undoubtedly."

"And," Brev continued, "you aren't on the best of terms with your mother."

"Evidently."

"So, if it's yourself only I've to deal with, why—we were good friends before, weren't we? With the danger yet to come and troubles all about us?"

"True. Well—I have had little to do with friendship, except that of a dog or a horse. But I might learn, having nothing else to occupy me at present."

At that moment Myrrha could be heard saying, "If you must go in the chicken house, Cory, I suppose you must."

The lady Anthea hung in the upper air. From her lofty dragon's-eye view, spanning time as well as distance, she saw many things.

Far out to sea she watched the fisherfolk who fled the Four Ports—undulating flotillas following the currents of the Western Ocean, water-wanderers who never dared gain a foothold on land again.

She saw mountain wolves denning in the caves of the vanished Barak-Shar, grey woolly cubs playing hide-and-seek among the tumbled spoils.

She saw the Hopgangers hauling stones with their oxen, stubbornly rebuilding their villages exactly as they were before, but singing new ballads as they worked.

Even farther she saw, to the rolling grasslands of the far north, where the Horsemen tested the temper of the land that gave them refuge and pondered whether to treat with other folk as householder to householder.

Closer at hand the Isles sank ever deeper in their bird-haunted jungles, a dreamy sleep unbroken now by the gongs and drums of empire.

But most she focussed her far-sighted eyes on Calabrinia, navel of the world; and these are the words she spoke, as they were passed down to succeeding generations:

"The City decays. The statue of his Benign Supremacy still stands, stripped of gold, but the aqueduct has fallen, and the dome of the Temple. The wells are dry, Ca wanders from his channel and is lost in the sand for long stretches.

"The jackal hunts where the ruined houses harbor rats, and the wild gazelle of the desert finds only a mouthful of dry grass where orchards and fields once spread.

"Travelers camp for a time in the Marketplace, and tell each other fabulous stories of the city in its heyday.

"Law and medicine, music and poetry, painting and architecture are gone, half-remembered ideas like dandelion fluff on the wind. Who knows where or whether they shall take root elsewhere?

"I played a game of solitaire, and could not make the cards come out. I never cheat—for then what is the game? I lost, and soften nothing in the telling, not even my own miscalculations. It is my whim to tell the truth, a thing so strange that no one is likely to believe it: that a mere girl should distinguish freedom from power and love from vanity, confounding all magicks and probabilities.

"Shall it be my part at last to deliver the funeral oration of a fishwife, dead in fullness of mortal age and justly famed in life for her eel pies and ten stalwart sons, all with a tongue fit to flay a sandshark?

"Or shall posterity, to whom this peroration may seem excessive in its length, refuse to mind its own affairs, be they eel-traps or wagon-tongues, and clamor successfully at the doors of Firstport begging for the chains of empire to be re-strung?

"Or shall I, Anthea, remind you all that I have still the dried heart of his Benign Supremacy, salted down and packed in a box with orrisroot and tansy? It has shrunk to the size of an acorn, but contains still the magicks I put there in the beginning. I can if I choose bestow it where I will. Alina chooses for herself, in the heat of temper, but what if she bears a daughter?"

The End.